THE EARTHWORM WAS
NO ANGEL, BUT SHE THOUGHT
SHE WAS BORN TO FLY . . .

Jeff flew below us for a while, then climbed. It suited me to have two of us watching Ariel; I was beginning to fret that she might not realize the way down was going to be just as tiring as the way up. I could glide until forced down by starvation. But a beginner gets tense.

We were halfway up and I decided to call uncle. So, I called out, "Ariel? Lean right and get out of the circle."

I couldn't find her.

I don't know how it happened. Maybe she leaned too far and started to struggle. I seemed to hang there frozen for an hour while I watched her. I spilled my wings completely— but couldn't manage to fall fast enough; she was as far below me as ever.

Baen Books by Robert A. Heinlein

Glory Road
Podkayne of Mars
Farnham's Freehold
The Menace From Earth
Sixth Column
Take Back Your Government *(nonfiction)*
Revolt in 2100 & Methuselah's Children

THE
MENACE
from
EARTH

THE MENACE FROM EARTH
This is a work of fiction. All the characters and events portrayed in this book are fictional, and any resemblance to real people or events is purely coincidental.

A Baen Books Original

Baen Publishing Enterprises
P.O. Box 1403
Riverdale NY 10471

ISBN 0-671-57802-2

First Baen printing, May 1987
Third Printing, February 1999

Acknowledgements:
The Menace from Earth, Fantasy House, Inc. 1957; *Water is for Washing*, Popular Publications, Inc. 1947; *Project Nightmare*, Ziff-Davis Publishing Co. 1953; *Sky Lift*, Greenleaf Publishing Co. 1953; *By His Bootstraps*, Street & Smith Publications, Inc. 1941; *Goldfish Bowl*, Street & Smith Publications, Inc. 1942; *Columbus Was a Dope*, Better Publications, Inc. 1947; *The Year of the Jackpot*, Galaxy Publishing Corp. 1952.

Printed in the United States of America

Distributed by Simon & Schuster
1230 Ave of the Americas
New York, NY 10020

TO HERMANN B. DEUTSCH

Robert A.
HEINLEIN

Table of Contents

The Year of the Jackpot

The Year of the Jackpot

At first Potiphar Breen did not notice the girl who was undressing.

She was standing at a bus stop only ten feet away. He was indoors but that would not have kept him from noticing; he was seated in a drugstore booth adjacent to the bus stop; there was nothing between Potiphar and the young lady but plate glass and an occasional pedestrian.

Nevertheless he did not look up when she began to peel. Propped up in front of him was a Los Angeles *Times;* beside it, still unopened, were the *Herald-Express* and the *Daily News*. He was scanning the newspaper carefully but the headline stories got only a passing glance. He noted the maximum and minimum temperatures in Brownsville, Texas and entered them in a neat black notebook; he did the same with the closing prices of three blue chips and two dogs on the New York Exchange, as well as the total number of shares. He then began a rapid sifting of minor news stories, from time to time entering briefs of them in his little book; the items he recorded seemed randomly unrelated—among them a publicity release in which Miss National Cottage Cheese

3

Week announced that she intended to marry and have twelve children by a man who could prove that he had been a life-long vegetarian, a circumstantial but wildly unlikely flying saucer report, and a call for prayers for rain throughout Southern California.

Potiphar had just written down the names and addresses of three residents of Watts, California who had been miraculously healed at a tent meeting of the God-is-All First Truth Brethren by the Reverend Dickie Bottomley, the eight-year-old evangelist, and was preparing to tackle the *Herald-Express*, when he glanced over his reading glasses and saw the amateur ecdysiast on the street corner outside. He stood up, placed his glasses in their case, folded the newspapers and put them carefully in his right coat pocket, counted out the exact amount of his check and added twenty-five cents. He then took his raincoat from a hook, placed it over his arm, and went outside.

By now the girl was practically down to the buff. It seemed to Potiphar Breen that she had quite a lot of buff. Nevertheless she had not pulled much of a house. The corner newsboy had stopped hawking his disasters and was grinning at her, and a mixed pair of transvestites who were apparently waiting for the bus had their eyes on her. None of the passers-by stopped. They glanced at her, then with the self-conscious indifference to the unusual of the true Southern Californian, they went on their various ways. The transvestites were frankly staring. The male member of the team wore a frilly feminine blouse but his skirt was a conservative Scottish kilt—his female companion wore a business suit and Homburg hat; she stared with lively interest.

As Breen approached the girl hung a scrap of nylon on the bus stop bench, then reached for her shoes. A police officer, looking hot and unhappy, crossed with the lights and came up to them. "Okay," he said in a tired voice, "that'll be all, lady. Get them duds back on and clear out of here."

The female transvestite took a cigar out of her mouth. "Just," she said, "what business is it of yours, officer?"

The cop turned to her. "Keep out of this!" He ran his eyes over her get up, that of her companion. "I ought to run both of you in, too."

The transvestite raised her eyebrows. "Arrest us for being clothed, arrest her for not being. I think I'm going to like this." She turned to the girl, who was standing still and saying nothing, as if she were puzzled by what was going on. "I'm a lawyer, dear." She pulled a card from her vest pocket. "If this uniformed Neanderthal persists in annoying you, I'll be delighted to handle him."

The man in the kilt said, "Grace! Please!"

She shook him off. "Quiet, Norman—this *is* our business." She went on to the policeman, "Well? Call the wagon. In the meantime my client will answer no questions."

The officer looked unhappy enough to cry and his face was getting dangerously red. Breen quietly stepped forward and slipped his raincoat around the shoulders of the girl. She looked startled and spoke for the first time. "Uh—thanks." She pulled the coat about her, cape fashion.

The female attorney glanced at Breen then back to the cop. "Well, officer? Ready to arrest us?"

He shoved his face close to hers. "I ain't going to give you the satisfaction!" He sighed and added, "Thanks, Mr. Breen—you know this lady?"

"I'll take care of her. You can forget it, Kawonski."

"I sure hope so. If she's with you, I'll do just that. But get her out of here, Mr. Breen—please!"

The lawyer interrupted. "Just a moment—you're interfering with my client."

Kawonski said, "Shut up, you! You heard Mr. Breen—she's with him. Right, Mr. Breen?"

"Well—yes. I'm a friend. I'll take care of her."

The transvestite said suspiciously, "I didn't hear *her* say that."

Her companion said, "Grace—please! There's our bus."

"And I didn't hear her say she was your client," the cop retorted. "You look like a—" His words were drowned out by the bus's brakes. "—and besides that, if you don't climb on that bus and get off my territory, I'll . . . I'll . . ."

"You'll what?"

"Grace! We'll miss our bus."

"Just a moment, Norman. Dear, is this man really a friend of yours? Are you with him?"

The girl looked uncertainly at Breen, then said in a low voice, "Uh, yes. That's right."

"Well . . ." The lawyer's companion pulled at her arm. She shoved her card into Breen's hand and got on the bus; it pulled away.

Breen pocketed the card. Kawonski wiped his forehead. "Why did you do it, lady?" he said peevishly.

The girl looked puzzled. "I . . . I don't know."

"You hear that, Mr. Breen? That's what they all say. And if you pull 'em in, there's six more the next day. The Chief said—" He sighed. "The Chief said—well, if I had arrested her like that female shyster wanted me to, I'd be out at a hundred and ninety-sixth and Ploughed Ground tomorrow morning, thinking about retirement. So get her out of here, will you?"

The girl said, "But—"

"No 'buts,' lady. Just be glad a real gentleman like Mr. Breen is willing to help you." He gathered up her clothes, handed them to her. When she reached for them she again exposed an uncustomary amount of skin; Kawonski hastily gave them to Breen instead, who crowded them into his coat pockets.

She let Breen lead her to where his car was parked, got in and tucked the raincoat around her so that she was rather more dressed than a girl usually is. She looked at him.

She saw a medium-sized and undistinguished man who was slipping down the wrong side of thirty-five and looked older. His eyes had that mild and slightly naked look of the habitual spectacles wearer who is not at the moment with glasses; his hair was gray at the temples and thin on top. His herringbone suit, black shoes, white shirt, and neat tie smacked more of the East than of California.

He saw a face which he classified as "pretty" and "wholesome" rather than "beautiful" and "glamorous." It was topped by a healthy mop of light brown hair. He set her age at twenty-five, give or take eighteen months. He smiled gently, climbed in without speaking and started his car.

He turned up Doheny Drive and east on Sunset. Near La Cienega he slowed down. "Feeling better?"

"Uh, I guess so Mr.—'Breen'?"

"Call me Potiphar. What's your name? Don't tell me if you don't want to."

"Me? I'm . . . I'm Meade Barstow."

"Thank you, Meade. Where do you want to go? Home?"

"I suppose so. I—Oh my no! I can't go home like *this*." She clutched the coat tightly to her.

"Parents?"

"No. My landlady. She'd be shocked to death."

"Where, then?"

She thought. "Maybe we could stop at a filling station and I could sneak into the ladies' room."

"Mmm . . .. maybe. See here, Meade—my house is six blocks from here and has a garage entrance. You could get inside without being seen." He looked at her.

She stared back. "Potiphar—you don't *look* like a wolf?"

"Oh, but I am! The worst sort." He whistled and

gnashed his teeth. "See? But Wednesday is my day off from it."

She looked at him and dimpled. "Oh, well! I'd rather wrestle with you than with Mrs. Megeath. Let's go."

He turned up into the hills. His bachelor diggings were one of the many little frame houses clinging like fungus to the brown slopes of the Santa Monica Mountains. The garage was notched into this hill; the house sat on it. He drove in, cut the ignition, and led her up a teetery inside stairway into the living room. "In there," he said, pointing. "Help yourself." He pulled her clothes out of his coat pockets and handed them to her.

She blushed and took them, disappeared into his bedroom. He heard her turn the key in the lock. He settled down in his easy chair, took out his notebook, and opened the *Herald-Express*.

He was finishing the *Daily News* and had added several notes to his collection when she came out. Her hair was neatly rolled; her face was restored; she had brushed most of the wrinkles out of her skirt. Her sweater was neither too tight nor deep cut, but it was pleasantly filled. She reminded him of well water and farm breakfasts.

He took his raincoat from her, hung it up, and said, "Sit down, Meade."

She said uncertainly, "I had better go."

"Go if you must—but I had hoped to talk with you."

"Well—" She sat down on the edge of his couch and looked around. The room was small but as neat as his necktie, clean as his collar. The fireplace was swept; the floor was bare and polished. Books crowded bookshelves in every possible space. One corner was filled by an elderly flat-top desk; the papers on it were neatly in order. Near it, on its own stand, was a small electric calculator. To her right, French windows gave out on a tiny porch over the garage. Beyond it she could see the sprawling city; a few neon signs were already blinking.

She sat back a little. "This is a nice room—Potiphar. It looks like you."

"I take that as a compliment. Thank you." She did not answer; he went on, "Would you like a drink?"

"Oh, would I!" She shivered. "I guess I've got the jitters."

He got up. "Not surprising. What'll it be?"

She took Scotch and water, no ice; he was a Bourbon-and-ginger-ale man. She had soaked up half her highball in silence, then put it down, squared her shoulders and said, "Potiphar?"

"Yes, Meade?"

"Look—if you brought me here to make a pass, I wish you'd go ahead and make it. It won't do you a bit of good, but it makes me nervous to wait for it."

He said nothing and did not change his expression. She went on uneasily, "Not that I'd blame you for trying—under the circumstances. And I *am* grateful. But . . . well—it's just that I don't—"

He came over and took both her hands. "My dear, I haven't the slightest thought of making a pass at you. Nor need you feel grateful. I butted in because I was interested in your case."

"My case? Are you a doctor? A psychiatrist?"

He shook his head. "I'm a mathematician. A statistician, to be precise."

"Huh? I don't get it."

"Don't worry about it. But I would like to ask some questions. May I?"

"Uh, sure, sure! I owe you that much—and then some."

"You owe me nothing. Want your drink sweetened?"

She gulped it and handed him her glass, then followed him out into the kitchen. He did an exact job of measuring and gave it back. "Now tell me why you took your clothes off?"

She frowned. "I don't know. I *don't* know. I don't *know*. I guess I just went crazy." She added round-eyed, "But I don't feel crazy. Could I go off my rocker and not know it?"

"You're not crazy . . . not more so than the rest of us," he amended. "Tell me—where did you see some-one else do this?"

"Huh? But I never have."

"Where did you read about it?"

"But I haven't. Wait a minute—those people up in Canada. Dooka-somethings."

"Doukhobors. That's all? No bareskin swimming parties? No strip poker?"

She shook her head. "No. You may not believe it but I was the kind of a little girl who undressed under her nightie." She colored and added, "I still do—unless I remember to tell myself it's silly."

"I believe it. No news stories?"

"No. Yes, there was too! About two weeks ago, I think it was. Some girl in a theater, in the audience, I mean. But I thought it was just publicity. You know the stunts they pull here."

He shook his head. "It wasn't. February 3rd, the Grand Theater, Mrs. Alvin Copley. Charges dismiss-ed."

"Huh? How did *you* know?"

"Excuse me." He went to his desk, dialed the City News Bureau. "Alf? This is Pot Breen. They still sitting on that story? . . . yes, yes, the Gypsy Rose file. Any new ones today?" He waited; Meade thought that she could make out swearing. "Take it easy, Alf—this hot weather can't last forever. Nine, eh? Well, add another—Santa Monica Boulevard, late this afternoon. No arrest." He added, "Nope, no-body got her name—a middle-aged woman with a cast in one eye. I happened to see it . . . who, me?

Why would I want to get mixed up? But it's rounding up into a very, very interesting picture." He put the phone down.

Meade said, "Cast in one eye, indeed!"

"Shall I call him back and give him your name?"

"Oh, no!"

"Very well. Now, Meade, we seemed to have located the point of contagion in your case—Mrs. Copley. What I'd like to know next is how you felt, what you were thinking about, when you did it?"

She was frowning intently. "Wait a minute, Potiphar—do I understand that *nine other* girls have pulled the stunt I pulled?"

"Oh, no—nine others *today*. You are—" He paused briefly. "—the three hundred and nineteenth case in Los Angeles county since the first of the year. I don't have figures on the rest of the country, but the suggestion to clamp down on the stories came from the eastern news services when the papers here put our first cases on the wire. That proves that it's a problem elsewhere, too."

"You mean that women all over the country are peeling off their clothes in public? Why, how shocking!"

He said nothing. She blushed again and insisted, "Well, it is shocking, even if it was me, this time."

"No, Meade. One case is shocking; over three hundred makes it scientifically interesting. That's why I want to know how it felt. Tell me about it."

"But— All right, I'll try. I told you I don't know why I did it; I still don't. I—"

"You remember it?"

"Oh, yes! I remember getting up off the bench and pulling up my sweater. I remember unzipping my skirt. I remember thinking I would have to hurry as I could see my bus stopped two blocks down the street. I remember how *good* it felt when I finally, uh—" She paused and looked puzzled. "But I still don't know why."

"What were you thinking about just before you stood up?"

"I don't remember."

"Visualize the street. What was passing by? Where were your hands? Were your legs crossed or uncrossed? Was there anybody near you? What were you thinking about?"

"Uh . . . nobody was on the bench with me. I had my hands in my lap. Those characters in the mixed-up clothes were standing near by, but I wasn't paying attention. I wasn't thinking much except that my feet hurt and I wanted to get home—and how unbearably hot and sultry it was. Then—" Her eyes became distant. "—suddenly I knew what I had to do and it was very urgent that I do it. So I stood up and I . . . and I—" Her voice became shrill.

"Take it easy!" he said. "Don't do it again."

"Huh? Why, Mr. Breen! I wouldn't do anything like that."

"Of course not. Then what?"

"Why, you put your raincoat around me and you know the rest." She faced him. "Say, Potiphar, what were you doing with a raincoat? It hasn't rained in weeks—this is the driest, hottest rainy season in years."

"In sixty-eight years, to be exact."

"Huh?"

"I carry a raincoat anyhow. Uh, just a notion of mine, but I feel that when it does rain, it's going to rain awfully hard." He added, "Forty days and forty nights, maybe."

She decided that he was being humorous and laughed. He went on, "Can you remember how you got the idea?"

She swirled her glass and thought. "I simply don't know."

He nodded. "That's what I expected."

"I don't understand you—unless you think I'm crazy. Do you?"

"No. I think you had to do it and could not help it and don't know why and can't know why."

"But *you* know." She said it accusingly.

"Maybe. At least I have some figures. Ever take any interest in statistics, Meade?"

She shook her head. "Figures confuse me. Never mind statistics—*I want to know why I did what I did!*"

He looked at her very soberly. "I think we're lemmings, Meade."

She looked puzzled, then horrified. "You mean those little furry mouselike creatures? The ones that—"

"Yes. The ones that periodically make a death migration, until millions, hundreds of millions of them drown themselves in the sea. Ask a lemming why he does it. If you could get him to slow up his rush toward death, even money says he would rationalize his answer as well as any college graduate. But he does it because he has to—and so do we."

"That's a horrid idea, Potiphar."

"Maybe. Come here, Meade. I'll show you figures that confuse me, too." He went to his desk and opened a drawer, took out a packet of cards. "Here's one. Two weeks ago—a man sues an entire state legislature for alienation of his wife's affection—and the judge lets the suit be tried. Or this one—a patent application for a device to lay the globe over on its side and warm up the arctic regions. Patent denied, but the inventor took in over three hundred thousand dollars in down payments on South Pole real estate before the postal authorities stepped in. Now he's fighting the case and it looks as if he might win. And here—prominent bishop proposes applied courses in the so-called facts of life in high schools." He put the card away hastily. "Here's a dilly: a bill introduced in the Alabama lower house to repeal the laws of atomic energy—not the present statutes, but the natural laws concerning nuclear physics; the wording makes that plain." He shrugged. "How silly can you get?"

"They're crazy."

"No, Meade. One such is crazy; a lot of them is a lemming death march. No, don't object—I've plotted them on a curve. The last time we had anything like this was the so-called Era of Wonderful Nonsense. But this one is much worse." He delved into a lower drawer, hauled out a graph. "The amplitude is more than twice as great and we haven't reached peak. What the peak will be I don't dare guess— three separate rhythms, reinforcing."

She peered at the curves. "You mean that the laddy with the arctic real estate deal is somewhere on this line?"

"He adds to it. And back here on the last crest are the flag-pole sitters and the goldfish swallowers and the Ponzi hoax and the marathon dancers and the man who pushed a peanut up Pikes Peak with his nose. You're on the new crest—or you will be when I add you in."

She made a face. "I don't like it."

"Neither do I. But it's as clear as a bank statement. This year the human race is letting down its hair, flipping its lip with a finger, and saying, 'Wubba, wubba, wubba.'"

She shivered. "Do you suppose I could have another drink? Then I'll go."

"I have a better idea. I owe you a dinner for answering questions. Pick a place and we'll have a cocktail before."

She chewed her lip. "You don't owe me anything. And I don't feel up to facing a restaurant crowd. I might . . . I might—"

"No, you wouldn't," he said sharply. "It doesn't hit twice."

"You're sure? Anyhow, I don't want to face a crowd."

She glanced at his kitchen door. "Have you anything to eat in there? I can cook."

"Um, breakfast things. And there's a pound of ground round in the freezer compartment and some rolls. I sometimes make hamburgers when I don't want to go out."

She headed for the kitchen. "Drunk or sober, fully dressed or—or naked, I can cook. You'll see."

He did see. Open-faced sandwiches with the meat married to toasted buns and the flavor garnished rather than suppressed by scraped Bermuda onion and thin-sliced dill, a salad made from things she had scrounged out of his refrigerator, potatoes crisp but not vulcanized. They ate it on the tiny balcony, sopping it down with cold beer.

He sighed and wiped his mouth. "Yes, Meade, you can cook."

"Some day I'll arrive with proper materials and pay you back. Then I'll prove it."

"You've already proved it. Nevertheless I accept. But I tell you three times, you owe me nothing."

"No? If you hadn't been a Boy Scout, I'd be in jail."

Breen shook his head. "The police have orders to keep it quiet at all costs—to keep it from growing. You saw that. And, my dear, you weren't a person to me at the time. I didn't even see your face; I—"

"You saw plenty else!"

"Truthfully, I didn't look. You were just a—a statistic."

She toyed with her knife and said slowly, "I'm not sure, but I think I've just been insulted. In all the twenty-five years that I've fought men off, more or less successfully, I've been called a lot of names—but a 'statistic'—why I ought to take your slide rule and beat you to death with it."

"My dear young lady—"

"I'm not a lady, that's for sure. But I'm *not* a statistic."

"My dear Meade, then. I wanted to tell you, before you did anything hasty, that in college I wrestled varsity middle-weight."

She grinned and dimpled. "That's more the talk a girl likes to hear. I was beginning to be afraid you had been assembled in an adding machine factory. Potty, you're rather a dear."

"If that is a diminutive of my given name, I like it. But if it refers to my waist line, I resent it."

She reached across and patted his stomach. "I like your waist line; lean and hungry men are difficult. If I were cooking for you regularly, I'd really pad it."

"Is that a proposal?"

"Let it lie, let it lie—Potty, do you really think the whole country is losing its buttons?"

He sobered at once. "It's worse than that."

"Huh?"

"Come inside. I'll show you." They gathered up dishes and dumped them in the sink, Breen talking all the while. "As a kid I was fascinated by numbers. Numbers are pretty things and they combine in such interesting configurations. I took my degree in math, of course, and got a job as a junior actuary with Midwestern Mutual—the insurance outfit. That was fun—no way on earth to tell when a particular man is going to die, but an absolute certainty that so many men of a certain age group would die before a certain date. The curves were so lovely—and they always worked out. Always. You didn't have to know *why;* you could predict with dead certainty and never know why. The equations worked; the curves were right.

"I was interested in astronomy too; it was the one science where individual figures worked out neatly, completely, and accurately, down to the last decimal point the instruments were good for. Compared with astronomy the other sciences were mere carpentry and kitchen chemistry.

"I found there were nooks and crannies in astronomy where individual numbers won't do, where you have to go over to statistics, and I became even more interested. I joined the Variable Star Association and I might have gone into astronomy professionally, instead of what I'm in now—business consultation—if I hadn't gotten interested in something else."

"'Business consultation'?" repeated Meade. "Income tax work?"

"Oh, no—that's too elementary. I'm the numbers boy for a firm of industrial engineers. I can tell a rancher exactly how many of his Hereford bull calves will be sterile. Or I tell a motion picture producer how much rain insurance to carry on location. Or maybe how big a company in a particular line must be to carry its own risk in industrial accidents. And I'm right. I'm always right."

"Wait a minute. Seems to me a big company would *have* to have insurance."

"Contrariwise. A really big corporation begins to resemble a statistical universe."

"Huh?"

"Never mind. I got interested in something else—cycles. Cycles are everything, Meade. And everywhere. The tides. The seasons. Wars. Love. Everybody knows that in the spring the young man's fancy lightly turns to what the girls never stopped thinking about, but did you know that it runs in an eighteen-year-plus cycle as well? And that a girl born at the wrong swing of the curve doesn't stand nearly as good a chance as her older or younger sister?"

"What? Is *that* why I'm a doddering old maid?"

"You're twenty-five?" He pondered. "Maybe—but your chances are picking up again; the curve is swinging up. Anyhow, remember you are just one statistic; the curve applies to the group. Some girls get married every year anyhow."

"Don't call me a statistic."

"Sorry. And marriages match up with acreage

planted to wheat, with wheat cresting ahead. You could almost say that planting wheat makes people get married."

"Sounds silly."

"It *is* silly. The whole notion of cause-and-effect is probably superstition. But the same cycle shows a peak in house building right after a peak in marriages, every time."

"Now that makes sense."

"Does it? How many newlyweds do you know who can afford to build a house? You might as well blame it on wheat acreage. We don't know *why*; it just *is*."

"Sun spots, maybe?"

"You can correlate sun spots with stock prices, or Columbia River salmon, or women's skirts. And you are just as much justified in blaming short skirts for sun spots as you are in blaming sun spots for salmon. We don't know. But the curves go on just the same."

"But there has to be some *reason* behind it."

"Does there? That's mere assumption. A fact has no 'why.' There it stands, self demonstrating. Why did you take your clothes off today?"

She frowned. "That's not fair."

"Maybe not. But I want to show you why I'm worried." He went into the bedroom, came out with a large roll of tracing paper. "We'll spread it on the floor. Here they are, all of them. The 54-year cycle—see the Civil War there? See how it matches in? The 18 & ⅓ year cycle, the 9-plus cycle, the 41-month shorty, the three rhythms of sun spots—everything, all combined in one grand chart. Mississippi River floods, fur catches in Canada, stock market prices, marriages, epidemics, freight-car loadings, bank clearings, locust plagues, divorces, tree growth, wars, rainfall, earth magnetism, building construction, patents applied for, murders—you name it; I've got it there."

She stared at the bewildering array of wavy lines. "But, Potty, what does it mean?"

"It means that these things all happen, in regular rhythm, whether we like it or not. It means that when skirts are due to go up, all the sylists in Paris can't make 'em go down. It means that when prices are going down, all the controls and supports and government planning can't make 'em go up." He pointed to a curve. "Take a look at the grocery ads. Then turn to the financial page and read how the Big Brains try to double-talk their way out of it. It means that when an epidemic is due, it happens, despite all the public health efforts. It means we're lemmings."

She pulled her lip. "I don't like it. 'I am the master of my fate,' and so forth. I've got free will, Potty. I know I have—I can feel it."

"I imagine every little neutron in an atom bomb feels the same way. He can go *spung!* or he can sit still, just as he pleases. But statistical mechanics work out anyhow. And the bomb goes off—which is what I'm leading up to. See anything odd there, Meade?"

She studied the chart, trying not to let the curving lines confuse her. "They sort of bunch up over at the right end."

"You're dern tootin' they do! See that dotted vertical line? That's right now—and things are bad enough. But take a look at that solid vertical; that's about six months from now—and that's when we get it. Look at the cycles—the long ones, the short ones, all of them. Every single last one of them reaches either a trough or a crest exactly on—or almost on—that line."

"That's bad?"

"What do you think? Three of the big ones troughed in 1929 and the depression almost ruined us . . . even with the big 54-year cycle supporting things. Now we've got the big one troughing—and the few crests are not things that help. I mean to say, tent caterpillars and influenza don't do us any good. Meade, if statistics mean anything, this tired old planet hasn't seen a jackpot like this since Eve went into the apple business. I'm scared."

She searched his face. "Potty—you're not simply having fun with me? You know I can't check up on you."

"I wish to heaven I were. No, Meade, I can't fool about numbers; I wouldn't know how. This is it. The Year of the Jackpot."

She was very silent as he drove her home. As they approached West Los Angeles, she said, "Potty?"

"Yes, Meade?"

"What do we *do* about it?"

"What do you do about a hurricane? You pull in your ears. What can you do about an atom bomb? You try to out-guess it, not be there when it goes off. What else can you do?"

"Oh." She was silent for a few moments, then added, "Potty? Will you tell me which way to jump?"

"Huh? Oh, sure! If I can figure it out."

He took her to her door, turned to go. She said, "Potty!"

He faced her. "Yes, Meade?"

She grabbed his head, shook it—then kissed him fiercely on the mouth. "There—is that just a statistic?"

"Uh, no."

"It had better not be," she said dangerously. "Potty, I think I'm going to have to change your curve."

II

"RUSSIANS REJECT UN NOTE"

"MISSOURI FLOOD DAMAGE EXCEEDS 1951 RECORD"

"MISSISSIPPI MESSIAH DEFIES COURT"

"NUDIST CONVENTION STORMS BAILEY'S BEACH"

"BRITISH-IRAN TALKS STILL DEAD-LOCKED"

"FASTER-THAN-LIGHT WEAPON PROMISED"

"TYPHOON DOUBLING BACK ON MANILA"

"MARRIAGE SOLEMNIZED ON FLOOR OF HUDSON—New York, 13 July, *In a specially-constructed diving suit built for two, Merydith Smithe, café society headline girl, and Prince Augie Schleswieg of New York and the Riviera were united today by Bishop Dalton in a service televised with the aid of the Navy's ultra-new—*"

As the Year of the Jackpot progressed Breen took melancholy pleasure in adding to the data which proved that the curve was sagging as predicted. The undeclared World War continued its bloody, blundering way at half a dozen spots around a tortured globe. Breen did not chart it; the headlines were there for anyone to read. He concentrated on the odd facts in the other pages of the papers, facts which, taken singly, meant nothing, but taken together showed a disastrous trend.

He listed stock market prices, rainfall, wheat futures, but it was the "silly season" items which fascinated him. To be sure, some humans were always doing silly things—but at what point had prime damfoolishness become commonplace? When, for example, had the zombie-like professional models become accepted ideals of American womanhood? What were the gradations between National Cancer Week and National Athlete's Foot Week? On what day had the American people finally taken leave of horse sense?

Take transvestism—male-and-female dress customs were arbitrary, but they had seemed to be deeply rooted in the culture. When did the breakdown start? With Marlene Dietrich's tailored suits? By the late forties there was no "male" article of clothing that a woman could not wear in public—but when had men started to slip over the line? Should he count the psychological cripples who had made the word "drag" a byword in Greenwich Village and Hollywood long before this outbreak? Or were they "wild shots" not belonging on the curve? Did it start with some unknown normal man attending a masquerade and there discovering that skirts actually were more comfortable and practical than trousers? Or had it started with the resurgence of Scottish nationalism reflected in the wearing of kilts by many Scottish-Americans?

Ask a lemming to state his motives! The outcome was in front of him, a news story. Transvestism by draft-dodgers had at last resulted in a mass arrest in Chicago which was to have ended in a giant joint trial—only to have the deputy prosecutor show up in a pinafore and defy the judge to submit to an examination to determine the judge's true sex. The judge suffered a stroke and died and the trial was postponed—postponed forever in Breen's opinion; he doubted that this particular blue law would ever again be enforced.

Or the laws about indecent exposure, for that matter. The attempt to limit the Gypsy-Rose syndrome by ignoring it had taken the starch out of enforcement; now here was a report about the All Souls Community Church of Springfield: the pastor had reinstituted ceremonial nudity. Probably the first time this thousand years, Breen thought, aside from some screwball cults in Los Angeles. The reverend gentleman claimed that the ceremony was identical with the "dance of the high priestess" in the ancient temple of Karnak.

Could be—but Breen had private information that the "priestess" had been working the burlesque & nightclub circuit before her present engagement. In any case the holy leader was packing them in and had not been arrested.

Two weeks later a hundred and nine churches in

thirty-three states offered equivalent attractions. Breen entered them on his curves.

This queasy oddity seemed to him to have no relation to the startling rise in the dissident evangelical cults throughout the country. These churches were sincere, earnest and poor—but growing, ever since the War. Now they were multiplying like yeast. It seemed a statistical cinch that the United States was about to become godstruck again. He correlated it with Transcendentalism and the trek of the Latter Day Saints—hmm . . . yes, it fitted. And the curve was pushing toward a crest.

Billions in war bonds were now falling due; wartime marriages were reflected in the swollen peak of the Los Angeles school population. The Colorado River was at a record low and the towers in Lake Mead stood high out of the water. But the Angelenos committed slow suicide by watering lawns as usual. The Metropolitan Water District commissioners tried to stop it—it fell between the stools of the police powers of fifty "sovereign" cities. The taps remained open, trickling away the life blood of the desert paradise.

The four regular party conventions—Dixiecrats, Regular Republicans, the other Regular Republicans, and the Democrats—attracted scant attention, as the Know-Nothings had not yet met. The fact that the "American Rally," as the Know-Nothings preferred to be called, claimed not to be a party but an educational society did not detract from their strength. But what was their strength? Their beginnings had been so obscure that Breen had had to go back and dig into the December 1951 files—but he had been approached twice this very week to join them, right inside his own office—once by his boss, once by the janitor.

He hadn't been able to chart the Know-Nothings. They gave him chills in his spine. He kept column-inches on them, found that their publicity was shrinking while their numbers were obviously zooming.

Krakatau blew up on July 18th. It provided the first important transPacific TV-cast; its effect on sunsets, on solar constant, on mean temperature, and on rainfall would not be felt until later in the year. The San Andreas fault, its stresses unrelieved since the Long Beach disaster of 1933, continued to build up imbalance—an unhealed wound running the full length of the West Coast. Pelée and Etna erupted; Mauna Loa was still quiet.

Flying saucers seemed to be landing daily in every state. No one had exhibited one on the ground—or had the Department of Defense sat on them? Breen was unsatisfied with the off-the-record reports he had been able to get; the alcoholic content of some of them had been high. But the sea serpent on Ventura Beach was real; he had seen it. The troglodyte in Tennessee he was not in a position to verify.

Thirty-one domestic air crashes the last week in July . . . was it sabotage? Or was it a sagging curve on a chart? And that neo-polio epidemic that skipped from Seattle to New York? Time for a big epidemic? Breen's chart said it was. But how about B.W.? Could a chart *know* that a Slav biochemist would perfect an efficient virus-and-vector at the right time? Nonsense!

But the curves, if they meant anything at all, included "free will;" they averaged in all the individual "wills" of a statistical universe—and came out as a smooth function. Every morning three million "free wills" flowed toward the center of the New York megapolis; every evening they flowed out again—all by "free will," and on a smooth and predictable curve.

Ask a lemming! Ask *all* the lemmings, dead and alive—let them take a vote on it! Breen tossed his notebook aside and called Meade. "Is this my favorite statistic?"

"Potty! I was thinking about you."

"Naturally. This is your night off."

"Yes, but another reason, too. Potiphar, have you ever taken a look at the Great Pyramid?"

"I haven't even been to Niagara Falls. I'm looking for a rich woman, so I can travel."

"Yes, yes, I'll let you know when I get my first million, but—"

"That's the first time you've proposed to me this week."

"Shut up. Have you ever looked into the prophecies they found inside the pyramid?"

"Huh? Look, Meade, that's in the same class with astrology—strictly for squirrels. Grow up."

"Yes, of course. But Potty, I thought you were interested in anything odd. This is odd."

"Oh. Sorry. If it's 'silly season' stuff, let's see it."

"All right. Am I cooking for you tonight?"

"It's Wednesday, isn't it?"

"How soon?"

He glanced at his watch. "Pick you up in eleven minutes." He felt his whiskers. "No, twelve and a half."

"I'll be ready. Mrs. Megeath says that these regular dates mean that you are going to marry me."

"Pay no attention to her. She's just a statistic. And I'm a wild datum."

"Oh, well, I've got two hundred and forty-seven dollars toward that million. 'Bye!"

Meade's prize was the usual Rosicrucian come-on, elaborately printed, and including a photograph (retouched, he was sure) of the much disputed line on the corridor wall which was alleged to prophesy, by its various discontinuities, the entire future. This one had an unusual time scale but the major events were all marked on it—the fall of Rome, the Norman Invasion, the Discovery of America, Napoleon, the World Wars.

What made it interesting was that it suddenly stopped—now.

"What about it, Potty?"

"I guess the stonecutter got tired. Or got fired. Or they got a new head priest with new ideas." He tucked it into his desk. "Thanks. I'll think about how to list it." But he got it out again, applied dividers and a magnifying glass. "It says here," he announced, "that the end comes late in August—unless that's a fly speck."

"Morning or afternoon? I have to know how to dress."

"Shoes will be worn. All God's chilluns got shoes." He put it away.

She was quiet for a moment, then said, "Potty, isn't it about time to jump?"

"Huh? Girl, don't let *that* thing affect you! That's 'silly season' stuff."

"Yes. But take a look at *your* chart."

Nevertheless he took the next afternoon off, spent it in the reference room of the main library, confirmed his opinion of soothsayers. Nostradamus was pretentiously silly, Mother Shippey was worse. In any of them you could find what you looked for.

He did find one item in Nostradamus that he liked: "The Oriental shall come forth from his seat . . . he shall pass through the sky, through the waters and the snow, and he shall strike each one with his weapon."

That sounded like what the Department of Defense expected the commies to try to do to the Western Allies.

But it was also a description of every invasion that had come out of the "heartland" in the memory of mankind. Nuts!

When he got home he found himself taking down his father's Bible and turning to Revelations. He could not find anything that he could understand but he got fascinated by the recurring use of precise numbers. Presently he thumbed through the Book at random; his eye lit on: "Boast not thyself of tomorrow; for thou knowest not what a day may bring forth." He put the Book away, feeling humbled but not cheered.

The rains started the next morning. The Master Plumbers elected Miss Star Morning "Miss Sanitary Engineering" on the same day that the morticians designated her as "The Body I would Like Best to Prepare," and her option was dropped by Fragrant Features. Congress voted $1.37 to compensate Thomas Jefferson Meeks for losses incurred while an emergency postman for the Christmas rush of 1936, approved the appointment of five lieutenant generals and one ambassador and adjourned in eight minutes. The fire extinguishers in a midwest orphanage turned out to be filled with air. The chancellor of the leading football institution sponsored a fund to send peace messages and vitamins to the Politburo. The stock market slumped nineteen points and the tickers ran two hours late. Wichita, Kansas, remained flooded while Phoenix, Arizona, cut off drinking water to areas outside city limits. And Potiphar Breen found that he had left his raincoat at Meade Barstow's rooming house.

He phoned her landlady, but Mrs. Megeath turned him over to Meade. "What are you doing home on a Friday?" he demanded.

"The theater manager laid me off. Now you'll have to marry me."

"You can't afford me. Meade—seriously, baby, what happened?"

"I was ready to leave the dump anyway. For the last six weeks the popcorn machine has been carrying the place. Today I sat through *I Was A Teen-Age Beatnik* twice. Nothing to do."

"I'll be along."

"Eleven minutes?"

"It's raining. Twenty—with luck."

It was more nearly sixty. Santa Monica Boulevard was a navigable stream; Sunset Boulevard was a subway jam. When he tried to ford the streams leading to Mrs. Megeath's house, he found that changing tires with the wheel wedged against a storm drain presented problems.

"Potty! You look like a drowned rat."

"I'll live." But presently he found himself wrapped in a blanket robe belonging to the late Mr. Megeath and sipping hot cocoa while Mrs. Megeath dried his clothing in the kitchen.

"Meade . . . I'm 'at liberty,' too."

"Huh? You quit your job?"

"Not exactly. Old Man Wiley and I have been having differences of opinion about my answers for months—too much 'Jackpot factor' in the figures I give him to turn over to clients. Not that I call it that, but he has felt that I was unduly pessimistic."

"But you were right!"

"Since when has being right endeared a man to his boss? But that wasn't why he fired me; that was just the excuse. He wants a man willing to back up the Know-Nothing program with scientific double-talk. And I wouldn't join." He went to the window. "It's raining harder."

"But they haven't got any program."

"I know that."

"Potty, you should have joined. It doesn't mean anything—I joined three months ago."

"The hell you did!"

She shrugged. "You pay your dollar and you turn up for two meetings and they leave you alone. It kept my job for another three months. What of it?"

"Uh, well—I'm sorry you did it; that's all. Forget it. Meade, the water is over the curbs out there."

"You had better stay here overnight."

"Mmm . . . I don't like to leave 'Entropy' parked out in this stuff all night. Meade?"

"Yes, Potty?"

"We're both out of jobs. How would you like to duck north into the Mojave and find a dry spot?"

"I'd love it. But look, Potty—is this a proposal, or just a proposition?"

"Don't pull that 'either-or' stuff on me. It's just a suggestion for a vacation. Do you want to take a chaperone?"

"No."

"Then pack a bag."

"Right away. But look, Potiphar—pack a bag *how?* Are you trying to tell me it's *time to jump?*"

He faced her, then looked back at the window. "I don't know," he said slowly, "but this rain might go on quite a while. Don't take anything you don't have to have—but don't leave anything behind you can't get along without."

He repossessed his clothing from Mrs. Megeath while Meade was upstairs. She came down dressed in slacks and carrying two large bags; under one arm was a battered and rakish Teddy bear. "This is Winnie."

"Winnie the Pooh?"

"No, Winnie Churchill. When I feel bad he promises me 'blood, toil, tears, and sweat;' then I feel better. You said to bring anything I couldn't do without?" She looked at him anxiously.

"Right." He took the bags. Mrs. Megeath had seemed satisfied with his explanation that they were going to visit his (mythical) aunt in Bakersfield before looking for jobs; nevertheless she embarrassed him by kissing nim good-by and telling him to "take care of my little girl."

Santa Monica Boulevard was blocked off from use. While stalled in traffic in Beverly Hills he fiddled with the car radio, getting squawks and crackling noises, then finally one station nearby: "—in effect," a harsh, high, staccato voice was saying, "the Kremlin has given us till sundown to get out of town. This is your New York Reporter, who thinks that in days like these every American must personally keep his powder dry. And now for a word from—" Breen switched it off and glanced at her face. "Don't worry," he said. "They've been talking that way for years."

"You think they are bluffing?"

"I didn't say that. I said, 'don't worry.' "

But his own packing, with her help, was clearly on a "Survival Kit" basis—canned goods, all his warm clothing, a sporting rifle he had not fired in over two years, a first-aid kit and the contents of his medicine chest. He dumped the stuff from his desk into a carton, shoved it into the back seat along with cans and books and coats and covered the plunder with all the blankets in the house. They went back up the rickety stairs for a last check.

"Potty—where's your chart?"

"Rolled up on the back seat shelf. I guess that's all—hey, wait a minute!" He went to a shelf over his desk and began taking down small, sober-looking magazines. "I dern near left behind my file of *The Western Astronomer* and of the *Proceedings of the Variable Star Association*."

"Why take them?"

"Huh? I must be nearly a year behind on both of them. Now maybe I'll have time to read."

"Hmm . . . Potty, watching you read professional journals is not my notion of a vacation."

"Quiet, woman! You took Winnie; I take these."

She shut up and helped him. He cast a longing eye at his electric calculator but decided it was too much like the White Knight's mouse trap. He could get by with his slide rule.

As the car splashed out into the street she said, "Potty, how are you fixed for cash?"

"Huh? Okay, I guess."

"I mean, leaving while the banks are closed and everything." She held up her purse. "Here's my bank. It isn't much, but we can use it."

He smiled and patted her knee. "Stout fellow! I'm sitting on my bank; I started turning everything to cash about the first of the year."

"Oh. I closed out my bank account right after we met."

"You did? You must have taken my maunderings seriously."

"I always take you seriously."

Mint Canyon was a five-mile-an-hour nightmare, with visibility limited to the tail lights of the truck ahead. When they stopped for coffee at Halfway, they confirmed what seemed evident: Cajon Pass was closed and long-haul traffic for Route 66 was being detoured through the secondary pass. At long, long last they reached the Victorville cut-off and lost some of the traffic—a good thing, as the windshield wiper on his side had quit working and they were driving by the committee system. Just short of Lancaster she said suddenly, "Potty, is this buggy equipped with a snorkel?"

"Nope."

"Then we had better stop. But I see a light off the road."

The light was an auto court. Meade settled the matter of economy versus convention by signing the book herself; they were placed in one cabin. He saw that it had twin beds and let the matter ride. Meade went to bed with her Teddy bear without even asking to be kissed goodnight. It was already gray, wet dawn.

They got up in the late afternoon and decided to stay over one more night, then push north toward Bakersfield. A high pressure area was alleged to be moving south, crowding the warm, wet mass that

smothered Southern California. They wanted to get
into it. Breen had the wiper repaired and bought two
new tires to replace his ruined spare, added some
camping items to his cargo, and bought for Meade a
.32 automatic, a lady's social-purposes gun; he gave
it to her somewhat sheepishly.

"What's this for?"

"Well, you're carrying quite a bit of cash."

"Oh. I thought maybe I was to use it to fight you
off."

"Now, Meade—"

"Never mind. Thanks, Potty."

They had finished supper and were packing the
car with their afternoon's purchases when the quake
struck. Five inches of rain in twenty-four hours,
more than three billion tons of mass suddenly loaded
on a fault already overstrained, all cut loose in one
subsonic, stomach-twisting rumble.

Meade sat down on the wet ground very suddenly;
Breen stayed upright by dancing like a logroller.
When the ground quieted down somewhat, thirty
seconds later, he helped her up. "You all right?"

"My slacks are soaked." She added pettishly, "But,
Potty, it never quakes in wet weather. *Never.*"

"It did this time."

"But—"

"Keep quiet, can't you?" He opened the car door
and switched on the radio, waited impatiently for it
to warm up. Shortly he was searching the entire dial.
"Not a confounded Los Angeles station on the air!"

"Maybe the shock busted one of your tubes?"

"Pipe down." He passed a squeal and dialed back
to it:

"—your Sunshine Station in Riverside, California.
Keep tuned to this station for the latest develop-
ments. It is as of now impossible to tell the size of
the disaster. The Colorado River aqueduct is broken;
nothing is known of the extent of the damage nor

how long it will take to repair it. So far as we know the Owens River Valley aqueduct may be intact, but all persons in the Los Angeles area are advised to conserve water. My personal advice is to stick your washtubs out into this rain; it can't last forever. If we had time, we'd play *Cool Water*, just to give you the idea. I now read from the standard disaster instructions, quote: 'Boil all water. Remain quietly in your homes and do not panic. Stay off the highways. Co-operate with the police and render—' Joe! Joe! Catch that phone! '—render aid where necessary. Do not use the telephone except for—' Flash! an uncon-firmed report from Long Beach states that the Wilmington and San Pedro waterfront is under five feet of water. I repeat, this is unconfirmed. Here's a message from the commanding general, March Field: 'official, all military personnel will report—' "

Breen switched it off. "Get in the car."

"Where are we going?"

"North."

"We've paid for the cabin. Should we—"

"Get in!"

He stopped in the town, managed to buy six five-gallon-tins and a jeep tank. He filled them with gasoline and packed them with blankets in the back seat, topping off the mess with a dozen cans of oil. Then they were rolling.

"What are we doing, Potiphar?"

"I want to get west on the valley highway."

"Any particular place west?"

"I think so. We'll see. You work the radio, but keep an eye on the road, too. That gas back there makes me nervous."

Through the town of Mojave and northwest on 466 into the Tehachapi Mountains— Reception was poor in the pass but what Meade could pick up confirmed the first impression—worse than the quake of '06, worse than San Francisco, Managua, and Long Beach taken together.

When they got down out of the mountains it was clearing locally; a few stars appeared. Breen swung left off the highway and ducked south of Bakersfield by the county road, reached the Route 99 superhighway just south of Greenfield. It was, as he had feared, already jammed with refugees; he was forced to go along with the flow for a couple of miles before he could cut west at Greenfield toward Taft. They stopped on the western outskirts of the town and ate at an all-night truckers' joint.

They were about to climb back into the car when there was suddenly "sunrise" due south. The rosy light swelled almost instantaneously, filled the sky, and died; where it had been a red-and-purple pillar of cloud was mounting, mounting—spreading to a mushroom top.

Breen stared at it, glanced at his watch, then said harshly, "Get in the car."

"Potty—that was . . . that was—"

"That was—that used to be—Los Angeles. Get in the car!"

He simply drove for several minutes. Meade seemed to be in a state of shock, unable to speak. When the sound reached them he again glanced at his watch. "Six minutes and nineteen seconds. That's about right."

"Potty—*we should have brought Mrs. Megeath.*"

"How was I to know?" he said angrily. "Anyhow, you can't transplant an old tree. If she got it, she never knew it."

"Oh, I hope so!"

"Forget it; straighten out and fly right. We're going to have all we can do to take care of ourselves. Take the flashlight and check the map. I want to turn north at Taft and over toward the coast."

"Yes, Potiphar."

"And try the radio."

She quieted down and did as she was told. The radio gave nothing, not even the Riverside station; the whole broadcast range was covered by a curious static, like rain on a window. He slowed down as they approached Taft, let her spot the turn north onto the state road, and turned into it. Almost at once a figure jumped out into the road in front of them, waved his arms violently. Breen tromped on the brake.

The man came up on the left side of the car, rapped on the window; Breen ran the glass down. Then he stared stupidly at the gun in the man's left hand. "Out of the car," the stranger said sharply. "I've got to have it." He reached inside with his right hand, groped for the door lever.

Meade reached across Breen, stuck her little lady's gun in the man's face, pulled the trigger. Breen could feel the flash on his own face, never noticed the report. The man looked puzzled, with a neat, not-yet-bloody hole in his upper lip—then slowly sagged away from the car.

"Drive on!" Meade said in a high voice.

Breen caught his breath. "Good girl—"

"Drive on! *Get rolling!*"

They followed the state road through Los Padres National Forest, stopping once to fill the tank from their cans. They turned off onto a dirt road. Meade kept trying the radio, got San Francisco once but it was too jammed with static to read. Then she got Salt Lake City, faint but clear: "—since there are no reports of anything passing our radar screen the Kansas City bomb must be assumed to have been planted rather than delivered. This is a tentative theory but—" They passed into a deep cut and lost the rest.

When the squawk box again came to life it was a new voice: "Conelrad," said a crisp voice, "coming to you over the combined networks. The rumor that Los Angeles has been hit by an atom bomb is totally unfounded. It is true that the western metropolis has suffered a severe earthquake shock but that is all. Government officials and the Red Cross are on the spot to care for the victims, but—and I repeat—there has *been no atomic bombing.* So relax and stay in your homes. Such wild rumors can damage the United States quite as much as enemy's bombs. Stay off the highways and listen for—" Breen snapped it off.

"Somebody," he said bitterly, "has again decided that 'Mama knows best.' They won't tell us any bad news."

"Potiphar," Meade said sharply, "that *was* an atom bomb . . . wasn't it?"

"It was. And now we don't know whether it was just Los Angeles—and Kansas City—or all the big cities in the country. All we know is that they are lying to us."

"Maybe I can get another station?"

"The hell with it." He concentrated on driving. The road was very bad.

As it began to get light she said, "Potty—do you know where we're going? Are we just keeping out of cities?"

"I think I do. If I'm not lost." He stared around them. "Nope, it's all right. See that hill up forward with the triple gendarmes on its profile?"

"Gendarmes?"

"Big rock pillars. That's a sure landmark. I'm looking for a private road now. It leads to a hunting lodge belonging to two of my friends—an old ranch house actually, but as a ranch it didn't pay."

"Oh. They won't mind us using it?"

He shrugged. "If they show up, we'll ask them. If they show up. They lived in Los Angeles, Meade."

"Oh. Yes, I guess so."

The private road had once been a poor grade of wagon trail; now it was almost impassable. But they finally topped a hogback from which they could see almost to the Pacific, then dropped down into a sheltered bowl where the cabin was. "All out, girl. End of the line."

Meade sighed. "It looks heavenly."

"Think you can rustle breakfast while I unload? There's probably wood in the shed. Or can you manage a wood range?"

"Just try me."

Two hours later Breen was standing on the hogback, smoking a cigarette, and staring off down to the west. He wondered if that was a mushroom cloud up San Francisco way? Probably his imagination, he decided, in view of the distance. Certainly there was nothing to be seen to the south.

Meade came out of the cabin. "Potty!"

"Up here."

She joined him, took his hand, and smiled, then snitched his cigarette and took a deep drag. She expelled it and said, "I know it's sinful of me, but I feel more peaceful than I have in months and months."

"I know."

"Did you see the canned goods in that pantry? We could pull through a hard winter here."

"We might have to."

"I suppose. I wish we had a cow."

"What would you do with a cow?"

"I used to milk four cows before I caught the school bus, every morning. I can butcher a hog, too."

"I'll try to find one."

"You do and I'll manage to smoke it." She yawned. "I'm suddenly terribly sleepy."

"So am I. And small wonder."

"Let's go to bed."

"Uh, yes. Meade?"

"Yes, Potty?"

"We may be here quite a while. You know that, don't you?"

"Yes, Potty."

"In fact it might be smart to stay put until those curves all start turning up again. They will, you know."

"Yes. I had figured that out."

He hesitated, then went on, "Meade . . . will you marry me?"

"Yes." She moved up to him.

After a time he pushed her gently away and said, "My dear, my very dear, uh—we could drive down and find a minister in some little town?"

She looked at him steadily. "That wouldn't be very bright, would it? I mean, nobody knows we're here and that's the way we want it. And besides, your car might not make it back up that road."

"No, it wouldn't be very bright. But I want to do the right thing."

"It's all right, Potty. It's *all right*."

"Well, then . . . kneel down here with me. We'll say them together."

"Yes, Potiphar." She knelt and he took her hand. He closed his eyes and prayed wordlessly.

When he opened them he said, "What's the matter?"

"Uh, the gravel hurts my knees."

"We'll stand up, then."

"No. Look, Potty, why don't we just go in the house and say them there?"

"Huh? Hell's bells, woman, we might forget to say them entirely. Now repeat after me: I, Potiphar, take thee, Meade—"

"Yes, Potiphar. I, Meade, take thee, Potiphar—"

III

"OFFICIAL: STATIONS WITHIN RANGE RELAY TWICE. EX-
ECUTIVE BULLETIN NUMBER NINE—ROAD LAWS PRE-
VIOUSLY PUBLISHED HAVE BEEN IGNORED IN MANY

INSTANCES. PATROLS ARE ORDERED TO SHOOT WITHOUT
WARNING AND PROVOST MARSHALS ARE DIRECTED TO
USE DEATH PENALTY FOR UNAUTHORIZED POSSESSION OF
GASOLINE. B.W. AND RADIATION QUARANTINE REGULA-
TIONS PREVIOUSLY ISSUED WILL BE RIGIDLY ENFORCED.
LONG LIVE THE UNITED STATES! HARLEY J. NEAL, LIEU-
TENANT GENERAL, ACTING CHIEF OF GOVERNMENT.
ALL STATIONS RELAY TWICE."

"THIS IS THE FREE RADIO AMERICA RELAY NETWORK,
PASS THIS ALONG, BOYS! GOVERNOR BRANDLEY WAS
SWORN IN TODAY AS PRESIDENT BY ACTING CHIEF JUS-
TICE ROBERTS UNDER THE RULE-OF-SUCCESSION. THE
PRESIDENT NAMED THOMAS DEWEY AS SECRETARY OF
STATE AND PAUL DOUGLAS AS SECRETARY OF DEFENSE.
HIS SECOND OFFICIAL ACT WAS TO STRIP THE RENEGADE
NEAL OF RANK AND TO DIRECT HIS ARREST BY ANY CITIZEN
OR OFFICIAL. MORE LATER, PASS THE WORD ALONG.

"HELLO, CQ, CQ, CQ. THIS IS W5KMR, FREEPORT. QRR,
QRR! ANYBODY READ ME? ANYBODY? WE'RE DYING LIKE
FLIES DOWN HERE. WHAT'S HAPPENED? STARTS WITH
FEVER AND A BURNING THIRST BUT YOU CAN'T SWALLOW.
WE NEED HELP. ANYBODY READ ME? HELLO, CQ 75 CQ
75 THIS IS W5 KILO METRO ROMEO CALLING QRR AND
CQ 75. BY FOR SOMEBODY. . . .ANYBODY!!!"

"THIS IS THE LORD'S TIME, SPONSORED BY SWAN'S ELIXIR,
THE TONIC THAT MAKES WAITING FOR THE KINGDOM OF
GOD WORTHWHILE. YOU ARE ABOUT TO HEAR A MES-
SAGE OF CHEER FROM JUDGE BROOMFIELD, ANOINTED
VICAR OF THE KINGDOM ON EARTH. BUT FIRST A BULLE-
TIN: SEND YOUR CONTRIBUTIONS TO 'MESSIAH,' CLINT,
TEXAS. DON'T TRY TO MAIL THEM: SEND THEM BY A KING-
DOM MESSENGER OR BY SOME PILGRIM JOURNEYING THIS
WAY. AND NOW THE TABERNACLE CHOIR FOLLOWED BY
THE VOICE OF THE VICAR ON EARTH—"

"—THE FIRST SYMPTOM IS LITTLE RED SPOTS IN THE ARMPITS. THEY ITCH. PUT 'EM TO BED AT ONCE AND KEEP 'EM COVERED UP WARM. THEN GO SCRUB YOURSELF AND WEAR A MASK: WE DON'T KNOW YET HOW YOU CATCH IT. PASS IT ALONG, ED."

"—NO NEW LANDINGS REPORTED ANYWHERE ON THIS CONTINENT. THE PARATROOPERS WHO ESCAPED THE ORIGINAL SLAUGHTER ARE THOUGHT TO BE HIDING OUT IN THE POCONOS. SHOOT—BUT BE CAREFUL; IT MIGHT BE AUNT TESSIE. OFF AND CLEAR, UNTIL NOON TOMORROW—"

The curves were turning up again. There was no longer doubt in Breen's mind about that. It might not even be necessary to stay up here in the Sierra Madres through the winter—though he rather thought they would. He had picked their spot to keep them west of the fallout; it would be silly to be mowed down by the tail of a dying epidemic, or be shot by a nervous vigilante, when a few months' wait would take care of everything.

Besides, he had chopped all that firewood. He looked at his calloused hands—he had done all that work and, by George, he was going to enjoy the benefits!

He was headed out to the hogback to wait for sunset and do an hour's reading; he glanced at his car as he passed it, thinking that he would like to try the radio. He suppressed the yen; two thirds of his reserve gasoline was gone already just from keeping the battery charged for the radio—and here it was only December. He really ought to cut it down to twice a week. But it meant a lot to catch the noon bulletin of Free America and then twiddle the dial a few minutes to see what else he could pick up.

But for the past three days Free America had not been on the air—solar static maybe, or perhaps just a power failure. But that rumor that President Brandley had been assassinated—while it hadn't come from the Free radio . . . and it hadn't been denied by them, either, which was a good sign. Still, it worried him.

And that other story that lost Atlantis had pushed up during the quake period and that the Azores were now a little continent—almost certainly a hang-over of the "silly season"—but it would be nice to hear a follow-up.

Rather sheepishly he let his feet carry him to the car. It wasn't fair to listen when Meade wasn't around. He warmed it up, slowly spun the dial, once around and back. Not a peep at full gain, nothing but a terrible amount of static. Served him right.

He climbed the hogback, sat down on the bench he had dragged up there—their "memorial bench," sacred to the memory of the time Meade had hurt her knees on the gravel—sat down and sighed. His lean belly was stuffed with venison and corn fritters; he lacked only tobacco to make him completely happy. The evening cloud colors were spectacularly beautiful and the weather was extremely balmy for December; both, he thought, caused by volcanic dust, with perhaps an assist from atom bombs.

Surprising how fast things went to pieces when they started to skid! And surprising how quickly they were going back together, judging by the signs. A curve reaches trough and then starts right back up. World War III was the shortest big war on record—forty cities gone, counting Moscow and the other slave cities as well as the American ones—and then *whoosh!* neither side fit to fight. Of course, the fact that both sides had thrown their ICBMs over the pole through the most freakish arctic weather since Peary invented the place had a lot to do with it, he supposed. It was amazing that any of the Russians paratroop transports had gotten through at all.

He sighed and pulled the November 1951 copy of

the *Western Astronomer* out of his pocket. Where
was he? Oh, yes, *Some Notes on the Stability of
G-Type Stars with Especial Reference to Sol,* by A.
G. M. Dynkowski, Lenin Institute, translated by
Heinrich Ley, F. R. A. S. Good boy, Ski—sound
mathematician. Very clever application of harmonic
series and tightly reasoned. He started to thumb for
his place when he noticed a footnote that he had
missed. Dynkowski's own name carried down to it:
"This monograph was denounced by *Pravda* as romantic reactionariism shortly after it was published.
Professor Dynkowski has been unreported since and
must be presumed to be liquidated."

The poor geek! Well, he probably would have
been atomized by now anyway, along with the goons
who did him in. He wondered if they really had
gotten all the Russki paratroopers? Well, he had
killed his quota; if he hadn't gotten that doe within a
quarter mile of the cabin and headed right back,
Meade would have had a bad time. He had shot
them in the back, the swine! and buried them beyond
the woodpile—and then it had seemed a shame to
skin and eat an innocent deer while those lice got
decent burial.

Aside from mathematics, just two things worth
doing—kill a man and love a woman. He had done
both; he was rich.

He settled down to some solid pleasure. Dynkowski
was a treat. Of course, it was old stuff that a G-type
star, such as the sun, was potentially unstable; a
G-O star could explode, slide right off the Russell
diagram, and end up as a white dwarf. But no one
before Dynkowski had defined the exact conditions
for such a catastrophe, nor had anyone else devised
mathematical means of diagnosing the instability and
describing its progress.

He looked up to rest his eyes from the fine print
and saw that the sun was obscured by a thin low

cloud—one of those unusual conditions where the
filtering effect is just right to permit a man to view
the sun clearly with the naked eye. Probably volcanic dust in the air, he decided, acting almost like
smoked glass.

He looked again. Either he had spots before his
eyes or that was one fancy big sun spot. He had
heard of being able to see them with the naked eye,
but it had never happened to him. He longed for a
telescope.

He blinked. Yep, it was still there, upper right. A
big spot—no wonder the car radio sounded like a
Hitler speech.

He turned back and continued on to the end of the
article, being anxious to finish before the light failed.
At first his mood was sheerest intellectual pleasure at
the man's tight mathematical reasoning. A 3% imbalance in the solar constant—yes, that was standard
stuff; the sun would *nova* with that much change.
But Dynkowski went further; by means of a novel
mathematical operator which he had dubbed "yokes"
he bracketed the period in a star's history when this
could happen and tied it down further with secondary, tertiary, and quaternary yokes, showing exactly
the time of highest probablility. Beautiful! Dynkowski
even assigned dates to the extreme limit of his primary yoke, as a good statistician should.

But, as he went back and reviewed the equations,
his mood changed from intellectual to personal.
Dynkowski was not talking about just any G-O star;
in the latter part he meant old Sol himself, Breen's
personal sun, the big boy out there with the oversized freckle on his face.

That was one hell of a big freckle! It was a hole you
could chuck Jupiter into and not make a splash. He
could see it very clearly now.

Everybody talks about "when the stars grow old
and the sun grows cold"—but it's an impersonal con-

cept, like one's own death. Breen started thinking
about it very personally. How long would it take,
from the instant the imbalance was triggered until
the expanding wave front engulfed earth? The mechanics couldn't be solved without a calculator even
though they were implicit in the equations in front of
him. Half an hour, for a horseback guess, from in-
citement until the earth went *phutt!*

It hit him with gentle melancholy. No more? Never
again? Colorado on a cool morning . . . the Boston
Post road with autumn wood smoke tanging the air
. . . Bucks county bursting in the spring. The wet
smells of the Fulton Fish Market—no, that was gone
already. Coffee at the *Morning Call*. No more wild
strawberries on a hillside in Jersey, hot and sweet as
lips. Dawn in the South Pacific with the light airs
cool velvet under your shirt and never a sound but
the chuckling of the water against the sides of the old
rust bucket—what was her name? That was a long
time ago—the *S. S. Mary Brewster*.

No more moon if the earth was gone. Stars—but
no one to look at them.

He looked back at the dates bracketing Dynkowski's
probability yoke. "Thine Alabaster Cities gleam, un-
dimmed by—"

He suddenly felt the need for Meade and stood up.

She was coming out to meet him. "Hello, Potty!
Safe to come in now—I've finished the dishes."

"I should help."

"You do the man's work; I'll do the woman's work.
That's fair." She shaded her eyes. "What a sunset!
We ought to have volcanoes blowing their tops every
year."

"Sit down and we'll watch it."

She sat beside him and he took her hand. "Notice
the sun spot? You can see it with your naked eye."

She stared. "Is that a sun spot? It looks as if
somebody had taken a bite out of it."

He squinted his eyes at it again. Damned if it didn't look bigger!

Meade shivered. "I'm chilly. Put your arm around me." He did so with his free arm, continuing to hold hands with the other. It *was* bigger—the thing was growing.

What good is the race of man? Monkeys, he thought, monkeys with a spot of poetry in them, cluttering and wasting a second-string planet near a third-string star. But sometimes they finish in style.

She snuggled to him. "Keep me warm."

"It will be warmer soon. I mean I'll keep you warm."

"Dear Potty."

She looked up. "Potty—something funny is happening to the sunset."

"No darling—to the sun."

"I'm frightened."

"I'm here, dear."

He glanced down at the journal, still open beside him. He did not need to add up the two figures and divide by two to reach the answer. Instead he clutched fiercely at her hand, knowing with an unexpected and overpowering burst of sorrow that this was

The End

By His Bootstraps

By His Bootstraps

Bob Wilson did not see the circle grow.

Nor, for that matter, did he see the stranger who stepped out of the circle and stood staring at the back of Wilson's neck—stared, and breathed heavily, as if laboring under strong and unusual emotion.

Wilson had no reason to suspect that anyone else was in his room; he had every reason to expect the contrary. He had locked himself in his room for the purpose of completing his thesis in one sustained drive. He *had* to—tomorrow was the last day for submission, yesterday the thesis had been no more than a title: "An Investigation into Certain Mathematical Aspects of a Rigor of Metaphysics."

Fifty-two cigarettes, four pots of coffee, and thirteen hours of continuous work had added seven thousand words to the title. As to the validity of his thesis he was far too groggy to give a damn. Get it done, was his only thought, get it done, turn it in, take three stiff drinks and sleep for a week.

He glanced up and let his eyes rest on his wardrobe door, behind which he had cached a gin bottle, nearly full. No, he admonished himself, one more drink and you'll never finish it, Bob, old son.

49

The stranger behind him said nothing.

Wilson resumed typing. "—nor is it valid to assume that a conceivable proposition is necessarily a possible proposition, even when it is possible to formulate mathematics which describes the proposition with exactness. A case in point is the concept 'Time Travel.' Time travel may be imagined and its necessities may be formulated under any and all theories of time, formulae which resolve the paradoxes of each theory. Nevertheless, we know certain things about the empirical nature of time which preclude the possibility of the conceivable proposition. Duration is an attribute of consciousness and not of the plenum. It has no *Ding an Sich*. Therefore—"

A key of the typewriter stuck, three more jammed up on top of it. Wilson swore dully and reached forward to straighten out the cantankerous machinery. "Don't bother with it," he heard a voice say. "It's a lot of utter hogwash anyhow."

Wilson sat up with a jerk, then turned his head slowly around. He fervently hoped that there was someone behind him. Otherwise—

He perceived the stranger with relief. "Thank God," he said to himself. "For a moment I thought I had come unstuck." His relief turned to extreme annoyance. "What the devil are you doing in my room?" he demanded. He shoved back his chair, got up and strode over to the one door. It was still locked, and bolted on the inside.

The windows were no help; they were adjacent to his desk and three stories above a busy street. "How *did* you get in?" he added.

"Through that," answered the stranger, hooking a thumb toward the circle. Wilson noticed it for the first time, blinked his eyes and looked again. There it hung between them and the wall, a great disk of nothing, of the color one sees when the eyes are shut tight.

Wilson shook his head vigorously. The circle remained. "Gosh," he thought, "I was right the first time. I wonder when I slipped my trolley?" He advanced toward the disk, put out a hand to touch it.

"Don't!" snapped the stranger.

"Why not?" said Wilson edgily. Nevertheless he paused.

"I'll explain. But let's have a drink first." He walked directly to the wardrobe, opened it, reached in and took out the bottle of gin without looking.

"Hey!" yelled Wilson. "What are you doing there? That's *my* liquor."

"*Your* liquor—" The stranger paused for a moment. "Sorry. You don't mind if I have a drink, do you?"

"I suppose not," Bob Wilson conceded in a surly tone. "Pour me one while you're about it."

"O. K.," agreed the stranger, "then I'll explain."

"It had better be good," Wilson said ominously. Nevertheless he drank his drink and looked the stranger over.

He saw a chap about the same size as himself and much the same age—perhaps a little older, though a three-day growth of beard may have accounted for that impression. The stranger had a black eye and a freshly cut and badly swollen upper lip. Wilson decided he did not like the chap's face. Still, there was something familiar about the face; he felt that he should have recognized it, that he had seen it many times before under different circumstances.

"Who are you?" he asked suddenly.

"Me?" said his guest. "Don't you recognize me?"

"I'm not sure," admitted Wilson. "Have I ever seen you before?"

"Well—not exactly," the other temporized. "Skip it—you wouldn't know about it."

"What's your name?"

"My name? Uh . . . just call me Joe."

Wilson set down his glass. "O. K., Joe Whatever-your-name-is, trot out that explanation and make it snappy."

"I'll do that," agreed Joe. "That dingus I came through"—he pointed to the circle—"that's a Time Gate."

"A what?"

"A Time Gate. Time flows along side by side on each side of the Gate, but some thousands of years apart—just how many thousands I don't know. But for the next couple of hours that Gate is open. You can walk into the future just by stepping through that circle." The stranger paused.

Bob drummed on the desk. "Go ahead. I'm listening. It's a nice story."

"You don't believe me, do you? I'll show you." Joe got up, went again to the wardrobe and obtained Bob's hat, his prized and only hat, which he had mistreated into its present battered grandeur through six years of undergraduate and graduate life. Joe chucked it toward the impalpable disk.

It struck the surface, went on through with no apparent resistance, disappeared from sight.

Wilson got up, walked carefully around the circle and examined the bare floor. "A neat trick," he conceded. "Now I'll thank you to return to me my hat."

The stranger shook his head. "You can get it for yourself when you pass through."

"Huh?"

"That's right. Listen—" Briefly the stranger repeated his explanation about the Time Gate. Wilson, he insisted, had an opportunity that comes once in a millennium—if he would only hurry up and climb through that circle. Furthermore, though Joe could not explain in detail at the moment, it was very important that Wilson go through.

* * *

Bob Wilson helped himself to a second drink, and then a third. He was beginning to feel both good and argumentative. "Why?" he said flatly.

Joe looked exasperated. "Dammit, if you'd just step through once, explanations wouldn't be necessary. However—" According to Joe, there was an old guy on the other side who needed Wilson's help. With Wilson's help the three of them would run the country. The exact nature of the help Joe could not or would not specify. Instead he bore down on the unique possibilities for high adventure. "You don't want to slave your life away teaching numskulls in some freshwater college," he insisted. "This is your chance. Grab it!"

Bob Wilson admitted to himself that a Ph.D. and an appointment as an instructor was not his idea of existence. Still, it beat working for a living. His eye fell on the gin bottle, its level now deplorably lowered. That explained it. He got up unsteadily.

"No, my dear fellow," he stated, "I'm not going to climb on your merry-go-round. You know why?"

"Why?"

"Because I'm drunk, that's why. You're not there at all. *That* ain't there." He gestured widely at the circle. "There ain't anybody here but me, and I'm drunk. Been working too hard," he added apologetically. "I'm goin' to bed."

"You're not drunk."

"I *am* drunk. Peter Piper pepped a pick of pippered peckles." He moved toward his bed.

Joe grabbed his arm. "You can't do that," he said. "Let him alone!"

They both swung around. Facing them, standing directly in front of the circle was a third man. Bob looked at the newcomer, looked back at Joe, blinked his eyes and tried to focus them. The two looked a good bit alike, he thought, enough alike to be brothers. Or maybe he was seeing double. Bad stuff, gin.

Should 'ave switched to rum a long time ago. Good stuff, rum. You could drink it, or take a bath in it. No, that was gin—he meant Joe.

How silly! Joe was the one with the black eye. He wondered why he had ever been confused.

Then who was this other lug? Couldn't a couple of friends have a quiet drink together without people butting in?

"Who are you?" he said with quiet dignity.

The newcomer turned his head, then looked at Joe. "*He* knows me," he said meaningly.

Joe looked him over slowly. "Yes," he said, "yes, I suppose I do. But what the deuce are you here for? And why are you trying to bust up the plan?"

"No time for long-winded explanations. I know more about it than you do—you'll concede that—and my judgment is bound to be better than yours. He doesn't go through the Gate."

"I don't concede anything of the sort—"

The telephone rang.

"Answer it!" snapped the newcomer.

Bob was about to protest the peremptory tone, but decided he wouldn't. He lacked the phlegmatic temperament necessary to ignore a ringing telephone. "Hello?"

"Hello," he was answered. "Is that Bob Wilson?"

"Yes. Who is this?"

"Never mind. I just wanted to be sure you were there. I *thought* you would be. You're right in the groove, kid, right in the groove."

Wilson heard a chuckle, then the click of the disconnection. "Hello," he said. "Hello!" He jiggled the bar a couple of times, then hung up.

"What was it?" asked Joe.

"Nothing. Some nut with a misplaced sense of humor." The telephone bell rang again. Wilson added, "There he is again," and picked up the receiver.

"Listen, you butterfly-brained ape! I'm a busy man, and this is *not* a public telephone."

"Why, Bob!" came a hurt feminine voice.

"Huh? Oh, it's you, Genevieve. Look—I'm sorry. I apologize—"

"Well, I should think you would!"

"You don't understand, honey. A guy has been pestering me over the phone and I thought it was him. You know I wouldn't talk that way to you, Babe."

"Well, I should think not. Particularly after all you said to me this afternoon, and all we *meant* to each other."

"Huh? This afternoon? Did you say *this* afternoon?"

"Of course. But what I called up about was this: You left your hat in my apartment. I noticed it a few minutes after you had gone and just thought I'd call and tell you where it is. Anyhow," she added coyly, "it gave me an excuse to hear your voice again."

"Sure. Fine," he said mechanically. "Look, Babe, I'm a little mixed up about this. Trouble I've had all day long, and more trouble now. I'll look you up tonight and straighten it out. But I *know* I didn't leave your hat in my apartment—"

"*Your* hat, silly!"

"Huh? Oh, sure! Anyhow, I'll see you tonight. 'Bye." He rang off hurriedly. Gosh, he thought, that woman is getting to be a problem. Hallucinations. He turned to his two companions.

"Very well, Joe. I'm ready to go if you are." He was not sure just when or why he had decided to go through the time gadget, but he had. Who did this other mug think he was, anyhow, trying to interfere with a man's freedom of choice?

"Fine!" said Joe, in a relieved voice. "Just step through. That's all there is to it."

"No, you don't!" It was the ubiquitous stranger. He stepped between Wilson and the Gate.

Bob Wilson faced him. "Listen, you! You come butting in here like you think I was a bum. If you don't like it, go jump in the lake—and I'm just the kind of guy who can do it! You and who else?"

The stranger reached out and tried to collar him. Wilson let go a swing, but not a good one. It went by nothing faster than parcel post. The stranger walked under it and let him have a mouthful of knuckles— large, hard ones. Joe closed in rapidly, coming to Bob's aid. They traded punches in a free-for-all, with Bob joining in enthusiastically but inefficiently. The only punch he landed was on Joe, theoretically his ally. However, he had intended it for the third man.

It was this *faux pas* which gave the stranger an opportunity to land a clean left jab on Wilson's face. It was inches higher than the button, but in Bob's bemused condition it was sufficient to cause him to cease taking part in the activities.

Bob Wilson came slowly to awareness of his surroundings. He was seated on a floor which seemed a little unsteady. Someone was bending over him. "Are you all right?" the figure inquired.

"I guess so," he answered thickly. His mouth pained him; he put his hand to it, got it sticky with blood. "My head hurts."

"I should think it would. You came through head over heels. I think you hit your head when you landed."

Wilson's thoughts were coming back into confused focus. Came through? He looked more closely at his succorer. He saw a middle-aged man with gray-shot bushy hair and a short, neatly trimmed beard. He was dressed in what Wilson took to be purple lounging pajamas.

But the room in which he found himself bothered him even more. It was circular and the ceiling was arched so subtly that it was difficult to say how high it was. A steady glareless light filled the room from no apparent source. There was no furniture save for a high dais or pulpit-shaped object near the wall facing him. "Came through? Came through what?"

"The Gate, of course." There was something odd about the man's accent. Wilson could not place it, save for a feeling that English was not a tongue he was accustomed to speaking.

Wilson looked over his shoulder in the direction of the other's gaze, and saw the circle.

That made his head ache even more. "Oh, Lord," he thought, "now I really am nuts. Why don't I wake up?" He shook his head to clear it.

That was a mistake. The top of his head did not quite come off—not quite. And the circle stayed where it was, a simple locus hanging in the air, its flat depth filled with the amorphous colors and shapes of no-vision. "Did I come through that?"

"Yes."

"Where am I?"

"In the Hall of the Gate in the High Palace of Norkaal. But what is more important is *when* you are. You have gone forward a little more than thirty thousand years."

"Now I know I'm crazy," thought Wilson. He got up unsteadily and moved toward the Gate.

The older man put a hand on his shoulder. "Where are you going?"

"Back!"

"Not so fast. You will go back all right—I give you my word on that. But let me dress your wounds first. And you should rest. I have some explanations to make to you, and there is an errand you can do for me when you get back—to our mutual advantage. There is a great future in store for you and me, my boy—a great future!"

Wilson paused uncertainly. The elder man's insistence was vaguely disquieting. "I don't like this."

The other eyed him narrowly. "Wouldn't you like a drink before you go?"

Wilson most assuredly would. Right at the moment a stiff drink seemed the most desirable thing on earth—or in time. "O.K."

"Come with me." The older man led him back of the structure near the wall and through a door which led into a passageway. He walked briskly; Wilson hurried to keep up.

"By the way," he asked, as they continued down the long passage, "what is your name?"

"My name? You may call me Diktor—everyone else does."

"O. K., Diktor. Do you want my name?"

"Your name?" Diktor chuckled. "I know your name. It's Bob Wilson."

"Huh? Oh—I suppose Joe told you."

"Joe? I know no one by that name."

"You don't? He seemed to know you. Say—maybe you aren't that guy I was supposed to see."

"But I am. I have been expecting you—in a way. Joe . . . Joe—Oh!" Diktor chuckled. "It had slipped my mind for a moment. He told you to call him Joe, didn't he?"

"Isn't it his name?"

"It's as good a name as any other. Here we are." He ushered Wilson into a small, but cheerful room. It contained no furniture of any sort, but the floor was soft and warm as live flesh. "Sit down. I'll be back in a moment."

Bob looked around for something to sit on, then turned to ask Diktor for a chair. But Diktor was gone, furthermore the door through which they had entered was gone. Bob sat down on the comfortable floor and tried not to worry.

Diktor returned promptly. Wilson saw the door dilate to let him in, but did not catch on to how it was done. Diktor was carrying a carafe, which gurgled pleasantly, and a cup. "Mud in your eye," he said heartily and poured a good four fingers. "Drink up."

Bob accepted the cup. "Aren't you drinking?"

"Presently. I want to attend to your wounds first."

"O.K." Wilson tossed off the first drink in almost indecent haste—it was good stuff, a little like Scotch, he decided, but smoother and not as dry—while Diktor worked deftly with salves that smarted at first, then soothed. "Mind if I have another?"

"Help yourself."

Bob drank more slowly the second cup. He did not finish it; it slipped from relaxed fingers, spilling a ruddy, brown stain across the floor. He snored.

Bob Wilson woke up feeling fine and completely rested. He was cheerful without knowing why. He lay relaxed, eyes still closed, for a few moments and let his soul snuggle back into his body. This was going to be a good day, he felt. Oh, yes—he had finished that double-damned thesis. No, he hadn't either! He sat up with a start.

The sight of the strange walls around him brought him back into continuity. But before he had time to worry—at once, in fact—the door relaxed and Diktor stepped in. "Feeling better?"

"Why, yes, I do. Say, what is this?"

"We'll get to that. How about some breakfast?"

In Wilson's scale of evaluations breakfast rated just after life itself and ahead of the chance of immortality. Diktor conducted him to another room—the first that he had seen possessing windows. As a matter of fact half the room was open, a balcony hanging high over a green countryside. A soft, warm, summer breeze wafted through the place. They broke their fast in luxury, Roman style, while Diktor explained.

Bob Wilson did not follow the explanations as closely as he might have done, because his attention was diverted by the maidservants who served the meal. The first came in bearing a great tray of fruit on her head. The fruit was gorgeous. So was the girl. Search as he would he could discern no fault in her.

Her costume lent itself to the search.

She came first to Diktor, and with a single, graceful movement dropped to one knee, removed the tray from her head, and offered it to him. He helped himself to a small, red fruit and waved her away. She then offered it to Bob in the same delightful manner.

"As I was saying," continued Diktor, "it is not certain where the High Ones came from or where they went when they left Earth. I am inclined to think they went away into Time. In any case they ruled more than twenty thousand years and completely obliterated human culture as you knew it. What is more important to you and to me is the effect they had on the human psyche. One twentieth-century style go-getter can accomplish just about anything he wants to accomplish around here—Aren't you listening?"

"Huh? Oh, yes, sure. Say, that's one mighty pretty girl." His eyes still rested on the exit through which she had disappeared.

"Who? Oh, yes, I suppose so. She's not exceptionally beautiful as women go around here."

"That's hard to believe. I could learn to get along with a girl like that."

"You like her? Very well, she is yours."

"Huh?"

"She's a slave. Don't get indignant. They are slaves by nature. If you like her, I'll make you a present of her. It will make her happy." The girl had just returned. Diktor called to her in a language strange to Bob. "Her name is Arma," he said in an aside, then spoke to her briefly.

Arma giggled. She composed her face quickly, and, moving over to where Wilson reclined, dropped on both knees to the floor and lowered her head, with both hands cupped before her. "Touch her forehead," Diktor instructed.

Bob did so. The girl arose and stood waiting placidly by his side. Diktor spoke to her. She looked puzzled, but moved out of the room. "I told her that, notwithstanding her new status, you wished her to continue serving breakfast."

Diktor resumed his explanations while the service of the meal continued. The next course was brought in by Arma and another girl. When Bob saw the second girl he let out a low whistle. He realized he had been a little hasty in letting Diktor give him Arma. Either the standard of pulchritude had gone up incredibly, he decided, or Diktor went to a lot of trouble in selecting his servants.

"—for that reason," Diktor was saying, "it is necessary that you go back through the Time Gate at once. Your first job is to bring this other chap back. Then there is one other task for you to do, and we'll be sitting pretty. After that it is share and share alike for you and me. And there is plenty to share, I—You aren't listening!"

"Sure I was, chief. I heard every word you said." He fingered his chin. "Say, have you got a razor I could borrow? I'd like to shave."

Diktor swore softly in two languages. "Keep your eyes off those wenches and listen to me! There's work to be done."

"Sure, sure. I understand that—and I'm your man. When do we start?" Wilson had made up his mind some time ago—just shortly after Arma had entered with the tray of fruit, in fact. He felt as if he had walked into some extremely pleasant dream. If cooperation with Diktor would cause that dream to continue, so be it. To hell with an academic career!

Anyhow, all Diktor wanted was for him to go back

where he started and persuade another guy to go through the Gate. The worst that could happen was for him to find himself back in the twentieth century. What could he lose?

Diktor stood up. "Let's get on with it," he said shortly, "before you get your attention diverted again. Follow me." He set off at a brisk pace with Wilson behind him.

Diktor took him to the Hall of the Gate and stopped. "All you have to do," he said, "is to step through the Gate. You will find yourself back in your own room, in your own time. Persuade the man you find there to go through the Gate. We have need of him. Then come back yourself."

Bob held up a hand and pinched thumb and forefinger together. "It's in the bag, boss. Consider it done." He started to step through the Gate.

"Wait!" commanded Diktor. "You are not used to time travel. I warn you that you are going to get one hell of a shock when you step through. This other chap—you'll recognize him."

"Who is he?"

"I won't tell you because you wouldn't understand. But you will when you see him. Just remember this— There are some very strange paradoxes connected with time travel. Don't let anything you see throw you. You do what I tell you to and you'll be all right."

"Paradoxes don't worry me," Bob said confidently. "Is that all? I'm ready."

"One minute." Diktor stepped behind the raised dais. His head appeared above the side a moment later. "I've set the controls. O.K. Go!"

Bob Wilson stepped through the locus known as the Time Gate.

There was no particular sensation connected with the transition. It was like stepping through a curtained doorway into a darker room. He paused for a moment on the other side and let his eyes adjust to the dimmer light. He was, he saw, indeed in his own room.

There was a man in it, seated at his own desk. Diktor had been right about that. This, then, was the chap he was to send back through the Gate. Diktor had said he would recognize him. Well, let's see who it is.

He felt a passing resentment at finding someone at *his* desk in *his* room, then thought better of it. After all, it was just a rented room; when he disappeared, no doubt it had been rented again. He had no way of telling how long he had been gone—shucks, it might be the middle of next week!

The chap did look vaguely familiar, although all he could see was his back. Who was it? Should he speak to him, cause him to turn around? He felt vaguely reluctant to do so until he knew who it was. He rationalized the feeling by telling himself that it was desirable to know with whom he was dealing before he attempted anything as outlandish as persuading this man to go through the Gate.

The man at the desk continued typing, paused to snuff out a cigarette by laying it in an ash tray, then stamping it with a paper weight.

Bob Wilson knew that gesture.

Chills trickled down his back. "If he lights his next one," he whispered to himself, "the way I think he is going to—"

The man at the desk took out another cigarette, tamped it on one end, turned it and tamped the other, straightened and crimped the paper on one end carefully against his left thumbnail and placed that end in his mouth.

Wilson felt the blood beating in his neck. *Sitting there with his back to him was himself, Bob Wilson!*

He felt that he was going to faint. He closed his eyes and steadied himself on a chair back. "I knew it," he thought, "the whole thing is absurd. I'm crazy. I know I'm crazy. Some sort of split personality. I shouldn't have worked so hard."

The sound of typing continued.

He pulled himself together, and reconsidered the matter.

Diktor had warned him that he was due for a shock, a shock that could not be explained ahead of time, because it could not be believed. "All right—suppose I'm not crazy. If time travel can happen at all, there is no reason why I can't come back and see myself doing something I did in the past. If I'm sane, that is what I'm doing.

"And if I am crazy, it doesn't make a damn bit of difference what I do!

"And furthermore," he added to himself, "if I'm crazy, maybe I can stay crazy and go back through the Gate! No, that does not make sense. Neither does anything else—the hell with it!"

He crept forward softly and peered over the shoulder of his double. "Duration is an attribute of the consciousness," he read, "and not of the plenum."

"That tears it," he thought, "right back where I started, and watching myself write my thesis."

The typing continued. "It has no *Ding an Sich*. Therefore—" A key stuck, and others piled up on top of it. His double at the desk swore and reached out a hand to straighten the keys.

"Don't bother with it," Wilson said on sudden impulse. "It's a lot of utter hogwash anyhow."

The other Bob Wilson sat up with a jerk, then looked slowly around. An expression of surprise gave way to annoyance. "What the devil are you doing in my room?" he demanded. Without waiting for an answer he got up, went quickly to the door and examined the lock. "How did you get in?"

"This," thought Wilson, "is going to be difficult."

"Through that," Wilson answered, pointing to the

Time Gate. His double looked where he had pointed, did a double take, then advanced cautiously and started to touch it.

"Don't!" yelled Wilson.

The other checked himself. "Why not?" he demanded.

Just why he must not permit his other self to touch the Gate was not clear to Wilson, but he had had an unmistakable feeling of impending disaster when he saw it about to happen. He temporized by saying, "I'll explain. But let's have a drink." A drink was a good idea in any case. There had never been a time when he needed one more than he did right now. Quite automatically he went to his usual cache of liquor in the wardrobe and took out the bottle he expected to find there.

"Hey!" protested the other. "What are you doing there? That's *my* liquor."

"*Your* liquor—" Hell's bells! It was *his* liquor. No, it wasn't; it was—*their* liquor. Oh, the devil! It was much too mixed up to try to explain. "Sorry. You don't mind if I have a drink, do you?"

"I suppose not," his double said grudgingly. "Pour me one while you're about it."

"O. K.," Wilson assented, "then I'll explain." It was going to be much, much too difficult to explain until he had had a drink, he felt. As it was, he couldn't explain it fully to himself.

"It had better be good," the other warned him, and looked Wilson over carefully while he drank his drink.

Wilson watched his younger self scrutinizing him with confused and almost insupportable emotions. Couldn't the stupid fool recognize his own face when he saw it in front of him? If he could not *see* what the situation was, how in the world was he ever going to make it clear to him?

It had slipped his mind that his face was barely recognizable in any case, being decidedly battered and unshaven. Even more important, he failed to take into account the fact that a person does not look at his own face, even in mirrors, in the same frame of mind with which he regards another's face. No sane person ever expects to see his own face hanging on another.

Wilson could see that his companion was puzzled by his appearance, but it was equally clear that no recognition took place. "Who are you?" the other man asked suddenly.

"Me?" replied Wilson. "Don't you recognize me?"

"I'm not sure. Have I ever seen you before?"

"Well—not exactly," Wilson stalled. How did you go about telling another guy that the two of you were a trifle closer than twins? "Skip it—you wouldn't know about it."

"What's your name?"

"My name? Uh—" Oh, oh! This was going to be sticky! The whole situation was utterly ridiculous. He opened his mouth, tried to form the words "Bob Wilson," then gave up with a feeling of utter futility. Like many a man before him, he found himself forced into a lie because the truth simply would not be believed. "Just call me Joe," he finished lamely.

He felt suddenly startled at his own words. It was at this point that he realized that he was *in fact*, "Joe," the Joe whom he had encountered once before. That he had landed back in his own room at the very time at which he had ceased working on his thesis he already realized, but he had not had time to think the matter through. Hearing himself refer to himself as Joe slapped him in the face with the realization that this was not simply a similar scene, but the *same* scene he had lived through once before— save that he was living through it from a different viewpoint.

At least he thought it was the same scene. Did it differ in any respect? He could not be sure as he could not recall, word for word, what the conversation had been.

For a complete transcript of the scene that lay dormant in his memory he felt willing to pay twenty-five dollars cash, plus sales tax.

Wait a minute now—he was under no compulsion. He was sure of that. Everything he did and said was the result of his own free will. Even if he couldn't remember the script, there were some things he *knew* "Joe" hadn't said. "Mary had a little lamb," for example. He would recite a nursery rhyme and get off this damned repetitious treadmill. He opened his mouth—

"O. K., Joe Whatever-your-name-is," his alter ego remarked, setting down a glass which had contained, until recently, a quarter pint of gin, "trot out that explanation and make it snappy."

He opened his mouth again to answer the question, then closed it. "Steady, son, steady," he told himself. "You're a free agent. You want to recite a nursery rhyme—go ahead and do it. Don't answer him; go ahead and recite it—and break this vicious circle."

But under the unfriendly, suspicious eye of the man opposite him he found himself totally unable to recall any nursery rhyme. His mental processes stuck on dead center.

He capitulated. "I'll do that. That dingus I came through—that's a Time Gate."

"A what?"

"A Time Gate. Time flows along side by side on each side—" As he talked he felt sweat breaking out on him; he felt reasonably sure that he was explaining in exactly the same words in which explanation had first been offered to *him*. "—into the future just by stepping through that circle." He stopped and wiped his forehead.

"Go ahead," said the other implacably. "I'm listening. It's a nice story."

Bob suddenly wondered if the other man *could* be himself. The stupid arrogant dogmatism of the man's manner infuriated him. All right, all right! He'd show him. He strode suddenly over to the wardrobe, took out his hat and threw it through the Gate.

His opposite number watched the hat snuff out of existence with expressionless eyes, then stood up and went around in back of the Gate, walking with the careful steps of a man who is a little bit drunk, but determined not to show it. "A neat trick," he applauded, after satisfying himself that the hat was gone, "now I'll thank you to return to me my hat."

Wilson shook his head. "You can get it for yourself when you pass through," he answered absent-mindedly. He was pondering the problem of how many hats there were on the other side of the Gate.

"Huh?"

"That's right. Listen—" Wilson did his best to explain persuasively what it was he wanted his earlier *persona* to do. Or rather to cajole. Explanations were out of the question, in any honest sense of the word. He would have preferred attempting to explain tensor calculus to an Australian aborigine, even though he did not understand that esoteric mathematics himself.

The other man was not helpful. He seemed more interested in nursing the gin than be did in following Wilson's implausible protestations.

"Why?" he interrupted pugnaciously.

"Dammit," Wilson answered, "if you'd just step through once, explanations wouldn't be necessary. However—" He continued with a synopsis of Diktor's proposition. He realized with irritation that Diktor had been exceedingly sketchy with *his* explanations.

He was forced to hit only the high spots in the logical parts of his argument, and bear down on the emotional appeal. He was on safe ground there—no one knew better than he did himself how fed up the earlier Bob Wilson had been with the petty drudgery and stuffy atmosphere of an academic career. "You don't want to slave your life away teaching numskulls in some fresh-water college," he concluded. "This is your chance. Grab it!"

Wilson watched his companion narrowly and thought he detected a favorable response. He definitely seemed interested. But the other set his glass down carefully, stared at the gin bottle, and at last replied:

"My dear fellow, I am not going to climb on your merry-go-round. You know why?"

"Why?"

"Because I'm drunk, that's why. You're not there at all. *That* ain't there." He gestured widely at the Gate, nearly fell, and recovered himself with effort. "There ain't anybody here but me, and I'm drunk. Been working too hard," he mumbled, " 'm goin' to bed."

"You're not drunk," Wilson protested unhopefully. "Damnation," he thought, "a man who can't hold his liquor shouldn't drink."

"I *am* drunk. Peter Piper pepped a pick of pippered peckles." He lumbered over toward the bed.

Wilson grabbed his arm. "You can't do that."

"Let him alone!"

Wilson swung around, saw a third man standing in front of the Gate—recognized him with a sudden shock. His own recollection of the sequence of events was none too clear in his memory, since he had been somewhat intoxicated—damned near boiled, he admitted—the first time he had experienced this particular busy afternoon. He realized that he should have anticipated the arrival of a third party. But his memory had not prepared him for who the third party would turn out to be.

He recognized himself—another carbon copy.

He stood silent for a minute, trying to assimilate this new fact and force it into some reasonable integration. He closed his eyes helplessly. This was just a little too much. He felt that he wanted to have a few plain words with Diktor.

"Who the hell are you?" He opened his eyes to find that his other self, the drunk one, was addressing the latest edition. The newcomer turned away from his interrogator and looked sharply at Wilson.

"*He* knows me."

Wilson took his time about replying. This thing was getting out of hand. "Yes," he admitted, "yes, I suppose I do. But what the deuce are you here for? And why are you trying to bust up the plan?"

His facsimile cut him short. "No time for long-winded explanations. I know more about it than you do—you'll concede that—and my judgment is bound to be better than yours. He doesn't go through the Gate."

The offhand arrogance of the other antagonized Wilson. "I don't concede anything of the sort—" he began.

He was interrupted by the telephone bell. "Answer it!" snapped Number Three.

The tipsy Number One looked belligerent but picked up the handset. "Hello. . . . Yes. Who is this? . . . Hello. . . . Hello!" He tapped the bar of the instrument, then slammed the receiver back into its cradle.

"Who was that?" Wilson asked, somewhat annoyed that he had not had a chance to answer it himself.

"Nothing. Some nut with a misplaced sense of humor." At that instant the telephone rang again. "There he is again!" Wilson tried to answer it, but his alcoholic counterpart beat him to it, brushed him aside. "Listen, you butterfly-brained ape! I'm a busy man and this is *not* a public telephone. . . . Huh? Oh, it's you, Genevieve. Look—I'm sorry. I apologize— . . . You don't understand, honey. A guy has been pestering me over the phone and I thought it was him. You know I wouldn't talk to you that way, Babe. . . . Huh? This afternoon? Did you say *this* afternoon? Sure. Fine. Look, Babe, I'm a little mixed up about this. Trouble I've had all day long and more trouble now. I'll look you up tonight and straighten it out. But I *know* I didn't leave your hat in my apartment— . . . Huh? Oh, sure! Anyhow, I'll see you tonight. 'Bye."

It almost nauseated Wilson to hear his earlier self catering to the demands of that clinging female. Why didn't he just hang up on her? The contrast with Arma—there was a dish!—was acute; it made him more determined than ever to go ahead with the plan, despite the warning of the latest arrival.

After hanging up the phone his earlier self faced him, pointedly ignoring the presence of the third copy. "Very well, Joe," he announced. "I'm ready to go if you are."

"Fine!" Wilson agreed with relief. "Just step through. That's all there is to it."

"No, you don't!" Number Three barred the way.

Wilson started to argue, but his erratic comrade was ahead of him. "Listen, you! You come butting in here like you think I was a bum. If you don't like it, go jump in the lake—and I'm just the kind of a guy who can do it! You and who else?"

They started trading punches almost at once. Wilson stepped in warily, looking for an opening that would enable him to put the slug on Number Three with one decisive blow.

He should have watched his drunken ally as well. A wild swing from that quarter glanced off his already damaged features and caused him excruciating pain. His upper lip, cut, puffy, and tender from his other encounter, took the blow and became an area of pure agony. He flinched and jumped back.

A sound cut through his fog of pain, a dull *Smack!* He forced his eyes to track and saw the feet of a man disappear through the Gate. Number Three was still standing by the Gate. "Now you've done it!" he said bitterly to Wilson, and nursed the knuckles of his left hand.

The obviously unfair allegation reached Wilson at just the wrong moment. His face still felt like an experiment in sadism. "Me?" he said angrily. "*You* knocked him through. I never laid a finger on him."

"Yes, but it's your fault. If you hadn't interfered, I wouldn't have had to do it."

"*Me* interfere? Why, you bald-faced hypocrite—*you* butted in and tried to queer the pitch. Which reminds me—you owe me some explanations and I damn well mean to have 'em. What's the idea of—"

But his opposite number cut in on him. "Stow it," he said gloomily. "It's too late now. He's gone through."

"Too late for what?" Wilson wanted to know.

"Too late to put a stop to this chain of events."

"Why should we?"

"Because," Number Three said bitterly, "Diktor has played me—I mean has played *you* . . . *us*—for a dope, for a couple of dopes. Look, he told you that he was going to set you up as a big shot over *there*"—he indicated the Gate—"didn't he?"

"Yes," Wilson admitted.

"Well, that's a lot of malarkey. All he means to do is to get us so incredibly tangled up in this Time Gate thing that we'll never get straightened out again."

Wilson felt a sudden doubt nibbling at his mind. It *could* be true. Certainly there had not been much sense to what had happened so far. After all, why should Diktor want his help, want it bad enough to offer to split with him, even-Steven, what was obviously a cushy spot? "How do you know?" he demanded.

"Why go into it?" the other answered wearily. "Why don't you just take my word for it?"

"Why should I?"

His companion turned a look of complete exasperation on him. "If you can't take my word, whose word can you take?"

The inescapable logic of the question simply annoyed Wilson. He resented this interloping duplicate of himself anyhow; to be asked to follow his lead blindly irked him. "I'm from Missouri," he said. "I'll see for myself." He moved toward the Gate.

"Where are you going?"

"Through! I'm going to look up Diktor and have it out with him."

"Don't!" the other said. "Maybe we can break the chain even now." Wilson felt and looked stubborn. The other sighed. "Go ahead," he surrendered. "It's your funeral. I wash my hands of you."

Wilson paused as he was about to step through the Gate. "It is, eh? H-m-m-m—how can it be *my* funeral unless it's *your* funeral, too?"

The other man looked blank, then an expression of apprehension raced over his face. That was the last Wilson saw of him as he stepped through.

The Hall of the Gate was empty of other occupants when Bob Wilson came through on the other side. He looked for his hat, but did not find it, then stepped around back of the raised platform, seeking the exit he remembered. He nearly bumped into Diktor.

"Ah, there you are!" the older man greeted him. "Fine! Fine! Now there is just one more little thing to take care of, then we will be all squared away. I must say I am pleased with you, Bob, very pleased indeed."

"Oh, you are, are you?" Bob faced him truculently. "Well, it's too bad I can't say the same about you! I'm not a damn bit pleased. What was the idea of shoving me into that . . . that daisy chain without warning me? What's the meaning of all this nonsense? Why didn't you warn me?"

"Easy, easy," said the older man, "don't get excited. Tell the truth now—if I had told you that you were going back to meet yourself face to face, would you have believed me? Come now, 'fess up."

Wilson admitted that he would not have believed it.

"Well, then," Diktor continued with a shrug, "there was no point in me telling you, was there? If I had told you, you would not have believed me, which is another way of saying that you would have believed false data. Is it not better to be in ignorance than to believe falsely?"

"I suppose so, but—"

"Wait! I did not intentionally deceive you. I did not deceive you at all. But had I told you the full truth, you would have been deceived because you would have rejected the truth. It was better for you to learn the truth with your own eyes. Otherwise—"

"Wait a minute! Wait a minute!" Wilson cut in. "You're getting me all tangled up. I'm willing to let bygones be bygones, if you'll come clean with me. Why did you send me back at all?"

" 'Let bygones be bygones,' " Diktor repeated. "Ah, if we only could! But we can't. That's why I sent you back—in order that you might come through the Gate in the first place."

"Huh? Wait a minute—I already *had* come through the Gate."

Diktor shook his head. "Had you, now? Think a moment. When you got back into your own time and your own place you found your earlier self there, didn't you?"

"Mmmm—yes."

"*He*—your earlier self—had not yet been through the Gate, had he?"

"No. I—"

"How could you have *been* through the Gate, unless you persuaded him to *go* through the Gate?"

Bob Wilson's head was beginning to whirl. He was beginning to wonder who did what to whom and who got paid. "But that's impossible! You are telling me that I did something because I was going to do something."

"Well, didn't you? You were there."

"No, I didn't—no . . . well, maybe I did, but it didn't *feel* like it."

"Why should you expect it to? It was something totally new to your experience."

"But . . . but—" Wilson took a deep breath and got control of himself. Then he reached back into his academic philosophical concepts and produced the notion he had been struggling to express. "It denies all reasonable theories of causation. You would have me believe that causation can be completely circular. I went through because I came back from going through to persuade myself to go through. That's silly."

"Well, didn't you?"

Wilson did not have an answer ready for that one. Diktor continued with, "Don't worry about it. The causation you have been accustomed to is valid enough in its own field but is simply a special case under the general case. *Causation in a plenum need not be and is not limited by a man's perception of duration.*"

Wilson thought about that for a moment. It sounded nice, but there was something slippery about it. "Just a second," he said. "How about entropy? You can't get around entropy."

"Oh, for Heaven's sake," protested Diktor, "shut up, will you? You remind me of the mathematician who proved that airplanes couldn't fly." He turned and started out the door. "Come on. There's work to be done."

Wilson hurried after him. "Dammit, you can't do this to me. What happened to the other two?"

"The other two what?"

"The other two of me? Where are they? How am I ever going to get unsnarled?"

"You aren't snarled up. You don't feel like more than one person, do you?"

"No, but—"

"Then don't worry about it."

"But I've got to worry about it. What happened to the guy that came through just ahead of me?"

"You remember, don't you? However—" Diktor hurried on ahead, led him down a passageway, and dilated a door. "Take a look inside," he directed.

Wilson did so. He found himself looking into a small windowless unfurnished room, a room that he recognized. Sprawled on the floor, snoring steadily, was another edition of himself.

"When you first came through the Gate," explained Diktor at his elbow, "I brought you in here, atttended to your hurts, and gave you a drink. The drink contained a soporific which will cause you to sleep about thirty-six hours, sleep that you badly needed. When you wake up, I will give you breakfast and explain to you what needs to be done."

Wilson's head started to ache again. "Don't do that," he pleaded. "Don't refer to that guy as if he were me. *This* is *me*, standing here."

"Have it your own way," said Diktor. "That is the man you *were*. You remember the things that are about to happen to him, don't you?"

"Yes, but it makes me dizzy. Close the door, please."

"O. K.," said Diktor, and complied. "We've got to hurry, anyhow. Once a sequence like this is established there is no time to waste. Come on." He led the way back to the Hall of the Gate.

"I want you to return to the twentieth century and obtain certain things for us, things that can't be obtained on this side but which will be very useful to us in, ah, developing—yes, that is the word—developing this country."

"What sort of things?"

"Quite a number of items. I've prepared a list for you—certain reference books, certain items of commerce. Excuse me, please. I must adjust the controls of the Gate." He mounted the raised platform from the rear. Wilson followed him and found that the structure was boxlike, open at the top, and had a raised floor. The Gate could be seen by looking over the high sides.

The controls were unique.

Four colored spheres the size of marbles hung on crystal rods arranged with respect to each other as the four major axes of a tetrahedron. The three spheres which bounded the base of the tetrahedron were red, yellow, and blue; the fourth at the apex was white. "Three spatial controls, one time control," explained Diktor. "It's very simple. Using here-and-now as zero reference, displacing any control away from the center moves the other end of the Gate farther from here-and-now. Forward or back, right or left, up or down, past or future—they are all controlled by moving the proper sphere in or out on its rod."

Wilson studied the system. "Yes," he said, "but how do you tell where the other end of the Gate is? Or when? I don't see any graduations."

"You don't need them. You can see where you are.

Look." He touched a point under the control frame-work on the side toward the Gate. A panel rolled back and Wilson saw there was a small image of the Gate itself. Diktor made another adjustment and Wilson found that he could see through the image.

He was gazing into his own room, as if through the wrong end of a telescope. He could make out two figures, but the scale was too small for him to see clearly what they were doing, nor could he tell which editions of himself were there present—if they were in truth himself! He found it quite upsetting. "Shut it off," he said.

Diktor did so and said, "I must not forget to give you your list." He fumbled in his sleeve and pro-duced a slip of paper which he handed to Wilson. "Here—take it."

Wilson accepted it mechanically and stuffed it into his pocket. "See here," he began, "everywhere I go I keep running into myself. I don't like it at all. It's disconcerting. I feel like a whole batch of guinea pigs. I don't half understand what this is all about and now you want to rush me through the Gate again with a bunch of half-baked excuses. Come clean. Tell me what it's all about."

Diktor showed temper in his face for the first time. "You are a stupid and ignorant young fool. I've told you all that you are able to understand. This is a period in history entirely beyond your comprehen-sion. It would take weeks before you would even begin to understand it. I am offering you half a world in return for a few hours' cooperation and you stand there arguing about it. Stow it, I tell you. Now—where shall we set you down?" He reached for the controls.

"Get away from those controls!" Wilson rapped out. He was getting the glimmering of an idea. "Who are you, anyhow?"

"Me? I'm Diktor."

"That's not what I mean and you know it. How did you learn English?"

Diktor did not answer. His face became expressionless.

"Go on," Wilson persisted. "You didn't learn it here; that's a cinch. You're from the twentieth century, *aren't you?*"

Diktor smiled sourly. "I wondered how long it would take you to figure that out."

Wilson nodded. "Maybe I'm not bright, but I'm not as stupid as you think I am. Come on. Give me the rest of the story."

Diktor shook his head. "It's immaterial. Besides, we're wasting time."

Wilson laughed. "You've tried to hurry me with that excuse once too often. How can we waste time when we have *that?*" He pointed to the controls and to the Gate beyond it. "Unless you lied to me, we can use any slice of time we want to, any time. No, I think I know why you tried to rush me. Either you want to get me out of the picture here, or there is something devilishly dangerous about the job you want me to do. And I know how to settle it—you're going with me!"

"You don't know what you're saying," Diktor answered slowly. "That's impossible. I've got to stay here and manage the controls."

"That's just what you aren't going to do. You could send me through and lose me. I prefer to keep you in sight."

"Out of the question," answered Diktor. "You'll have to trust me." He bent over the controls again.

"Get away from there!" shouted Wilson. "Back out of there before I bop you one." Under Wilson's menacing fist Diktor withdrew from the control pulpit entirely. "There. That's better," he added when both of them were once more on the floor of the hall.

The idea which had been forming in his mind took

full shape. The controls, he knew, were still set on his room in the boardinghouse where he lived—or had lived—back in the twentieth century. From what he had seen through the speculum of the controls, the time control was set to take him right back to the day in 1952 from which he had started. "Stand there," he commanded Diktor, "I want to see something."

He walked over to the Gate as if to inspect it. Instead of stopping when he reached it, he stepped on through.

He was better prepared for what he found on the other side than he had been on the two earlier occasions of time translation—"earlier" in the sense of sequence in his memory track. Nevertheless it is never too easy on the nerves to catch up with one's self.

For he had done it again. He was back in his own room, but there were two of himself there before him. They were very much preoccupied with each other; he had a few seconds in which to get them straightened out in his mind. One of them had a beautiful black eye and a badly battered mouth. Beside that he was very much in need of a shave. That tagged him. He had been through the Gate at least once. The other, though somewhat in need of shaving himself, showed no marks of a fist fight.

He had them sorted out now, and knew where and *when* he was. It was all still mostly damnably confusing, but after former—no, not *former*, he amended—*other* experiences with time translation he knew better what to expect. He was back at the beginning again; this time he would put a stop to the crazy nonsense once and for all.

The other two were arguing. One of them swayed drunkenly toward the bed. The other grabbed him by the arm. "You can't do that," he said.

"Let him alone!" snapped Wilson.

The other two swung around and looked him over.

Wilson watched the more sober of the pair size him up, saw his expression of amazement change to startled recognition. The other, the earliest Wilson, seemed to have trouble in focusing on him at all. "This is going to be a job," thought Wilson. "The man is positively stinking." He wondered why anyone would be foolish enough to drink on an empty stomach. It was not only stupid, it was a waste of good liquor.

He wondered if they had left a drink for him.

"Who are you?" demanded his drunken double.

Wilson turned to "Joe." "He knows me," he said significantly.

"Joe," studied him. "Yes," he conceded, "yes, I suppose I do. But what the deuce are you here for? And why are you trying to bust up the plan?"

Wilson interrupted him. "No time for long-winded explanations. I know more about it than you do—you'll concede that—and my judgment is bound to be better than yours. He doesn't go through the Gate."

"I don't concede anything of the sort—"

The ringing of the telephone checked the argument. Wilson greeted the interruption with relief, for he realized that he had started out on the wrong tack. Was it possible that he was really as dense himself as this lug appeared to be? Did *he* look that way to other people? But the time was too short for self-doubts and soul-searching. "Answer it!" he commanded Bob (Boiled) Wilson.

The drunk looked belligerent, but acceded when he saw that Bob (Joe) Wilson was about to beat him to it. "Hello. . . . Yes. Who is this? . . . Hello. . . . Hello!"

"Who was that?" asked "Joe."

"Nothing. Some nut with a misplaced sense of humor." The telephone rang again. "There he is again." The drunk grabbed the phone before the others could reach it. "Listen, you butterfly-brained ape! I'm a busy man and this is *not* a public telephone. . . . Huh? Oh, it's you, Genevieve—" Wilson paid little attention to the telephone conversation—he had heard it too many times before, and he had too much on his mind. His earliest *persona* was much too drunk to be reasonable, he realized; he must concentrate on some argument that would appeal to "Joe"—otherwise he was outnumbered. "—Huh? Oh, sure!" the call concluded. "Anyhow, I'll see you tonight. 'Bye."

Now was the time, thought Wilson, before this dumb yap can open his mouth. What would he say? What would sound convincing?

But the boiled edition spoke first. "Very well, Joe," he stated, "I'm ready to go if you are."

"Fine!" said "Joe." "Just step through. That's all there is to it."

This was getting out of hand, not the way he had planned it at all. "No, you don't!" he barked and jumped in front of the Gate. He would have to make them realize, and quickly.

But he got no chance to do so. The drunk cussed him out, then swung on him; his temper snapped. He knew with sudden fierce exultation that he had been wanting to take a punch at someone for some time. Who did they think they were to be taking chances with his future?

The drunk was clumsy; Wilson stepped under his guard and hit him hard in the face. It was a solid enough punch to have convinced a sober man, but his opponent shook his head and came back for more. "Joe" closed in. Wilson decided that he would have to put his original opponent away in a hurry, and give his attention to "Joe;"—by far the more dangerous of the two.

A slight mix-up between the two allies gave him his chance. He stepped back, aimed carefully, and landed a long jab with his left, one of the hardest blows he had ever struck in his life. It lifted his target right off his feet.

As the blow landed, Wilson realized his orientation with respect to the Gate, knew with bitter certainty that he had again played through the scene to its inescapable climax.

He was alone with "Joe;" their companion had disappeared through the Gate.

His first impulse was the illogical but quite human and very common feeling of look-what-you-made-me-do. "Now you've done it!" he said angrily.

"Me?" "Joe" protested. "You knocked him through. I never laid a finger on him."

"Yes," Wilson was forced to admit. "But it's your fault," he added, "if you hadn't interfered, I wouldn't have had to do it."

"Me interfere? Why, you bald-faced hypocrite, you butted in and tried to queer the pitch. Which reminds me—you owe me some explanations and I damn well mean to have them. What's the idea of—"

"Stow it," Wilson headed him off. He hated to be wrong and he hated still more to have to admit that he was wrong. It had been hopeless from the start, he now realized. He felt bowed down by the utter futility of it. "It's too late now. He's gone through."

"Too late for what?"

"Too late to put a stop to this chain of events." He was aware now that it always had been too late, regardless of what time it was, what year it was, or how many times he came back and tried to stop it. He *remembered* having gone through the first time, he had *seen* himself asleep on the other side. Events would have to work out their weary way.

"Why should we?"

It was not worth while to explain, but he felt the need for self-justification. "Because," he said, "Diktor has played me—I mean has played *you* . . . us—for a dope, for a couple of dopes. Look, he told you that he was going to set you up as a big shot over there, didn't he?"

"Yes—"

"Well, that's a lot of malarkey. All he means to do is to get us so incredibly tangled up in this Gate thing that we'll never get straightened out again."

"Joe" looked at him sharply. "How do you know?"

Since it was largely hunch, he felt pressed for reasonable explanation. "Why go into it?" he evaded. "Why don't you just take my word for it?"

"Why should I?"

"Why should you? Why, you lunk, can't you see? I'm yourself, older and more experienced—you *have* to believe me." Aloud he answered, "If you can't take my word, whose word can you take?"

"Joe" grunted. "I'm from Missouri," he said. "I'll see for myself."

Wilson was suddenly aware that "Joe" was about to step through the Gate. "Where are you going?"

"Through! I'm going to look up Diktor and have it out with him."

"Don't!" Wilson pleaded. "Maybe we can break the chain even now." But the stubborn sulky look on the other's face made him realize how futile it was. He was still enmeshed in inevitability; it *had* to happen. "Go ahead," he shrugged. "It's your funeral. I wash my hands of you."

"Joe" paused at the Gate. "It is, eh? Hm-m-m-how can it be *my* funeral unless it's *your* funeral, too?"

Wilson stared speechlessly while "Joe" stepped through the Gate. Whose funeral? He had not thought of it in quite that way. He felt a sudden impulse to rush through the Gate, catch up with his alter ego, and watch over him. The stupid fool might do anything. Suppose he got himself killed? Where would that leave Bob Wilson? Dead, of course.

Or would it? Could the death of a man thousands

of years in the future kill *him* in the year 1952? He saw the absurdity of the situation suddenly, and felt very much relieved. "Joe's" actions could not endanger him; he remembered everything that "Joe" had done—was going to do. "Joe" would get into an argument with Diktor and, in due course of events, would come back through the Time Gate. No, *had* come back through the Time Gate. He was "Joe." It was hard to remember that.

Yes, he was "Joe." As well as the first guy. They would thread their courses, in and out and round-about, and end up here, with *him*. Had to.

Wait a minute—in that case the whole crazy business was straightened out. He had gotten away from Diktor, had all of his various personalities sorted out, and was back where he started from, no worse for the wear except for a crop of whiskers and, possibly, a scar on his lip. Well, he knew when to let well enough alone. Shave, and get back to work, kid.

As he shaved he stared at his face and wondered why he had failed to recognize it the first time. He had to admit that he had never looked at it objectively before. He had always taken it for granted.

He acquired a crick in his neck from trying to look at his own profile through the corner of one eye.

On leaving the bathroom the Gate caught his eye forcibly. For some reason he had assumed that it would be gone. It was not. He inspected it, walked around it, carefully refrained from touching it. Wasn't the damned thing ever going to go away? It had served its purpose; why didn't Diktor shut it off?

He stood in front of it, felt a sudden surge of the compulsion that leads men to jump from high places. What would happen if he went through? What would he find? He thought of Arma. And the other one—what was her name? Perhaps Diktor had not told him. The other maidservant, anyhow, the second one.

But he restrained himself and forced himself to sit back down at the desk. If he was going to stay here—and of course he was, he was resolved on that point—he must finish the thesis. He had to eat; he needed the degree to get a decent job. Now where was he?

Twenty minutes later he had come to the conclusion that the thesis would have to be rewritten from one end to the other. His prime theme, the application of the empirical method to the problems of speculative metaphysics and its expression in rigorous formulae, was still valid, he decided, but he had acquired a mass of new and not yet digested data to incorporate in it. In re-reading his manuscript he was amazed to find how dogmatic he had been. Time after time he had fallen into the Cartesian fallacy, mistaking clear reasoning for correct reasoning.

He tried to brief a new version of the thesis, but discovered that there were two problems he was forced to deal with which were decidedly not clear in his mind: the problem of the ego and the problem of free will. When there had been three of him in the room, which one was the ego—was *himself*? And how was it that he had been unable to change the course of events?

An absurdly obvious answer to the first question occurred to him at once. The ego was himself. Self is self, an unproved and unprovable first statement, directly experienced. What, then, of the other two? Surely they had been equally sure of ego-being—he remembered it. He thought of a way to state it: Ego is the point of consciousness, the latest term in a continuously expanding series along the line of memory duration. That sounded like a general statement, but he was not sure; he would have to try to formulate it mathematically before he could trust it. Verbal language had such queer booby traps in it.

The telephone rang.

He answered it absent-mindedly. "Yes?"

"Is that you, Bob?"

"Yes. Who is this?"

"Why, it's Genevieve, of course, darling. What's come over you today? That's the second time you've failed to recognize my voice."

Annoyance and frustration rose up in him. Here was another problem he had failed to settle—well, he'd settle it now. He ignored her complaint. "Look here, Genevieve, I've told you not to telephone me while I'm working. Good-bye!"

"Well, of all the— You can't talk that way to me, Bob Wilson! In the first place, you weren't working today. In the second place, what makes you think you can use honey and sweet words on me and two hours later snarl at me? I'm not any too sure I want to marry you."

"Marry you? What put that silly idea in your head?"

The phone sputtered for several seconds. When it had abated somewhat he resumed with, "Now just calm down. This isn't the Gay Nineties, you know. You can't assume that a fellow who takes you out a few times intends to marry you."

There was a short silence. "So that's the game, is it?" came an answer at last in a voice so cold and hard and completely shrewish that he almost failed to recognize it. "Well, there's a way to handle men like you. A woman isn't unprotected in this State!"

"You ought to know," he answered savagely. "You've hung around the campus enough years."

The receiver clicked in his ear.

He wiped the sweat from his forehead. That dame, he knew, was quite capable of causing him lots of trouble. He had been warned before he ever started running around with her, but he had been so sure of his own ability to take care of himself. He should have known better—but then he had not expected anything quite as raw as this.

He tried to get back to work on his thesis, but found himself unable to concentrate. The deadline of 10 A.M. the next morning seemed to be racing toward him. He looked at his watch. It had stopped. He set it by the desk clock—four fifteen in the afternoon. Even if he sat up all night he could not possibly finish it properly.

Besides there was Genevieve—

The telephone rang again. He let it ring. It continued; he took the receiver off the cradle. He would *not* talk to her again.

He thought of Arma. There was a proper girl with the right attitude. He walked over to the window and stared down into the dusty, noisy street. Half subconsciously he compared it with the green and placid countryside he had seen from the balcony where he and Diktor had breakfasted. This was a crummy world full of crummy people. He wished poignantly that Diktor had been on the up-and-up with him.

An idea broke surface in his brain and plunged around frantically. The Gate was still open. *The Gate was still open!* Why worry about Diktor? He was his own master. Go back and play it out—everything to gain, nothing to lose.

He stepped up to the Gate, then hesitated. Was he wise to do it? After all, how much did he know about the future?

He heard footsteps climbing the stairs, coming down the hall, no—yes, stopping at his door. He was suddenly convinced that it was Genevieve; that decided him. He stepped through.

The Hall of the Gate was empty on his arrival. He hurried around the control box to the door and was just in time to hear, "Come on. There's work to be done." Two figures were retreating down the corridor. He recognized both of them and stopped suddenly.

That was a near thing, he told himself; I'll just have to wait until they get clear. He looked around for a place to conceal himself, but found nothing but the control box. That was useless; they were coming back. Still—

He entered the control box with a plan vaguely forming in his mind. If he found that he could dope out the controls, the Gate might give him all the advantage he needed. First he needed to turn on the speculum gadget. He felt around where he recalled having seen Diktor reach to turn it on, then reached in his pocket for a match.

Instead he pulled out a piece of paper. It was the list that Diktor had given him, the things he was to obtain in the twentieth century. Up to the present moment there had been too much going on for him to look it over.

His eyebrows crawled up his forehead as he read. It was a funny list, he decided. He had subconsciously expected it to call for technical reference books, samples of modern gadgets, weapons. There was nothing of the sort. Still, there was a sort of mad logic to the assortment. After all, Diktor knew these people better than he did. It might be just what was needed.

He revised his plans, subject to being able to work the Gate. He decided to make one more trip back and do the shopping Diktor's list called for—but for his own benefit, not Diktor's. He fumbled in the semidarkness of the control booth, seeking the switch or control for the speculum. His hand encountered a soft mass. He grasped it, and pulled it out.

It was his hat.

He placed it on his head, guessing idly that Diktor had stowed it there, and reached again. This time he brought forth a small notebook. It looked like a find— very possibly Diktor's own notes on the operation of the controls. He opened it eagerly.

It was not what he had hoped. But it did contain page after page of handwritten notes. There were three columns to the page; the first was in English, the second in international phonetic symbols, the third in a completely strange sort of writing. It took no brilliance for him to identify it as a vocabulary. He slipped it into a pocket with a broad smile; it might have taken Diktor months or even years to work out the relationship between the two languages; he would be able to ride on Diktor's shoulders in the matter.

The third try located the control and the speculum lighted up. He felt again the curious uneasiness he had felt before, for he was gazing again into his own room and again it was inhabited by two figures. He did not want to break into that scene again, he was sure. Cautiously he touched one of the colored beads.

The scene shifted, panned out through the walls of the boardinghouse and came to rest in the air, three stories above the campus. He was pleased to have gotten the Gate out of the house, but three stories was too much of a jump. He fiddled with the other two colored beads and established that one of them caused the scene in the speculum to move toward him or away from him while the other moved it up or down.

He wanted a reasonably inconspicuous place to locate the Gate, some place where it would not attract the attention of the curious. This bothered him a bit; there was no ideal place, but he compromised on a blind alley, a little court formed by the campus powerhouse and the rear wall of the library. Cautiously and clumsily he maneuvered his flying eye to the neighborhood he wanted and set it down carefully between the two buildings. He then readjusted his position so that he stared right into a blank wall. Good enough!

Leaving the controls as they were, he hurried out

of the booth and stepped unceremoniously back into his own period.

He bumped his nose against the brick wall. "I cut that a little too fine," he mused as he slid cautiously out from between the confining limits of the wall and the Gate. The Gate hung in the air, about fifteen inches from the wall and roughly parallel to it. But there was room enough, he decided—no need to go back and readjust the controls. He ducked out of the areaway and cut across the campus toward the Students' Co-op, wasting no time. He entered and went to the cashier's window.

"Hi, Bob."

"H'lo, Soupy. Cash a check for me?"

"How much?"

"Twenty dollars."

"Well—I suppose so. Is it a good check?"

"Not very. It's my own."

"Well, I might invest in it as a curiosity." He counted out a ten, a five, and five ones.

"Do that," advised Wilson. "My autographs are going to be rare collectors' items." He passed over the check, took the money, and proceeded to the bookstore in the same building. Most of the books on the list were for sale there. Ten minutes later he had acquired title to:

"The Prince," by Niccolò Machiavelli.

"Behind the Ballots," by James Farley.

"Mein Kampf" (unexpurgated), by Adolf Schickelgruber.

"How to Make Friends and Influence People," by Dale Carnegie.

The other titles he wanted were not available in the bookstore; he went from there to the university library where he drew out "Real Estate Broker's Manual," "History of Musical Instruments," and a quarto titled "Evolution of Dress Styles." The latter was a handsome volume with beautiful colored plates

and was classified as reference. He had to argue a
little to get a twenty-four hour permission for it.

He was fairly well loaded down by then; he left
the campus, went to a pawnshop and purchased two
used, but sturdy, suitcases into one of which he
packed the books. From there he went to the largest
music store in the town and spent forty-five minutes
in selecting and rejecting phonograph records, with
emphasis on swing and torch—highly emotional stuff,
all of it. He did not neglect classical and semi-classical,
but he applied the same rule to those categories—a
piece of music had to be sensuous and compelling,
rather than cerebral. In consequence his collection
included such strangely assorted items as the "Mar-
seillaise," Ravel's "Bolero," four Cole Porters, and
"L'Après-midi d'un Faune."

He insisted on buying the best mechanical repro-
ducer on the market in the face of the clerk's insistence that what he needed was an electrical one. But
he finally got his own way, wrote a check for the
order, packed it all in his suitcases, and had the clerk
get a taxi for him.

He had a bad moment over the check. It was pure
rubber, as the one he had cashed at the Students'
Co-op had cleaned out his balance. He had urged
them to phone the bank, since that was what he
wished them not to do. It had worked. He had
established, he reflected, the all-time record for kit-
ing checks—thirty thousand years.

When the taxi drew up opposite the court where
he had located the Gate, he jumped out and hurried
in.

The Gate was gone.

He stood there for several minutes, whistling softly,
and assessing—unfavorably—his own abilities, mental processes, et cetera. The consequences of writing
bad checks no longer seemed quite so hypothetical.

He felt a touch at his sleeve. "See here, Bud, do

you want my hack, or don't you? The meter's still clicking."

"'Huh? Oh, sure." He followed the driver, climbed back in.

"Where to?"

That was a problem. He glanced at his watch, then realized that the usually reliable instrument had been through a process which rendered its reading irrelevant. "What time is it?"

"Two fifteen." He reset his watch.

Two fifteen. There would be a jamboree going on in his room at that time of a particularly confusing sort. He did not want to go *there*—not yet. Not until his blood brothers got through playing happy fun games with the Gate.

The Gate!

It would be in his room until sometime after four fifteen. If he timed it right—"Drive to the corner of Fourth and McKinley," he directed, naming the intersection closest to his boardinghouse.

He paid off the taxi driver there, and lugged his bags into the filling station at that corner, where he obtained permission from the attendant to leave them and assurance that they would be safe. He had nearly two hours to kill. He was reluctant to go very far from the house for fear some hitch would upset his timing.

It occurred to him that there was one piece of unfinished business in the immediate neighborhood— and time enough to take care of it. He walked briskly to a point two streets away, whistling cheerfully, and turned in at an apartment house.

In response to his knock the door of Apartment 211 was opened a crack, then wider. "Bob darling! I thought you were working today."

"Hi, Genevieve. Not at all—I've got time to burn."

She glanced back over her shoulder. "I don't know whether I should let you come in—I wasn't expecting you. I haven't washed the dishes, or made the bed. I was just putting on my make-up."

"Don't be coy." He pushed the door open wide, and went on in.

When he came out he glanced at his watch. Three thirty—plenty of time. He went down the street wearing the expression of the canary that ate the cat.

He thanked the service station salesman and gave him a quarter for his trouble, which left him with a lone dime. He looked at this coin, grinned to himself, and inserted it in the pay phone in the office of the station. He dialed his own number.

"Hello," he heard.

"Hello," he replied. "Is that Bob Wilson?"

"Yes. Who is this?"

"Never mind," he chuckled. "I just wanted to be sure you were there. I *thought* you would be. You're right in the groove, kid, right in the groove." He replaced the receiver with a grin.

At four ten he was too nervous to wait any longer. Struggling under the load of the heavy suitcases he made his way to the boardinghouse. He let himself in and heard a telephone ringing upstairs. He glanced at his watch—four fifteen. He waited in the hall for three interminable minutes, then labored up the stairs and down the upper hallway to his own door. He unlocked the door and let himself in.

The room was empty, the Gate still there.

Without stopping for anything, filled with apprehension lest the Gate should flicker and disappear while he crossed the floor, he hurried to it, took a firm grip on his bags, and strode through it.

The Hall of the Gate was empty, to his great relief. What a break, he told himself thankfully. Just five minutes, that's all I ask. Five uninterrupted minutes. He set the suitcases down near the Gate to be ready for a quick departure. As he did so he noticed that a large chunk was missing from a corner of one case. Half a book showed through the opening, sheared as neatly as with a printer's trimmer. He identified it as "Mein Kampf."

He did not mind the loss of the book but the implications made him slightly sick at his stomach. Suppose he had not described a clear arc when he had first been knocked through the Gate, had hit the edge, half in and half out? Man Sawed in Half—and no illusion!

He wiped his face and went to the control booth. Following Diktor's simple instructions he brought all four spheres together at the center of the tetrahedron. He glanced over the side of the booth and saw that the Gate had disappeared entirely. "Check!" he thought. "Everything on zero—no Gate." He moved the white sphere slightly. The Gate reappeared. Turning on the speculum he was able to see that the miniature scene showed the inside of the Hall of the Gate itself. So far so good—but he would not be able to tell what time the Gate was set for by looking into the Hall. He displaced a space control slightly; the scene flickered past the walls of the palace and hung in the open air. Returning the white time control to zero he then displaced it very, very slightly. In the miniature scene the sun became a streak of brightness across the sky; the days flickered past like light from a low frequency source of illumination. He increased the displacement a little, saw the ground become sear and brown, then snow covered, and finally green again.

Working cautiously, steadying his right hand with his left, he made the seasons march past. He had counted ten winters when he became aware of voices somewhere in the distance. He stopped and listened, then very hastily returned the space controls to zero, leaving the time control as it was—set for ten years in the past—and rushed out of the booth.

He hardly had time to grasp his bags, lift them,

and swing them through the Gate, himself with them. This time he was exceedingly careful not to touch the edge of the circle.

He found himself, as he had planned to, still in the Hall of the Gate, but, if he had interpreted the controls correctly, ten years away from the events he had recently participated in. He had intended to give Diktor a wider berth than that, but there had been no time for it. However, he reflected, since Diktor was, by his own statement and the evidence of the little notebook Wilson had lifted from him, a native of the twentieth century, it was quite possible that ten years was enough. Diktor might not be in this era. If he was, there was always the Time Gate for a getaway. But it was reasonable to scout out the situation first before making any more jumps.

It suddenly occurred to him that Diktor might be looking at him through the speculum of the Time Gate. Without stopping to consider that speed was no protection—since the speculum could be used to view *any* time sector—he hurriedly dragged his two suitcases into the cover of the control booth. Once inside the protecting walls of the booth he calmed down a bit. Spying could work both ways. He found the controls set at zero; making use of the same process he had used once before, he ran the scene in the speculum forward through ten years, then cautiously hunted with the space controls on zero. It was a very difficult task; the time scale necessary to hunt through several months in a few minutes caused any figure which might appear in the speculum to flash past at an apparent speed too fast for his eye to follow. Several times he thought he detected flitting shadows which might be human beings but he was never able to find them when he stopped moving the time control.

He wondered in great exasperation why whoever had built the double-damned gadget had failed to provide it with graduations and some sort of delicate control mechanism—a vernier, or the like. It was not until much later that it occurred to him that the creator of the Time Gate might have no need of such gross aids to his senses. He would have given up, was about to give up, when, purely by accident, one more fruitless scanning happened to terminate with a figure in the field.

It was himself, carrying two suitcases. He saw himself walking directly into the field of view, grow large, disappear. He looked over the rail, half expecting to see himself step out of the Gate.

But nothing came out of the Gate. It puzzled him, until he recalled that it was the setting at *that* end, ten years in the future, which controlled the time of egress. But he had what he wanted; he sat back and watched. Almost immediately Diktor and another edition of himself appeared in the scene. He recalled the situation when he saw it portrayed in the speculum. It was Bob Wilson number three, about to quarrel with Diktor and make his escape back to the twentieth century.

That was that—Diktor had not seen him, did not know that he had made unauthorized use of the Gate, did not know that he was hiding ten years in the "past," would not look for him there. He returned the controls to zero, and dismissed the matter.

But other matters needed his attention—food, especially. It seemed obvious, in retrospect, that he should have brought along food to last him for a day or two at least. And maybe a .45. He had to admit that he had not been very foresighted. But he easily forgave himself—it was hard to be foresighted when the future kept slipping up behind one. "All right, Bob, old boy," he told himself aloud, "let's see if the natives are friendly—as advertised."

A cautious reconnoiter of the small part of the Palace with which he was acquainted turned up no

human beings nor life of any sort, not even insect
life. The place was dead, sterile, as static and
unlived-in as a window display. He shouted once just
to hear a voice. The echoes caused him to shiver; he
did not do it again.

The architecture of the place confused him. Not
only was it strange to his experience—he had expected that—but the place, with minor exceptions,
seemed totally unadapted to the uses of human beings.
Great halls large enough to hold ten thousand people
at once—had there been floors for them to stand on.
For there frequently were no floors in the accepted
meaning of a level or reasonably level platform. In
following a passageway he came suddenly to one of
the great mysterious openings in the structure and
almost fell in before he realized that his path had
terminated. He crawled gingerly forward and looked
over the edge. The mouth of the passage debouched
high up on a wall of the place; below him the wall
was cut back so that there was not even a vertical
surface for the eye to follow. Far below him, the wall
curved back and met its mate of the opposite side—
not decently, in a horizontal plane, but at an acute
angle.

There were other openings scattered around the
walls, openings as unserviceable to human beings as
the one in which he crouched. "The High Ones," he
whispered to himself. All his cockiness was gone out
of him. He retraced his steps through the fine dust
and reached the almost friendly familiarity of the
Hall of the Gate.

On his second try he attempted only those pas-
sages and compartments which seemed obviously
adapted to men. He had already decided what such
parts of the Palace must be—servants' quarters, or,
more probably, slaves' quarters. He regained his courage by sticking to such areas. Though deserted completely, by contrast with the rest of the great structure

a room or a passage which seemed to have been built for men was friendly and cheerful. The sourceless ever-present illuminations and the unbroken silence still bothered him, but not to the degree to which he had been upset by the Gargantuan and mysteriously convoluted chambers of the "High Ones."

He had almost despaired of finding his way out of the Palace and was thinking of retracing his steps when the corridor he was following turned and he found himself in bright sunlight.

He was standing at the top of a broad steep ramp which spread fanlike down to the base of the building. Ahead of him and below him, distant at least five hundred yards, the pavement of the ramp met the green of sod and bush and tree. It was the same placid, lush, and familiar scene he had looked out over when he breakfasted with Diktor—a few hours ago and ten years in the future.

He stood quietly for a short time, drinking in the sunshine, soaking up the heart-lifting beauty of the warm, spring day. "This is going to be all right," he exulted. "It's a grand place."

He moved slowly down the ramp, his eyes searching for human beings. He was halfway down when he saw a small figure emerge from the trees into a clearing near the foot of the ramp. He called out to it in joyous excitement. The child—it was a child he saw—looked up, stared at him for a moment, then fled back into the shelter of the trees.

"Impetuous, Robert—that's what you are," he chided himself. "Don't scare 'em. Take it easy." But he was not made downhearted by the incident. Where there were children there would be parents, society, opportunities for a bright, young fellow who took a broad view of things. He moved on down at a leisurely pace.

A man showed up at the point where the child had disappeared. Wilson stood still. The man looked him over and advanced hesitantly a step or two. "Come here!" Wilson invited in a friendly voice. "I won't hurt you."

The man could hardly have understood his words, but he advanced slowly. At the edge of the pavement he stopped, eyed it and would not proceed farther.

Something about the behavior pattern clicked in Wilson's brain, fitted in with what he had seen in the Palace, and with the little that Diktor had told him. "Unless," he told himself, "the time I spent in 'Anthropology I' was totally wasted, this Palace is tabu, the ramp I'm standing on is tabu, and, by contagion, I'm tabu. Play your cards, son, play your cards!"

He advanced to the edge of the pavement, being careful not to step off it. The man dropped to his knees and cupped his hands in front of him, head bowed. Without hesitation Wilson touched him on the forehead. The man got back to his feet, his face radiant.

"This isn't even sporting," Wilson said. "I ought to shoot him on the rise."

His Man Friday cocked his head, looked puzzled, and answered in a deep, melodious voice. The words were liquid and strange and sounded like a phrase from a song. "You ought to commercialize that voice," Wilson said admiringly. "Some stars get by on less. However— Get along now, and fetch something to eat. Food." He pointed to his mouth.

The man looked hesitant, spoke again. Bob Wilson reached into his pocket and took out the stolen notebook. He looked up "eat," than looked up "food." It was the same word. "Blellan," he said carefully.

"Blellaaaan?"

"Blellaaaaaaaan," agreed Wilson. "You'll have to excuse my accent. Hurry up." He tried to find "hurry" in the vocabulary, but it was not there. Either the language did not contain the idea or Diktor had not thought it worth while to record it. But we'll soon fix that, Wilson thought—if there isn't such a word, I'll give 'em one.

The man departed.

Wilson sat himself down Turk-fashion and passed the time by studying the notebook. The speed of his rise in these parts, he decided, was limited only by the time it took him to get into full communication. But he had only time enough to look up a few common substantives when his first acquaintance returned, in company.

The procession was headed by an extremely elderly man, white-haired but beardless. All of the men were beardless. He walked under a canopy carried by four male striplings. Only he of all the crowd wore enough clothes to get by anywhere but on a beach. He was looking uncomfortable in a sort of toga effect which appeared to have started life as a Roman-striped awning. That he was the head man was evident.

Wilson hurriedly looked up the word for "chief."

The word for chief was "Diktor."

It should not have surprised him, but it did. It was, of course, a logical probability that the word "Diktor" was a title rather than a proper name. It simply had not occurred to him.

Diktor—*the* Diktor—had added a note under the word. "One of the few words," Wilson read, "which shows some probability of having been derived from the dead languages. This word, a few dozen others, and the grammatical structure of the language itself, appear to be the only link between the language of the 'Forsaken Ones' and the English language."

The chief stopped in front of Wilson, just short of the pavement. "O.K., Diktor," Wilson ordered, "kneel down. You're not exempt." He pointed to the ground. The chief knelt down. Wilson touched his forehead.

The food that had been fetched along was plentiful and very palatable. Wilson ate slowly and with dignity, keeping in mind the importance of face. While he ate he was serenaded by the entire assemblage. The singing was excellent he was bound to admit. Their ideas of harmony he found a little strange and the performance, as a whole, seemed primitive, but their voices were all clear and mellow and they sang as if they enjoyed it.

The concert gave Wilson an idea. After he had satisfied his hunger he made the chief understand, with the aid of the indispensable little notebook, that he and his flock were to wait where they were. He then returned to the Hall of the Gate and brought back from there the phonograph and a dozen assorted records. He treated them to a recorded concert of "modern" music.

The reaction exceeded his hopes. "Begin the Beguine" caused tears to stream down the face of the old chief. The first movement of Tschaikowsky's "Concerto Number One in B Flat Minor" practically stampeded them. They jerked. They held their heads and moaned. They shouted their applause. Wilson refrained from giving them the second movement, tapered them off instead with the compelling monotony of the "Bolero."

"Diktor," he said—he was not thinking of the old chief—"Diktor, old chum, you certainly had these people doped out when you sent me shopping. By the time you show up—if you ever do—I'll own the place."

Wilson's rise to power was more in the nature of a triumphal progress than a struggle for supremacy; it contained little that was dramatic. Whatever it was that the High Ones had done to the human race it had left them with only physical resemblance and with temperament largely changed. The docile friendly children with whom Wilson dealt had little in common with the brawling, vulgar, lusty, dynamic swarms who had once called themselves the People of the United States.

The relationship was like that of Jersey cattle to longhorns, or cocker spaniels to wolves. The fight was gone out of them. It was not that they lacked intelligence, nor civilized arts; it was the competitive spirit that was gone, the will-to-power.

Wilson had a monopoly on that.

But even he lost interest in playing a game that he always won. Having established himself as boss man by taking up residence in the Palace and representing himself as the viceroy of the departed High Ones, he, for a time, busied himself in organizing certain projects intended to bring the culture "up-to-date" —the reinvention of musical instruments, establishment of a systematic system of mail service, redevelopment of the idea of styles in dress and a tabu against wearing the same fashion more than one season. There was cunning in the latter project. He figured that arousing a hearty interest in display in the minds of the womenfolk would force the men to hustle to satisfy their wishes. What the culture lacked was drive—it was slipping downhill. He tried to give them the drive they lacked.

His subjects cooperated with his wishes, but in a bemused fashion, like a dog performing a trick, not because he understands it, but because his master and godhead desires it.

He soon tired of it.

But the mystery of the High Ones and especially the mystery of their Time Gate, still remained to occupy his mind. His was a mixed nature, half hustler, half philosopher. The philosopher had his inning.

It was intellectually necessary to him that he be able to construct in his mind a physio-mathematical model for the phenomena exhibited by the Time Gate. He achieved one, not a good one perhaps, but one which satisfied all of the requirements. Think of a plane surface, a sheet of paper, or, better yet, a silk handkerchief—silk, because it has no rigidity, folds easily, while maintaining all of the relational attributes of a two-dimensional continuum on the surface of the silk itself. Let the threads of the woof be the dimension—or direction—of time; let the threads of the warp represent all three of the space dimensions.

An ink spot on the handkerchief becomes the Time Gate. By folding the handkerchief that spot may be superposed on any other spot on the silk. Press the two spots together between thumb and forefinger; the controls are set, the Time Gate is open, a microscopic inhabitant of this piece of silk may crawl from one fold to the other without traversing any other part of the cloth.

The model is imperfect; the picture is static—but a physical picture is necessarily limited by the sensory experience of the person visualizing it.

He could not make up his mind whether or not the concept of folding the four-dimensional continuum —three of space, one of time—back on itself so that the Gate was "open" required the concept of higher dimensions through which to fold it. It seemed so, yet it might simply be an intellectual shortcoming of the human mind. Nothing but empty space was required for the "folding," but "empty space" was itself a term totally lacking in meaning—he was enough of a mathematician to know that.

If higher dimensions were required to "hold" a four-dimensional continuum, then the number of dimensions of space and of time were necessarily infinite; each order requires the next higher order to maintain it.

But "infinite" was another meaningless term. "Open series" was a little better, but not much.

Another consideration forced him to conclude that there was probably at least one more dimension than the four his senses could perceive—the Time Gate itself. He became quite skilled in handling its controls, but he never acquired the foggiest notion of how it worked, or how it had been built. It seemed to him that the creatures who built it must necessarily have been able to stand outside the limits that confined him in order to anchor the Gate to the structure of space time. The concept escaped him.

He suspected that the controls he saw were simply the part that stuck through into the space he knew. The very Palace itself might be no more than a three-dimensional section of a more involved structure. Such a condition would help to explain the otherwise inexplicable nature of its architecture.

He became possessed of an overpowering desire to know more about these strange creatures, the "High Ones," who had come and ruled the human race and built this Palace and this Gate, and gone away again— and in whose backwash he had been flung out of his setting some thirty millennia. To the human race they were no more than a sacred myth, a contradictory mass of tradition. No picture of them remained, no trace of their writing, nothing of their works save the High Palace of Norkaal and the Gate. And a sense of irreparable loss in the hearts of the race they had ruled, a loss expressed by their own term for themselves—the Forsaken Ones.

With controls and speculum he hunted back through time, seeking the Builders. It was slow work, as he had found before. A passing shadow, a tedious retracing—and failure.

Once he was sure that he had seen such a shadow in the speculum. He set the controls back far enough to be sure that he had repassed it, armed himself with food and drink and waited.

He waited three weeks.

The shadow might have passed during the hours he was forced to take out for sleep. But he felt sure that he was in the right period; he kept up the vigil.

He saw it.

It was moving toward the Gate.

When he pulled himself together he was halfway down the passageway leading away from the Hall. He realized that he had been screaming. He still had an attack of the shakes.

Somewhat later he forced himself to return to the Hall, and, with eyes averted, enter the control booth and return the spheres to zero. He backed out hastily and left the Hall for his apartment. He did not touch the controls nor enter the Hall for more than two years.

It had not been fear of physical menace that had shaken his reason, nor the appearance of the creature—he could recall nothing of *how* it looked. It had been a feeling of sadness infinitely compounded which had flooded through him at the instant, a sense of tragedy, of grief insupportable and unescapable, of infinite weariness. He had been flicked with emotions many times too strong for his spiritual fiber and which he was no more fitted to experience than an oyster is to play a violin.

He felt that he had learned all about the High Ones a man could learn and still endure. He was no longer curious. The shadow of that vicarious emotion ruined his sleep, brought him sweating out of dreams.

One other problem bothered him—the problem of himself and his meanders through time. It still worried him that he had met himself coming back, so to speak, had talked with himself, fought with himself.

Which one was *himself*?

He was all of them, he knew, for he remembered being each one. How about the times when there had been more than one present?

By sheer necessity he was forced to expand the principle of nonidentity—"Nothing is identical with anything else, not even with itself"—to include the ego. In a four-dimensional continuum each event is an absolute individual, it has its space coordinates and its date. The Bob Wilson he was right now was *not* the Bob Wilson he had been ten minutes ago. Each was a discrete section of a four-dimensional process. One resembled the other in many particulars, as one slice of bread resembles the slice next to it. But they were *not* the same Bob Wilson—they differed by a length of time.

When he had doubled back on himself, the difference had become apparent, for the separation was now in space rather than in time, and he happened to be so equipped as to be able to *see* a space length, whereas he could only remember a time difference. Thinking back he could remember a great many different Bob Wilsons, baby, small child, adolescent, young man. They were all different—he knew that. The only thing that bound them together into a feeling of identity was continuity of memory.

And that was the same thing that bound together the three—no, four, Bob Wilsons on a certain crowded afternoon, a memory track that ran through all of them. The only thing about it that remained remarkable was time travel itself.

And a few other little items—the nature of "free will," the problem of entropy, the law of the conservation of energy and mass. The last two, he now realized, needed to be extended or generalized to include the cases in which the Gate, or something like it, permitted a leak of mass, energy, or entropy from one neighborhood in the continuum to another. They were otherwise unchanged and valid. Free will was another matter. It could not be laughed off, because it could be directly experienced—yet his own free will had worked to create the same scene over and over again. Apparently human will must be considered as one of the factors which make up the processes in the continuum—"free" to the ego, mechanistic from the outside.

And yet his last act of evading Diktor had apparently changed the course of events. He was here and running the country, had been for many years, but Diktor had not showed up. Could it be that each act of "true" free will created a new and different future? Many philosophers had thought so.

This future appeared to have no such person as Diktor—*the* Diktor—in it, anywhere or anywhen.

As the end of his first ten years in the future approached, he became more and more nervous, less and less certain of his opinion. Damnation, he thought, if Diktor is going to show up it was high time that he did so. He was anxious to come to grips with him, establish which was to be boss.

He had agents posted throughout the country of the Forsaken Ones with instructions to arrest any man with hair on his face and fetch him forthwith to the Palace. The Hall of the Gate he watched himself.

He tried fishing the future for Diktor, but had no significant luck. He thrice located a shadow and tracked it down; each time it was himself. From tedium and partly from curiosity he attempted to see the other end of the process; he tried to relocate his original home, thirty thousand years in the past.

It was a long chore. The further the time button was displaced from the center, the poorer the control became. It took patient practice to be able to stop the image within a century or so of the period he wanted. It was in the course of this experimentation that he discovered what he had once looked for, a fractional control—a vernier, in effect. It was as simple as the primary control, but twist the bead instead of moving it directly.

He steadied down on the twentieth century, approximated the year by the models of automobiles, types of architecture, and other gross evidence, and stopped in what he believed to be 1952. Careful displacement of the space controls took him to the

university town where he had started—after several
false tries; the image did not enable him to read road
signs.

He located his boardinghouse, brought the Gate
into his own room. It was vacant, no furniture in it.

He panned away from the room, and tried again, a
year earlier. Success—his own room, his own furniture, but empty. He ran rapidly back, looking for
shadows.

There! He checked the swing of the image. There
were three figures in the room, the image was too
small, the light too poor for him to be sure whether
or not one of them was himself. He leaned over and
studied the scene.

He heard a dull thump outside the booth. He
straightened up and looked over the side.

Sprawled on the floor was a limp human figure.
Near it lay a crushed and battered hat.

He stood perfectly still for an uncounted time,
staring at the two redundant figures, hat and man,
while the winds of unreason swept through his mind
and shook it. He did not need to examine the uncon-
scious form to identify it. He knew . . . *he knew*—it
was his younger self, knocked willy-nilly through the
Time Gate.

It was not that fact in itself which shook him. He
had not particularly expected it to happen, having
come tentatively to the conclusion that he was living
in a different, an alternative, future from the one in
which he had originally transitted the Time Gate. He
had been aware that it might happen nevertheless,
that it did happen did not surprise him.

When it did happen, *he himself had been the only
spectator!*

He was Diktor. He was *the* Diktor. He was *the
only* Diktor!

He would never find Diktor, nor have it out with
him. He need never fear his coming. There never

had been, never would be, any other person called Diktor, because Diktor never had been nor ever would be anyone but himself.

In review, it seemed obvious that he must be Diktor; there were so many bits of evidence pointing to it. And yet it had not been obvious. Each point of similarity between himself and the Diktor, he recalled, had arisen from rational causes—usually from his desire to ape the gross characteristics of the "other" and thereby consolidate his own position of power and authority before the "other" Diktor showed up. For that reason he had established himself in the very apartments that "Diktor" had used—so that they would be "his" first.

To be sure his people called him Diktor, but he had thought nothing of that—they called anyone who ruled by that title, even the little subchieftains who were his local administrators.

He had grown a beard, such as Diktor had worn, partly in imitation of the "other" man's precedent, but more to set him apart from the hairless males of the Forsaken Ones. It gave him prestige, increased his tabu. He fingered his bearded chin. Still, it seemed strange that he had not recalled that his own present appearance checked with the appearance of "Diktor." "Diktor" had been an older man. He himself was only thirty-two, ten here, twenty-two *there*.

Diktor he had judged to be about forty-five. Perhaps an unprejudiced witness would believe himself to be that age. His hair and beard were shot with gray—had been, ever since the year he had succeeded too well in spying on the High Ones. His face was lined. Uneasy lies the head and so forth. Running a country, even a peaceful Arcadia, will worry a man, keep him awake nights.

Not that he was complaining—it had been a good life, a grand life, and it beat anything the ancient past had to offer.

In any case, he had been looking for a man in his middle forties, whose face he remembered dimly after ten years and whose picture he did not have. It had never occurred to him to connect that blurred face with his present one. Naturally not.

But there were other little things. Arma, for example. He had selected a likely-looking lass some three years back and made her one of his household staff, renaming her Arma in sentimental memory of the girl he had once fancied. It was logically necessary that they were the same girl, not two Armas, but one.

But, as he recalled her, the "first" Arma had been much prettier.

Hm-m-m—it must be his own point of view that had changed. He admitted that he had had much more opportunity to become bored with exquisite female beauty than his young friend over there on the floor. He recalled with a chuckle how he had found it necessary to surround himself with an elaborate system of tabus to keep the nubile daughters of his subjects out of his hair—most of the time. He had caused a particular pool in the river adjacent to the Palace to be dedicated to his use in order that he might swim without getting tangled up in mermaids.

The man on the floor groaned, but did not open his eyes.

Wilson, the Diktor, bent over him but made no effort to revive him. That the man was not seriously injured he had reason to be certain. He did not wish him to wake up until he had had time to get his own thoughts entirely in order.

For he had work to do, work which must be done meticulously, without mistake. Everyone, he thought with a wry smile, makes plans to provide for their future.

He was about to provide for his past.

There was the matter of the setting of the Time

Gate when he got around to sending his early self back. When he had tuned in on the scene in his room a few minutes ago, he had picked up the action just before his early self had been knocked through. In sending him back he must make a slight readjustment in the time setting to an instant around two o'clock of that particular afternoon. That would be simple enough; he need only search a short sector until he found his early self alone and working at his desk.

But the Time Gate had appeared in that room at a later hour; he had just caused it to do so. He felt confused.

Wait a minute, now—if he changed the setting of the time control, the Gate would appear in his room at the earlier time, remain there, and simply blend into its "reappearance" an hour or so later. Yes, that was right. To a person in the room it would simply be as if the Time Gate had been there all along, from about two o'clock.

Which it had been. He would see to that.

Experienced as he was with the phenomena exhibited by the Time Gate, it nevertheless required a strong and subtle intellectual effort to think other than in durational terms, to take an *eternal* viewpoint.

And there was the hat. He picked it up and tried it on. It did not fit very well, no doubt because he was wearing his hair longer now. The hat must be placed where it would be found—Oh, yes, in the control booth. And the notebook, too.

The notebook, the notebook—Mm-m-m—Something funny, there. When the notebook he had stolen had become dog-eared and tattered almost to illegibility some four years back, he had carefully recopied its contents in a new notebook—to refresh his memory of English rather than from any need for it as a guide. The worn-out notebook he had destroyed; it was the new one he intended to obtain, and leave to be found.

In that case, *there never had been two notebooks*. The one he had now would become, after being taken through the Gate to a point ten years in the past, the notebook from which he had copied it. They were simply different segments of the same physical process, manipulated by means of the Gate to run concurrently, side by side, for a certain length of time.

As he had himself—one afternoon.

He wished that he had not thrown away the worn-out notebook. If he had it at hand, he could compare them and convince himself that they were identical save for the wear and tear of increasing entropy.

But when had he learned the language, in order that he might prepare such a vocabulary? To be sure, when he copied it he then *knew* the language— copying had not actually been necessary.

But he *had* copied it.

The physical process he had all straightened out in his mind, but the intellectual process it represented was completely circular. His older self had taught his younger self a language which the older self knew because the younger self, after being taught, grew up to be the older self and was, therefore, capable of teaching.

But where had it started?

Which comes first, the hen or the egg?

You feed the rats to the cats, skin the cats, and feed the carcasses of the cats to the rats who are in turn fed to the cats. The perpetual motion fur farm.

If God created the world, who created God?

Who wrote the notebook? Who started the chain?

He felt the intellectual desperation of any honest philosopher. He knew that he had about as much chance of understanding such problems as a collie has of understanding how dog food gets into cans.

Applied psychology was more his size—which reminded him that there were certain books which his early self would find very useful in learning how to deal with the political affairs of the country he was to run. He made a mental note to make a list.

The man on the floor stirred again, sat up. Wilson knew that the time had come when he must insure his past. He was not worried; he felt the sure confidence of the gambler who is "hot," who *knows* what the next roll of the dice will show.

He bent over his alter ego. "Are you all right?" he asked.

"I guess so," the younger man mumbled. He put his hand to his bloody face. "My head hurts."

"I should think it would," Wilson agreed. "You came through head over heels. I think you hit your head when you landed."

His younger self did not appear fully to comprehend the words at first. He looked around dazedly, as if to get his bearings. Presently he said, "Came through? Came through what?"

"The Gate, of course," Wilson told him. He nodded his head toward the Gate, feeling that the sight of it would orient the still groggy younger Bob.

Young Wilson looked over his shoulder in the direction indicated, sat up with a jerk, shuddered and closed his eyes. He opened them again after what seemed to be a short period of prayer, looked again, and said, "Did I come through that?"

"Yes," Wilson assured him.

"Where am I?"

"In the Hall of the Gate in the High Palace of Norkaal. But what is more important," Wilson added, "is *when* you are. You have gone forward a little more than thirty thousand years."

The knowledge did not seem to reassure him. He got up and stumbled toward the Gate. Wilson put a restraining hand on his shoulder. "Where are you going?"

"Back!"

"Not so fast." He did not dare let him go back yet, not until the Gate had been reset. Besides he was still drunk—his breath was staggering. "You will go back all right—I give you my word on that. But let me dress your wounds first. And you should rest. I have some explanations to make to you, and there is an errand you can do for me when you get back—to our mutual advantage. There is a great future in store for you and me, my boy—a great future!"

A great future!

Colombus Was a Dope

Colombus Was a Dope

"I do like to wet down a sale," the fat man said happily, raising his voice above the sighing of the air-conditioner. "Drink up, Professor, I'm two ahead of you."

He glanced up from their table as the elevator door opposite them opened. A man stepped out into the cool dark of the bar and stood blinking, as if he had just come from the desert glare outside.

"Hey, Fred—Fred Nolan," the fat man called out. "Come over!" He turned to his guest. "Man I met on the hop from New York. Siddown, Fred. Shake hands with Professor Appleby, Chief Engineer of the Starship *Pegasus*—or will be when she's built. I just sold the Professor an order of bum steel for his crate. Have a drink on it."

"Glad to, Mr. Barnes," Nolan agreed. "I've met Dr. Appleby. On business—Climax Instrument Company."

"Huh?"

"Climax is supplying us with precision equipment," offered Appleby.

Barnes looked surprised, then grinned. "That's one on me. I took Fred for a government man, or one of

119

your scientific johnnies. What'll it be, Fred? Old-fashioned? The same, Professor?"

"Right. But please don't call me 'Professor.' I'm not one and it ages me. I'm still young."

"I'll say you are, uh—Doc, Pete! Two old-fashioneds and another double Manhattan! I guess I expected a comic book scientist, with a long white beard. But now that I've met you, I can't figure out one thing."

"Which is?"

"Well, at your age you bury yourself in this god-forsaken place—"

"We couldn't build the *Pegasus* on Long Island," Appleby pointed out, "and this is the ideal spot for the take-off."

"Yeah, sure, but that's not it. It's—well, mind you, I sell steel. You want special alloys for a starship; I sell it to you. But just the same, now that business is out of the way, why do you want to do it? Why try to go to Proxima Centauri, or any other star?"

Appleby looked amused. "It can't be explained. Why do men try to climb Mount Everest? What took Perry to the North Pole? Why did Columbus get the Queen to hock her jewels? Nobody has ever been to Proxima Centauri—so we're going."

Barnes turned to Nolan. "Do you get it, Fred?"

Nolan shrugged. "I sell precision instruments. Some people raise chrysanthemums; some build starships. I sell instruments."

Barnes' friendly face looked puzzled. "Well—" The bartender put down their drinks. "Say, Pete, tell me something. Would you go along on the *Pegasus* expedition if you could?"

"Nope."

"Why not?"

"I like it here."

Dr. Appleby nodded. "There's your answer, Barnes, in reverse. Some have the Columbus spirit and some haven't."

"It's all very well to talk about Columbus," Barnes persisted, "but he expected to come back. You guys don't expect to. Sixty years—you told me it would take sixty years. Why, you may not even live to get there."

"No, but our children will. And our grandchildren will come back."

"But—say, you're not *married?*"

"Certainly I am. Family men only on the expedition. It's a two-to-three generation job. You know that." He hauled out a wallet. "There's Mrs. Appleby with Diane. Diane is three and a half."

"She's a pretty baby," Barnes said soberly and passed it on to Nolan, who smiled at it and handed it back to Appleby. Barnes went on. "What happens to her?"

"She goes with us, naturally. You wouldn't want her put in an orphanage, would you?"

"No, but—" Barnes tossed off the rest of his drink, "I don't get it," he admitted. "Who'll have another drink?"

"Not for me, thanks," Appleby declined, finishing his more slowly and standing up. "I'm due home. Family man, you know." He smiled.

Barnes did not try to stop him. He said goodnight and watched Appleby leave.

"My round," said Nolan. "The same?"

"Huh? Yeah, sure." Barnes stood up. "Let's get up to the bar, Fred, where we can drink properly. I need about six."

"Okay," Nolan agreed, standing up. "What's the trouble?"

"Trouble? Did you see that picture?"

"Well?"

"Well, how do *you* feel about it? I'm a salesman too, Fred. I sell steel. It don't matter what the customer wants to use it for; I sell it to him. I'd sell a man a rope to hang himself. But I do love kids. I can't stand to think of that cute little kid going along on that—that crazy expedition!"

"Why not? She's better off with her parents. She'll get as used to steel decks as most kids are to sidewalks."

"But look, Fred. You don't have any silly idea they'll make it, do you?"

"They might."

"Well, they won't. They don't stand a chance. I know. I talked it over with our technical staff before I left the home office. Nine chances out of ten they'll burn up on the takeoff. That's the best that can happen to them. If they get out of the solar system, which ain't likely, they'll still never make it. They'll never reach the stars."

Pete put another drink down in front of Barnes. He drained it and said:

"Set up another one, Pete. They can't. It's a theoretical impossibility. They'll freeze—or they'll roast—or they'll starve. But they'll never get there."

"Maybe so."

"No maybe about it. They're *crazy*. Hurry up with that drink, Pete. Have one yourself."

"Coming up. Don't mind if I do, thanks." Pete mixed the cocktail, drew a glass of beer, and joined them.

"Pete, here, is a wise man," Barnes said confidentially. "You don't catch him monkeying around with any trips to the stars. Columbus—Pfui! Columbus was a dope. He shoulda stood in bed."

The bartender shook his head. "You got me wrong, Mr. Barnes. If it wasn't for men like Columbus, we wouldn't be here today—now, would we? I'm just not the explorer type. But I'm a believer. I got nothing against the *Pegasus* expedition."

"You don't approve of them taking kids on it, do you?"

"Well . . . there were kids on the *Mayflower*, so they tell me."

"It's not the same thing." Barnes looked at Nolan, then back to the bartender. "If the Lord had intended us to go to the stars, he would have equipped us with jet propulsion. Fix me another drink, Pete."

"You've had about enough for a while, Mr. Barnes."

The troubled fat man seemed about to argue, thought better of it.

"I'm going up to the Sky Room and find somebody that'll dance with me," he announced. "G'night." He swayed softly toward the elevator.

Nolan watched him leave. "Poor old Barnes." He shrugged. "I guess you and I are hard-hearted, Pete."

"No. I believe in progress, that's all. I remember my old man wanted a law passed about flying machines, keep 'em from breaking their fool necks. Claimed nobody ever could fly, and the government should put a stop to it. He was wrong. I'm not the adventurous type myself but I've seen enough people to know they'll try anything once, and that's how progress is made."

"You don't look old enough to remember when men couldn't fly."

"I've been around a long time. Ten years in this one spot."

"Ten years, eh? Don't you ever get a hankering for a job that'll let you breathe a little fresh air?"

"Nope. I didn't get any fresh air when I served drinks on Forty-second Street and I don't miss it now. I like it here. Always something new going on here, first the atom laboratories and then the big observatory and now the Starship. But that's not the real reason. I like it here. It's my home. Watch this."

He picked up a brandy inhaler, a great fragile crystal globe, spun it and threw it, straight up, toward the ceiling. It rose slowly and gracefully, paused for a long reluctant wait at the top of its rise, then settled slowly, slowly, like a diver in a slow-motion movie. Pete watched it float past his nose, then reached out with thumb and forefinger, nipped it easily by the stem, and returned it to the rack.

"See that," he said. "One-sixth gravity. When I was tending bar on earth my bunions gave me the dickens all the time. Here I weigh only thirty-five pounds. I like it on the Moon."

The Menace From Earth

The Menace From Earth

My name is Holly Jones and I'm fifteen. I'm very intelligent but it doesn't show, because I look like an underdone angel. Insipid.

I was born right here in Luna City, which seems to surprise Earthside types. Actually, I'm third generation; my grandparents pioneered in Site One, where the Memorial is. I live with my parents in Artemis Apartments, the new coop in Pressure Five, eight hundred feet down near City Hall. But I'm not there much; I'm too busy.

Mornings I attend Tech High and afternoons I study or go flying with Jeff Hardesty—he's my partner—or whenever a tourist ship is in I guide groundhogs. This day the *Gripsholm* grounded at noon so I went straight from school to American Express.

The first gaggle of tourists was trickling in from Quarantine but I didn't push forward as Mr. Dorcas, the manager, knows I'm the best. Guiding is just temporary (I'm really a spaceship designer), but if you're doing a job you ought to do it well.

Mr. Dorcas spotted me. "Holly! Here, please. Miss Brentwood, Holly Jones will be your guide."

" 'Holly,' " she repeated. "What a quaint name. Are you really a guide, dear?"

I'm tolerant of groundhogs—some of my best friends are from Earth. As Daddy says, being born on Luna is luck, not judgment, and most people Earthside are stuck there. After all, Jesus and Gautama Buddha and Dr. Einstein were all groundhogs.

But they can be irritating. If high school kids weren't guides, whom could they hire? "My license says so," I said briskly and looked her over the way she was looking me over.

Her face was sort of familiar and I thought perhaps I had seen her picture in those society things you see in Earthside magazines—one of the rich playgirls we get too many of. She was almost loathsomely lovely . . . nylon skin, soft, wavy, silver-blond hair, basic specs about 35-24-34 and enough this and that to make me feel like a matchstick drawing, a low intimate voice and everything necessary to make plainer females think about pacts with the Devil. But I did not feel apprehensive; she was a groundhog and groundhogs don't count.

"All city guides are girls," Mr. Dorcas explained. "Holly is very competent."

"Oh, I'm sure," she answered quickly and went into tourist routine number one: surprise that a guide was needed just to find her hotel, amazement at no taxicabs, same for no porters, and raised eyebrows at the prospect of two girls walking alone through "an underground city."

Mr. Dorcas was patient, ending with: "Miss Brentwood, Luna City is the only metropolis in the Solar System where a woman is really safe—no dark alleys, no deserted neighborhoods, no criminal element."

I didn't listen; I just held out my tariff card for Mr. Dorcas to stamp and picked up her bags. Guides shouldn't carry bags and most tourists are delighted to experience the fact that their thirty-pound allowance weighs only five pounds. But I wanted to get her moving.

We were in the tunnel outside and me with a foot on the slidebelt when she stopped. "I forgot! I want a city map."

"None available."

"Really?"

"There's only one. That's why you need a guide."

"But why don't they supply them? Or would that throw you guides out of work?"

See? "You think guiding is makework? Miss Brentwood, labor is so scarce they'd hire monkeys if they could."

"Then why not print maps?"

"Because Luna City isn't flat like—" I almost said, "—groundhog cities," but I caught myself.

"—like Earthside cities," I went on. "All you saw from space was the meteor shield. Underneath it spreads out and goes down for miles in a dozen pressure zones."

"Yes, I know, but why not a map for each level?"

Groundhogs always say, "Yes, I know, but—"

"I can show you the one city map. It's a stereo tank twenty feet high and even so all you see clearly are big things like the Hall of the Mountain King and hydroponics farms and the Bats' Cave."

" 'The Bats' Cave,' " she repeated. "That's where they fly, isn't it?"

"Yes, that's where we fly."

"Oh, I want to see it!"

"OK. It first . . . or the city map?"

She decided to go to her hotel first. The regular route to the Zurich is to slide up and west through Gray's Tunnel past the Martian Embassy, get off at the Mormon Temple, and take a pressure lock down to Diana Boulevard. But I know all the shortcuts; we got off at Macy-Gimbel Upper to go down their personnel hoist. I thought she would enjoy it.

But when I told her to grab a hand grip as it dropped past her, she peered down the shaft and edged back. "You're joking."

I was about to take her back the regular way when a neighbor of ours came down the hoist. I said, "Hello, Mrs. Greenberg," and she called back, "Hi, Holly. How are your folks?"

Susie Greenberg is more than plump. She was hanging by one hand with young David tucked in her other arm and holding the *Daily Lunatic*, reading as she dropped. Miss Brentwood stared, bit her lip, and said, "How do I do it?"

I said, "Oh, use both hands; I'll take the bags." I tied the handles together with my hanky and went first.

She was shaking when we got to the bottom. "Goodness, Holly, how do you stand it? Don't you get homesick?"

Tourist question number six. . . . I said, "I've been to Earth," and let it drop. Two years ago Mother made me visit my aunt in Omaha and I was *miserable*— hot and cold and dirty and beset by creepy-crawlies. I weighed a ton and I ached and my aunt was always chivvying me to go outdoors and exercise when all I wanted was to crawl into a tub and be quietly wretched. And I had hay fever. Probably you've never heard of hay fever—you don't die but you wish you could.

I was supposed to go to a girls' boarding school but I phoned Daddy and told him I was desperate and he let me come home. What groundhogs can't understand is that *they* live in savagery. But groundhogs are groundhogs and loonies are loonies and never the twain shall meet.

Like all the best hotels the Zurich is in Pressure One on the west side so that it can have a view of Earth. I helped Miss Brentwood register with the roboclerk and found her room; it had its own port.

She went straight to it, began staring at Earth and going *ooh!* and *ahh!*

I glanced past her and saw that it was a few minutes past thirteen; sunset sliced straight down the tip of India—early enough to snag another client. "Will that be all, Miss Brentwood?"

Instead of answering she said in an awed voice, "Holly, isn't that the most beautiful sight you ever saw?"

"It's nice," I agreed. The view on that side is monotonous except for earth hanging in the sky—but Earth is what tourists always look at even though they've just left it. Still, Earth is pretty. The changing weather is interesting if you don't have to be in it. Did you ever endure a summer in Omaha?

"It's gorgeous," she whispered.

"Sure," I agreed. "Do you want to go somewhere? Or will you sign my card?"

"What? Excuse me, I was daydreaming. No, not right now—yes, I do! Holly, I want to go out *there!* I must! Is there time? How much longer will it be light?"

"Huh? It's two days to sunset."

She looked startled. "How quaint. Holly, can you get us space suits? I've got to go outside."

I didn't wince—I'm used to tourist talk. I suppose a pressure suit looked like a space suit to them. I simply said, "We girls aren't licensed outside. But I can phone a friend."

Jeff Hardesty is my partner in spaceship designing, so I throw business his way. Jeff is eighteen and already in Goddard Institute, but I'm pushing hard to catch up so that we can set up offices for our firm: "Jones & Hardesty, Spaceship Engineers." I'm very bright in mathematics, which is everything in space engineering, so I'll get my degree pretty fast. Meanwhile we design ships anyhow.

I didn't tell Miss Brentwood this, as tourists think

that a girl my age can't possibly be a spaceship designer.

Jeff has arranged his classes to let him guide on Tuesdays and Thursdays; he waits at West City Lock and studies between clients. I reached him on the lockmaster's phone. Jeff grinned and said, "Hi, Scale Model."

"Hi, Penalty Weight. Free to take a client?"

"Well, I was supposed to guide a family party, but they're late."

"Cancel them. Miss Brentwood . . . step into pickup, please. This is Mr. Hardesty."

Jeff's eyes widened and I felt uneasy. But it did not occur to me that Jeff could be attracted by a *groundhog* . . . even though it is conceded that men are robot slaves of their body chemistry in such matters. I knew she was exceptionally decorative, but it was unthinkable that Jeff could be captivated by any groundhog, no matter how well designed. They don't speak our language!

I am not romantic about Jeff; we are simply partners. But anything that affects Jones & Hardesty affects me.

When we joined him at West Lock he almost stepped on his tongue in a disgusting display of adolescent rut. I was ashamed of him and, for the first time, apprehensive. Why are males so childish?

Miss Brentwood didn't seem to mind his behavior. Jeff is a big hulk; suited up for outside he looks like a Frost Giant from *Das Rheingold;* she smiled up at him and thanked him for changing his schedule. He looked even sillier and told her it was a pleasure.

I keep my pressure suit at West Lock so that when I switch a client to Jeff he can invite me to come along for the walk. This time he hardly spoke to me after that platinum menace was in sight. But I helped her pick out a suit and took her into the dressing room and fitted it. Those rental suits take careful adjusting or they will pinch you in tender places once out in vacuum . . . besides those things about them that one girl ought to explain to another.

When I came out with her, not wearing my own, Jeff didn't even ask why I hadn't suited up—he took her arm and started toward the lock. I had to butt in to get her to sign my tariff card.

The days that followed were the longest in my life. I saw Jeff only once . . . on the slidebelt in Diana Boulevard, going the other way. She was with him.

Though I saw him but once, I knew what was going on. He was cutting classes and three nights running he took her to the Earthview Room of the Duncan Hines. None of my business!—I hope she had more luck teaching him to dance than I had. Jeff is a free citizen and if he wanted to make an utter fool of himself neglecting school and losing sleep over an upholstered groundhog that was his business.

But he should not have neglected the firm's business!

Jones & Hardesty had a tremendous backlog because we were designing Starship *Prometheus*. This project we had been slaving over for a year, flying not more than twice a week in order to devote time to it—and that's a sacrifice.

Of course you can't build a starship today, because of the power plant. But Daddy thinks that there will soon be a technological break-through and mass-conversion power plants will be built—which means starships. Daddy ought to know—he's Luna Chief Engineer for Space Lanes and Fermi Lecturer at Goddard Institute. So Jeff and I are designing a self-supporting interstellar ship on that assumption: quarters, auxiliaries, surgery, labs—everything.

Daddy thinks it's just practice but Mother knows better—Mother is a mathematical chemist for General Synthetics of Luna and is nearly as smart as I am. She realizes that Jones & Hardesty plans to be ready with a finished proposal while other designers are still floundering.

Which was why I was furious with Jeff for wasting time over this creature. We had been working every possible chance. Jeff would show up after dinner, we would finish our homework, then get down to real work, the *Prometheus* . . . checking each other's computations, fighting bitterly over details, and having a wonderful time. But the very day I introduced him to Ariel Brentwood, he failed to appear. I had finished my lessons and was wondering whether to start or wait for him—we were making a radical change in power plant shielding—when his mother phoned me. "Jeff asked me to call you, dear. He's having dinner with a tourist client and can't come over."

Mrs. Hardesty was watching me so I looked puzzled and said, "Jeff thought I was expecting him? He has his dates mixed." I don't think she believed me; she agreed too quickly.

All that week I was slowly convinced against my will that Jones & Hardesty was being liquidated. Jeff didn't break any more dates—how can you break a date that hasn't been made?—but we always went flying Thursday afternoons unless one of us was guiding. He didn't call. Oh, I know where he was; he took her iceskating in Fingal's Cave.

I stayed home and worked on the *Prometheus*, recalculating masses and moment arms for hydroponics and stores on the basis of the shielding change. But I made mistakes and twice I had to look up logarithms instead of remembering . . . I was so used to wrangling with Jeff over everything that I just couldn't function.

Presently I looked at the name plate of the sheet I was revising. "Jones & Hardesty" it read, like all the rest. I said to myself, "Holly Jones, quit bluffing; this may be The End. You knew that someday Jeff would fall for somebody."

"Of course . . . but not a *groundhog*."

"But he *did*. What kind of an engineer are you if you can't face facts? She's beautiful and rich—she'll get her father to give him a job Earthside. You hear me? *Earthside!* So you look for another partner . . . or go into business on your own."

I erased "Jones & Hardesty" and lettered "Jones & Company" and stared at it. Then I started to erase that, too—but it smeared; I had dripped a tear on it. Which was ridiculous!

The following Tuesday both Daddy and Mother were home for lunch which was unusual as Daddy lunches at the spaceport. Now Daddy can't even see you unless you're a spaceship but that day he picked to notice that I had dialed only a salad and hadn't finished it. "That plate is about eight hundred calories short," he said, peering at it. "You can't boost without fuel—aren't you well?"

"Quite well, thank you," I answered with dignity.

"Mmm . . . now that I think back, you've been moping for several days. Maybe you need a checkup." He looked at Mother.

"I do not either need a checkup!" I had *not* been moping—doesn't a woman have a right not to chatter?

But I hate to have doctors poking at me so I added, "It happens I'm eating lightly because I'm going flying this afternoon. But if you insist, I'll order pot roast and potatoes and sleep instead!"

"Easy, punkin'," he answered gently. "I didn't mean to intrude. Get yourself a snack when you're through . . . and say hello to Jeff for me."

I simply answered, "OK," and asked to be excused; I was humiliated by the assumption that I couldn't fly without Mr. Jefferson Hardesty but did not wish to discuss it.

Daddy called after me, "Don't be late for dinner,"

and Mother said, "Now, Jacob—" and to me, "Fly until you're tired, dear; you haven't been getting much exercise. I'll leave your dinner in the warmer. Anything you'd like?"

"No, whatever you dial for yourself." I just wasn't interested in food, which isn't like me. As I headed for Bats' Cave I wondered if I had caught something. But my cheeks didn't feel warm and my stomach wasn't upset even if I wasn't hungry.

Then I had a horrible thought. Could it be that I was jealous? *Me?*

It was unthinkable. I am not romantic; I am a career woman. Jeff had been my partner and pal, and under my guidance he could have become a great spaceship designer, but our relationship was straightforward . . . a mutual respect for each other's abilities, with never any of that lovey-dovey stuff. A career woman can't afford such things—why look at all the professional time Mother had lost over having me!

No, I couldn't be jealous; I was simply worried sick because my partner had become involved with a groundhog. Jeff isn't bright about women and, besides, he's never been to Earth and has illusions about it. If she lured him Earthside, Jones & Hardesty was finished.

And somehow, "Jones & Company" wasn't a substitute: the *Prometheus* might never be built.

I was at Bats' Cave when I reached this dismal conclusion. I didn't feel like flying but I went to the locker room and got my wings anyhow.

Most of the stuff written about Bats' Cave gives a wrong impression. It's the air storage tank for the city, just like all the colonies have—the place where the scavenger pumps, deep down, deliver the air until it's needed. We just happen to be lucky enough to have one big enough to fly in. But it never was built, or anything like that; it's just a big volcanic bubble, two miles across, and if it had broken through, way back when, it would have been a crater.

Tourists sometimes pity us loonies because we have no chance to swim. Well, I tried it in Omaha and got water up my nose and scared myself silly. Water is for drinking, not playing in; I'll take flying. I've heard groundhogs say, oh yes, they had "flown" many times. But that's not *flying*. I did what they talk about, between White Sands and Omaha. I felt awful and got sick. Those things aren't safe.

I left my shoes and skirt in the locker room and slipped my tail surfaces on my feet, then zipped into my wings and got someone to tighten the shoulder straps. My wings aren't ready-made condors; they are Storer-Gulls, custom-made for my weight distribution and dimensions. I've cost Daddy a pretty penny in wings, outgrowing them so often, but these latest I bought myself with guide fees.

They're lovely!—titanalloy struts as light and strong as bird bones, tension-compensated wrist-pinion and shoulder joints, natural action in the alula slots, and automatic flap action in stalling. The wing skeleton is dressed in styrene feather-foils with individual quilling of scapulars and primaries. They almost fly themselves.

I folded my wings and went into the lock. While it was cycling I opened my left wing and thumbed the alula control—I had noticed a tendency to sideslip the last time I was airborne. But the alula opened properly and I decided I must have been overcontrolling, easy to do with Storer-Gulls; they're extremely maneuverable. Then the door showed green and I folded the wing and hurried out, while glancing at the barometer. Seventeen pounds—two more than Earth sea-level and nearly twice what we use in the city; even an ostrich could fly in that. I perked up and felt sorry for all groundhogs, tied down by six

times proper weight, who never, never, *never* could
fly.

Not even I could, on Earth. My wing loading is
less than a pound per square foot, as wings and all I
weigh less than twenty pounds. Earthside that would
be over a hundred pounds and I could flap forever
and never get off the ground.

I felt so good that I forgot about Jeff and his
weakness. I spread my wings, ran a few steps, warped
for lift and grabbed air—lifted my feet and was
airborne.

I sculled gently and let myself glide toward the air
intake at the middle of the floor—the Baby's Ladder,
we call it, because you can ride the updraft clear to
the roof, half a mile above, and never move a wing.
When I felt it I leaned right, spoiling with right
primaries, corrected, and settled in a counterclockwise soaring glide and let it carry me toward the
roof.

A couple of hundred feet up, I looked around. The
cave was almost empty, not more than two hundred
in the air and half that number perched or on the
ground—room enough for didoes. So as soon as I was
up five hundred feet I leaned out of the updraft and
began to beat. Gliding is no effort but flying is as
hard work as you care to make it. In gliding I support a mere ten pounds on each arm—shucks, on
Earth you work harder than that lying in bed. The lift
that keeps you in the air doesn't take any work; you
get it free from the shape of your wings just as long
as there is air pouring past them.

Even without an updraft all a level glide takes is
gentle sculling with your finger tips to maintain air
speed; a feeble old lady could do it. The lift comes
from differential air pressures but you don't have to
understand it; you just scull a little and the air supports you, as if you were lying in an utterly perfect
bed. Sculling keeps you moving forward just like

sculling a rowboat . . . or so I'm told; I've never
been in a rowboat. I had a chance to in Nebraska but
I'm not that foolhardy.

But when you're really flying, you scull with fore-
arms as well as hands and add power with your
shoulder muscles. Instead of only the outer quills of
your primaries changing pitch (as in gliding), now
your primaries and secondaries clear back to the
joint warp sharply on each downbeat and recovery;
they no longer lift, they force you forward—while
your weight is carried by your scapulars, up under
your armpits.

So you fly faster, or climb, or both, through controlling the angle of attack with your feet—with the
tail surfaces you wear on your feet, I mean.

Oh dear, this sounds complicated and isn't—you
just *do* it. You fly exactly as a bird flies. Baby birds
can learn it and they aren't very bright. Anyhow, it's
easy as breathing after you learn . . . and more fun
than you can imagine!

I climbed to the roof with powerful beats, increasing my angle of attack and slotting my alulae for lift
without burble—climbing at an angle that would stall
most fliers. I'm little but it's all muscle and I've been
flying since I was six. Once up there I glided and
looked around. Down at the floor near the south wall
tourists were trying guide wings—if you call those
things "wings." Along the west wall the visitors' gallery was loaded with goggling tourists. I wondered if
Jeff and his Circe character were there and decided
to go down and find out.

So I went into a steep dive and swooped toward
the gallery, leveled off and flew very fast along it. I
didn't spot Jeff and his groundhoggess but I wasn't
watching where I was going and overtook another
flier, almost collided. I glimpsed him just in time to
stall and drop under, and fell fifty feet before I got
control. Neither of us was in danger as the gallery is

two hundred feet up, but I looked silly and it was my own fault; I had violated a safety rule.

There aren't many rules but they are necesssary; the first is that orange wings always have the right of way—they're beginners. This flier did not have orange wings but I was overtaking. The flier underneath—or being overtaken—or nearer the wall—or turning counterclockwise, in that order, has the right of way.

I felt foolish and wondered who had seen me, so I went all the way back up, made sure I had clear air, then stooped like a hawk toward the gallery, spilling wings, lifting tail, and letting myself fall like a rock.

I completed my stoop in front of the gallery, lowering and spreading my tail so hard I could feel leg muscles knot and grabbing air with both wings, alulae slotted. I pulled level in an extremely fast glide along the gallery. I could see their eyes pop and thought smugly, "There! That'll show 'em!"

When darn if somebody didn't stoop on *me!* The blast from a flier braking right over me almost knocked me out of control. I grabbed air and stopped a sideslip, used some shipyard words and looked around to see who had blitzed me. I knew the black-and-gold wing pattern—Mary Muhlenburg, my best girl friend. She swung toward me, pivoting on a wing tip. "Hi, Holly! Scared you, didn't I?"

"You did not! You better be careful; the flightmaster'll ground you for a month."

"Slim chance! He's down for coffee."

I flew away, still annoyed, and started to climb. Mary called after me, but I ignored her, thinking, "Mary my girl, I'm going to get over you and fly you right out of the air."

This was a foolish thought as Mary flies every day and has shoulders and pectoral muscles like Mrs. Hercules. By the time she caught up with me I had cooled off and we flew side by side, still climbing. "Perch?" she called out.

"Perch," I agreed. Mary has lovely gossip and I could use a breather. We turned toward our usual perch, a ceiling brace for flood lamps—it isn't supposed to be a perch but the flightmaster hardly ever comes up there.

Mary flew in ahead of me, braked and stalled dead to a perfect landing. I skidded a little but Mary stuck out a wing and steadied me. It isn't easy to come into a perch, especially when you have to approach level. Two years ago a boy who had just graduated from orange wings tried it . . . knocked off his left alula and primaries on a strut—went fluttering and spinning down two thousand feet and crashed. He could have saved himself—you can come in safely with a badly damaged wing if you spill air with the other and accept the steeper glide, then stall as you land. But this poor kid didn't know how; he broke his neck, dead as Icarus. I haven't used that perch since.

We folded our wings and Mary sidled over. "Jeff is looking for you," she said with a sly grin.

My insides jumped but I answered coolly "So? I didn't know he was here."

"Sure. Down there," she added, pointing with her left wing. "Spot him?"

Jeff wears striped red and silver, but she was pointing at the tourist glide slope, a mile away. "No."

"He's there all right." She looked at me sidewise. "But I wouldn't look him up if I were you."

"Why not? Or for that matter, why should I?" Mary can be exasperating.

"Huh? You always run when he whistles. But he has that Earthside siren in tow again today; you might find it embarrassing."

"Mary, whatever are you talking about?"

"Huh? Don't kid me, Holly Jones; you know what I mean."

"I'm sure I don't," I answered with cold dignity.

"Humph! Then you're the only person in Luna City who doesn't. Everybody knows you're crazy about Jeff; everybody knows she's cut you out . . . and that you are simply simmering with jealousy."

Mary is my dearest friend but someday I'm going to skin her for a rug. "Mary, that's preposterously ridiculous! How can you even think such a thing?"

"Look, darling, you don't have to pretend. I'm for you." She patted my shoulders with her secondaries.

So I pushed her over backwards. She fell a hundred feet, straightened out, circled and climbed, and came in beside me, still grinning. It gave me time to decide what to say.

"Mary Muhlenburg, in the first place I am not crazy about anyone, least of all Jeff Hardesty. He and I are simply friends. So it's utterly nonsensical to talk about me being 'jealous.' In the second place Miss Brentwood is a lady and doesn't go around 'cutting out' anyone, least of all me. In the third place she is simply a tourist Jeff is guiding—business, nothing more."

"Sure, sure," Mary agreed placidly. "I was wrong. Still—" She shrugged her wings and shut up.

" 'Still' what? Mary, don't be mealy-mouthed."

"Mmm . . . I was wondering how you knew I was talking about Ariel Brentwood—since there isn't anything to it."

"Why, you mentioned her name."

"I did not."

I thought frantically. "Uh, maybe not. But it's perfectly simple. Miss Brentwood is a client I turned over to Jeff myself, so I assumed that she must be the tourist you meant."

"So? I don't recall even saying she was a tourist. But since she is just a tourist you two are splitting, why aren't you doing the inside guiding while Jeff sticks to outside work? I thought you guides had an agreement?"

"Huh? If he has been guiding her inside the city, I'm not aware of it—"

"You're the only one who isn't."

"—and I'm not interested; that's up to the grievance committee. But Jeff wouldn't take a fee for inside guiding in any case."

"Oh, sure!—not one he could *bank*. Well, Holly, seeing I was wrong, why don't you give him a hand with her? She wants to learn to glide."

Butting in on that pair was farthest from my mind. "If Mr. Hardesty wants my help, he will ask me. In the meantime I shall mind my own business . . . a practice I recommend to you!"

"Relax, shipmate," she answered, unruffled. "I was doing you a favor."

"Thank you, I don't need one."

"So I'll be on my way—got to practice for the gymkhana." She leaned forward and dropped off. But she didn't practice aerobatics; she dived straight for the tourist slope.

I watched her out of sight, then sneaked my left hand out the hand slit and got at my hanky—awkward when you are wearing wings but the floodlights had made my eyes water. I wiped them and blew my nose and put my hanky away and wiggled my hand back into place, then checked everything, thumbs, toes, and fingers, preparatory to dropping off.

But I didn't. I just sat there, wings drooping, and thought. I had to admit that Mary was partly right; Jeff's head was turned completely . . . over a *ground-hog*. So sooner or later he would go Earthside and Jones & Hardesty was finished.

Then I reminded myself that I had been planning to be a spaceship designer like Daddy long before Jeff and I teamed up. I wasn't dependent on anyone; I could stand alone, like Joan of Arc, or Lise Meitner.

I felt better . . . a cold, stern pride, like Lucifer in *Paradise Lost*.

I recognized the red and silver of Jeff's wings while he was far off and I thought about slipping quietly away. But Jeff can overtake me if he tries, so I decided, "Holly, don't be a fool! You've no reason to run . . . just be coolly polite."

He landed by me but didn't sidle up. "Hi, Decimal Point."

"Hi, Zero. Uh, stolen much lately?"

"Just the City Bank but they made me put it back." He frowned and added, "Holly, are you mad at me?"

"Why, Jeff, whatever gave you such a silly notion?"

"Uh . . . something Mary the Mouth said."

"Her? Don't pay any attention to what *she* says. Half of it's always wrong and she doesn't mean the rest."

"Yeah, a short circuit between her ears. Then you aren't mad?"

"Of *course* not. Why should I be?"

"No reason I know of. I haven't been around to work on the ship for a few days . . . but I've been awfully busy."

"Think nothing of it. I've been terribly busy myself."

"Uh, that's fine. Look, Test Sample, do me a favor. Help me out with a friend—a client, that is—well, she's a friend, too. She wants to learn to use glide wings."

I pretended to consider it. "Anyone I know?"

"Oh, yes. Fact is, you introduced us. Ariel Brentwood."

" 'Brentwood?' Jeff, there are so many tourists. Let me think. Tall girl? Blonde? Extremely pretty?"

He grinned like a goof and I almost pushed him off. "That's Ariel!"

"I recall her . . . she expected me to carry her

bags. But you don't need help, Jeff. She seemed very clever. Good sense of balance."

"Oh, yes, sure, all of that. Well, the fact is, I want you two to know each other. She's . . . well, she's just wonderful, Holly. A real person all the way through. You'll love her when you know her better. Uh . . . this seemed like a good chance."

I felt dizzy. "Why, that's very thoughtful, Jeff, but I doubt if she wants to know me better. I'm just a servant she hired—you know groundhogs."

"But she's not at all like the ordinary groundhog. And she *does* want to know you better—she *told* me so!"

After you told her to think so! I muttered. But I had talked myself into a corner. If I had not been hampered by polite upbringing I would have said, "On your way, vacuum skull! I'm not interested in your groundhog girl friends"—but what I did say was, "OK, Jeff," then gathered the fox to my bosom and dropped off into a glide.

So I taught Ariel Brentwood to "fly." Look, those so-called wings they let tourists wear have fifty square feet of lift surface, no controls except warp in the primaries, a built-in dihedral to make them stable as a table, and a few meaningless degrees of hinging to let the wearer think that he is "flying" by waving his arms. The tail is rigid, and canted so that if you stall (almost impossible) you land on your feet. All a tourist does is run a few yards, lift up his feet (he can't avoid it) and slide down a blanket of air. Then he can tell his grandchildren how he flew, really *flew*, "just like a bird."

An ape could learn to "fly" that much.

I put myself to the humiliation of strapping on a set of the silly things and had Ariel watch while I swung into the Baby's Ladder and let it carry me up a hundred feet to show her that you really and truly could "fly" with them. Then I thankfully got rid of them, strapped her into a larger set, and put on my beautiful Storer-Gulls. I had chased Jeff away (two instructors is too many), but when he saw her wing up, he swooped down and landed by us.

I looked up. "You again."

"Hello, Ariel. Hi, Blip. Say, you've got her shoulder straps too tight."

"Tut, tut," I said. "One coach at a time, remember? If you want to help, shuck those gaudy fins and put on some gliders . . . then I'll use you to show how not to. Otherwise get above two hundred feet and stay there; we don't need any dining-lounge pilots."

Jeff pouted like a brat but Ariel backed me up. "Do what teacher says, Jeff. That's a good boy."

He wouldn't put on gliders but he didn't stay clear, either. He circled around us, watching, and got bawled out by the flightmaster for cluttering the tourist area.

I admit Ariel was a good pupil. She didn't even get sore when I suggested that she was rather mature across the hips to balance well; she just said that she had noticed that I had the slimmest behind around there and she envied me. So I quit trying to get her goat, and found myself almost liking her as long as I kept my mind firmly on teaching. She tried hard and learned fast—good reflexes and (despite my dirty crack) good balance. I remarked on it and she admitted diffidently that she had had ballet training.

About mid-afternoon she said, "Could I possibly try real wings?"

"Huh? Gee, Ariel, I don't think so."

"Why not?"

There she had me. She had already done all that could be done with those atrocious gliders. If she was to learn more, she had to have real wings. "Ariel, it's dangerous. It's not what you've been doing, believe me. You might get hurt, even killed."

"Would you be held responsible?"

"No. You signed a release when you came in."

"Then I'd like to try it."

I bit my lip. If she had cracked up without my help, I wouldn't have shed a tear—but to let her do something too dangerous while she was my pupil . . . well, it smacked of David and Uriah. "Ariel, I can't stop you . . . but I should put my wings away and not have anything to do with it."

It was her turn to bite her lip. "If you feel that way, I can't ask you to coach me. But I still want to. Perhaps Jeff will help me."

"He probably will," I blurted out, "if he is as big a fool as I think he is!"

Her company face slipped but she didn't say anything because just then Jeff stalled in beside us. "What's the discussion?"

We both tried to tell him and confused him for he got the idea I had suggested it, and started bawling me out. Was I crazy? Was I trying to get Ariel hurt? Didn't I have any sense?

"*Shut up!*" I yelled, then added quietly but firmly, "Jefferson Hardesty, you wanted me to teach your girl friend, so I agreed. But don't butt in and don't think you can get away with talking to me like that. Now beat it! Take wing. Grab air!"

He swelled up and said slowly, "I absolutely forbid it."

Silence for five long counts. Then Ariel said quietly, "Come, Holly. Let's get me some wings."

"Right, Ariel."

But they don't rent real wings. Fliers have their own; they have to. However, there are second-hand ones for sale because kids outgrow them, or people shift to custom-made ones, or something. I found Mr. Schultz who keeps the key, and said that Ariel was thinking of buying but I wouldn't let her without a tryout. After picking over forty-odd pairs I found a set which Johnny Queveras had outgrown but which I knew were all right. Nevertheless I inspected them carefully. I could hardly reach the finger controls but they fitted Ariel.

While I was helping her into the tail surfaces I said, "Ariel? This is still a bad idea."

"I know. But we can't let men think they own us."

"I suppose not."

"The big toes spread them?"

"Yes. But don't do it. Just keep your feet together and toes pointed. Look, Ariel, you really aren't ready. Today all you will do is glide, just as you've been doing. Promise?"

She looked me in the eye. "I'll do exactly what you say . . . not even take wing unless you OK it."

"OK. Ready?"

"I'm ready."

"All right. Wups! I goofed. They aren't orange."

"Does it matter?"

"It sure does." There followed a weary argument because Mr. Schultz didn't want to spray them orange for a tryout. Ariel settled it by buying them, then we had to wait a bit while the solvent dried.

We went back to the tourist slope and I let her glide, cautioning her to hold both alulae open with her thumbs for more lift at slow speeds, while barely sculling with her fingers. She did fine, and stumbled in landing only once. Jeff stuck around, cutting figure eights above us, but we ignored him. Presently I taught her to turn in a wide, gentle bank—you can turn those awful glider things but it takes skill; they're only meant for straight glide.

Finally I landed by her and said, "Had enough?"

"I'll never have enough! But I'll unwing if you say."

"Tired?"

"No." She glanced over her wing at the Baby's Ladder; a dozen fliers were going up it, wings motionless, soaring lazily. "I wish I could do that just once. It must be heaven."

I chewed it over. "Actually, the higher you are, the safer you are."

"Then why not?"

"Mmm . . . safer *provided* you know what you're doing. Going up that draft is just gliding like you've been doing. You lie still and let it lift you half a mile high. Then you come down the same way, circling the wall in a gentle glide. But you're going to be tempted to do something you don't understand yet— flap your wings, or cut some caper."

She shook her head solemnly. "I won't do anything you haven't taught me."

I was still worried. "Look, it's only half a mile up but you cover five miles getting there and more getting down. Half an hour at least. Will your arms take it?"

"I'm sure they will."

"Well . . . you can start down anytime; you don't have to go all the way. Flex your arms a little now and then, so they won't cramp. Just don't flap your wings."

"I won't."

"OK." I spread my wings. "Follow me."

I led her into the updraft, leaned gently right, then back left to start the counterclockwise climb, all the while sculling very slowly so that she could keep up. Once we were in the groove I called out, "Steady as you are!" and cut out suddenly, climbed and took station thirty feet over and behind her. "Ariel?"

"Yes, Holly?"

"I'll stay over you. Don't crane your neck; you don't have to watch me, I have to watch you. You're doing fine."

"I feel fine!"

"Wiggle a little. Don't stiffen up. It's a long way to the roof. You can scull harder if you want to."

"Aye aye, Cap'n!"

"Not tired?"

"Heavens, no! Girl, I'm living!" She giggled. "And mama said I'd never be an angel!"

I didn't answer because red-and-silver wings came charging at me, braked suddenly and settled into the circle between me and Ariel. Jeff's face was almost as red as his wings. "What the devil do you think you are doing?"

"Orange wings!" I yelled. "Keep clear!"

"Get down out of here! Both of you!"

"Get out from between me and my pupil. You know the rules."

"Ariel!" Jeff shouted. "Lean out of the circle and glide down. I'll stay with you."

"Jeff Hardesty," I said savagely, "I give you three seconds to get out from between us—then I'm going to report you for violation of Rule One. For the third time—*Orange Wings!*"

Jeff growled something, dipped his right wing and dropped out of formation. The idiot sideslipped within five feet of Ariel's wing tip. I should have reported him for that; all the room you can give a beginner is none too much.

I said, "OK, Ariel?"

"OK, Holly. I'm sorry Jeff is angry."

"He'll get over it. Tell me if you feel tired."

"I'm not. I want to go all the way up. How high are we?"

"Four hundred feet, maybe."

Jeff flew below us a while, then climbed and flew over us . . . probably for the same reason I did: to see better. It suited me to have two of us watching her as long as he didn't interfere; I was beginning to fret that Ariel might not realize that the way down was going to be as long and tiring as the way up. I was hoping she would cry uncle. I knew I could glide until forced down by starvation. But a beginner gets tense.

Jeff stayed generally over us, sweeping back and forth—he's too active to glide very long—while Ariel and I continued to soar, winding slowly up toward the roof. It finally occurred to me when we were about halfway up that I could cry uncle myself; I didn't have to wait for Ariel to weaken. So I called out, "Ariel? Tired now?"

"No."

"Well, I am. Could we go down, please?"

She didn't argue, she just said, "All right. What am I to do?"

"Lean right and get out of the circle." I intended to have her move out five or six hundred feet, get into the return down draft, and circle the cave down instead of up. I glanced up, looking for Jeff. I finally spotted him some distance away and much higher but coming toward us. I called out, "Jeff! See you on the ground." He might not have heard me but he would see if he didn't hear; I glanced back at Ariel.

I couldn't find her.

Then I saw her, a hundred feet below—flailing her wings and falling, out of control.

I didn't know how it happened. Maybe she leaned too far, went into a sideslip and started to struggle, But I didn't try to figure it out; I was simply filled with horror. I seemed to hang there frozen for an hour while I watched her.

But the fact appears to be that I screamed *"Jeff!"* and broke into a stoop.

But I didn't seem to fall, couldn't overtake her. I spilled my wings completely—but couldn't manage to fall; she was as far away as ever.

You do start slowly, of course; our low gravity is the only thing that makes human flying possible.

Even a stone falls a scant three feet in the first second. But that first second seemed endless.

Then I knew I was falling. I could feel rushing air—but I still didn't seem to close on her. Her struggles must have slowed her somewhat, while I was in an intentional stoop, wings spilled and raised over my head, falling as fast as possible. I had a wild notion that if I could pull even with her, I could shout sense into her head, get her to dive, then straighten out in a glide. But I couldn't *reach* her.

This nightmare dragged on for hours.

Actually we didn't have room to fall for more than twenty seconds; that's all it takes to stoop a thousand feet. But twenty seconds can be horribly long . . . long enough to regret every foolish thing I had ever done or said, long enough to say a prayer for us both . . . and to say good-by to Jeff in my heart. Long enough to see the floor rushing toward us and knew that we were both going to crash if I didn't overtake her mighty quick.

I glanced up and Jeff was stooping right over us but a long way up. I looked down at once . . . and I was overtaking her . . . I was passing her—*I was under her!*

Then I was braking with everything I had, almost pulling my wings off. I grabbed air, held it, and started to beat without ever going to level flight. I beat once, twice, three times . . . and hit her from below, jarring us both.

Then the floor hit us.

I felt feeble and dreamily contented. I was on my back in a dim room. I think Mother was with me and I know Daddy was. My nose itched and I tried to scratch it, but my arms wouldn't work. I fell asleep again.

I woke up hungry and wide awake. I was in a hospital bed and my arms still wouldn't work, which wasn't surprising as they were both in casts. A nurse came in with a tray. "Hungry?" she asked.

"Starved," I admitted.

"We'll fix that." She started feeding me like a baby.

I dodged the third spoonful and demanded. "What happened to my arms?"

"Hush," she said and gagged me with a spoon.

But a nice doctor came in later and answered my question. "Nothing much. Three simple fractures. At your age you'll heal in no time. But we like your company so I'm holding you for observation of possible internal injury."

"I'm not hurt inside," I told him. "At least, I don't hurt."

"I told you it was just an excuse."

"Uh, Doctor?"

"Well?"

"Will I be able to fly again?" I waited, scared.

"Certainly. I've seen men hurt worse get up and go three rounds."

"Oh. Well, thanks. Doctor? What happened to the other girl? Is she . . . did she . . .?"

"Brentwood? She's here."

"She's right here," Ariel agreed from the door. "May I come in?"

My jaw dropped, then I said, "Yeah. Sure. Come in."

The doctor said, "Don't stay long," and left. I said, "Well, sit down."

"Thanks." She hopped instead of walked and I saw that one foot was bandaged. She got on the end of the bed.

"You hurt your foot."

She shrugged. "Nothing. A sprain and a torn ligament. Two cracked ribs. But I would have been dead. You know why I'm not?"

I didn't answer. She touched one of my casts.

"That's why. You broke my fall and I landed on top of you. You saved my life and I broke both your arms."

"You don't have to thank me. I would have done it for anybody."

"I believe you and I wasn't thanking you. You can't thank a person for saving your life. I just wanted to make sure you knew that I knew it."

I didn't have an answer so I said, "Where's Jeff? Is he all right?"

"He'll be along soon. Jeff's not hurt . . . though I'm surprised he didn't break both ankles. He stalled in beside us so hard that he should have. But Holly . . . Holly my very dear . . . I slipped in so that you and I could talk about him before he got here."

I changed the subject quickly. Whatever they had given me made me feel dreamy and good, but not beyond being embarrassed. "Ariel, what happened? You were getting along fine—then suddenly you were in trouble."

She looked sheepish. "My own fault. You said we were going down, so I looked down. Really looked, I mean. Before that, all my thoughts had been about climbing clear to the roof; I hadn't thought about how far down the floor was. Then I looked down . . . and got dizzy and panicky and went all to pieces." She shrugged. "You were right. I wasn't ready."

I thought about it and nodded. "I see. But don't worry—when my arms are well, I'll take you up again."

She touched my foot. "Dear Holly. But I won't be flying again; I'm going back where I belong."

"Earthside?"

"Yes. I'm taking the *Billy Mitchell* on Wednesday."

"Oh. I'm sorry."

She frowned slightly. "Are you? Holly, you don't like me, do you?"

I was startled silly. What can you say? Especially

when it's true? "Well," I said slowly, "I don't dislike you. I just don't know you very well."

She nodded. "And I don't know you very well . . . even though I got to know you a lot better in a very few seconds. But Holly . . . listen please and don't get angry. It's about Jeff. He hasn't treated you very well the last few days—while I've been here, I mean. But don't be angry with him. I'm leaving and everything will be the same."

That ripped it open and I couldn't ignore it, because if I did, she would assume all sorts of things that weren't so. So I had to explain . . . about me being a career woman . . . how, if I had seemed upset, it was simply distress at breaking up the firm of Jones & Hardesty before it even finished its first starship . . . how I was *not* in love with Jeff but simply valued him as a friend and associate . . . but if Jones & Hardesty couldn't carry on, then Jones & Company would. "So you see, Ariel, it isn't necessary for you to give up Jeff. If you feel you owe me something, just forget it. It isn't necessary."

She blinked and I saw with amazement that she was holding back tears. "Holly, Holly . . . you don't understand at all."

"I understand all right. I'm not a child."

"No, you're a grown woman . . . but you haven't found it out." She held up a finger. "One—Jeff doesn't love me."

"I don't believe it."

"Two . . . I don't love him."

"I don't believe that, either."

"Three . . . you say you don't love him—but I'll take that up when we come to it. Holly, am I beautiful?"

Changing the subject is a female trait but'll never learn to do it that fast. "Huh?"

"I said, 'Am I beautiful?' "

"You know darn well you are!"

"Yes. I can sing a bit and dance, but I would get few parts if I were not, because I'm no better than a third-rate actress. So I have to be beautiful. How old am I?"

I managed not to boggle. "Huh? Older than Jeff thinks you are. Twenty-one, at least. Maybe twenty-two."

She sighed. "Holly, I'm old enough to be your mother."

"Huh? I don't believe that, either."

"I'm glad it doesn't show. But that's why, though Jeff is a dear, there never was a chance that I could fall in love with him. But how I feel about him doesn't matter; the important thing is that *he* loves *you*."

"*What?* That's the silliest thing you've said yet! Oh, he *likes* me—or did. But that's all." I gulped. "And it's all I want. Why, you should hear the way he talks to me."

"I have. But boys that age can't say what they mean; they get embarrassed."

"But—"

"Wait, Holly. I saw something you didn't because you were knocked cold. When you and I bumped, do you know what happened?"

"Uh, no."

"Jeff arrived like an avenging angel, a split second behind us. He was ripping his wings off as he hit, getting his arms free. He didn't even look at me. He just stepped across me and picked you up and cradled you in his arms, all the while bawling his eyes out."

"He *did?*"

"He did."

I mulled it over. Maybe the big lunk did kind of like me, after all.

Ariel went on, "So you see, Holly, even if you

don't love him, you must be very gentle with him, because he loves you and you can hurt him terribly."

I tried to think. Romance was still something that a career woman should shun . . . but if Jeff really did feel that way—well . . . would it be compromising my ideals to marry him just to keep him happy? To keep the firm together? Eventually, that is?

But if I did, it wouldn't be Jones & Hardesty; it would be Hardesty & Hardesty.

Ariel was still talking: "—you might even fall in love with him. It does happen, hon, and if it did, you'd be sorry if you had chased him away. Some other girl would grab him; he's awfully nice."

"But—" I shut up for I heard Jeff's step—I can always tell it. He stopped in the door and looked at us, frowning.

"Hi, Ariel."

"Hi, Jeff."

"Hi, Fraction." He looked me over. "My, but you're a mess."

"You aren't pretty yourself. I hear you have flat feet."

"Permanently. How do you brush your teeth with those things on your arms?"

"I don't."

Ariel slid off the bed, balanced on one foot. "Must run. See you later, kids."

"So long, Ariel."

"Good-by, Ariel. Uh . . . thanks."

Jeff closed the door after she hopped away, came to the bed and said gruffly, "Hold still."

Then he put his arms around me and kissed me.

Well, I couldn't stop him, could I? With both arms broken? Besides, it was consonant with the new policy for the firm. I was startled speechless because Jeff never kisses me, except birthday kisses, which don't count. But I tried to kiss back and show that I appreciated it.

I don't know what the stuff was they had been giving me but my ears began to ring and I felt dizzy again.

Then he was leaning over me. "Runt," he said mournfully, "you sure give me a lot of grief."

"You're no bargain yourself, flathead," I answered with dignity.

"I suppose not." He looked me over sadly. "What are you crying for?"

I didn't know that I had been. Then I remembered why. "Oh, Jeff—I busted my pretty wings!"

"We'll get you more. Uh, brace yourself. I'm going to do it again."

"All right." He did.

I suppose Hardesty & Hardesty has more rhythm than Jones & Hardesty.

It really sounds better.

Sky Lift

Sky Lift

"All torch pilots! Report to the Commodore!" The call echoed through Earth Satellite Station.

Joe Appleby flipped off the shower to listen. "You don't mean me," he said happily, "I'm on leave—but I'd better shove before you change your mind."

He dressed and hurried along a passageway. He was in the outer ring of the Station; its slow revolution, a giant wheel in the sky, produced gravity-like force against his feet. As he reached his room the loud-speakers repeated, "All torch pilots, report to the Commodore," then added, "Lieutenant Appleby, report to the Commodore." Appleby uttered a rude monosyllable.

The Commodore's office was crowded. All present wore the torch, except a flight surgeon and Commodore Berrio himself, who wore the jets of a rocketship pilot. Berrio glanced up and went on talking: "—the situation. If we are to save Proserpina Station, an emergency run must be made out to Pluto. Any questions?"

No one spoke. Appleby wanted to, but did not wish to remind Berrio that he had been late. "Very well," Berrio went on. "Gentlemen, it's a job for torch pilots. I must ask for volunteers."

Good! thought Appleby. Let the eager lads volunteer and then adjourn. He decided that he might still catch the next shuttle to Earth. The Commodore continued, "Volunteers please remain. The rest are dismissed."

Excellent, Appleby decided. Don't rush for the door, me lad. Be dignified—sneak out between two taller men.

No one left. Joe Appleby felt swindled but lacked the nerve to start the exodus. The Commodore said soberly, "Thank you, gentlemen. Will you wait in the wardroom, please?" Muttering, Appleby left with the crowd. He wanted to go out to Pluto someday—sure!—but not now, not with Earthside leave papers in his pocket.

He held a torcher's contempt for the vast distance itself. Older pilots thought of interplanetary trips with a rocket man's bias, in terms of years—trips that a torch ship with steady acceleration covered in days. By the orbits that a rocketship must use the round trip to Jupiter takes over five years; Saturn is twice as far, Uranus twice again, Neptune still farther. No rocketship ever attempted Pluto; a round trip would take more than ninety years. But torch ships had won a foothold even there: Proserpina Station—cryology laboratory, cosmic radiation station, parallax observatory, physics laboratory, all in one quintuple dome against the unspeakable cold.

Nearly four billion miles from Proserpina Station Appleby followed a classmate into the wardroom. "Hey, Jerry," he said, "tell me what it is I seem to have volunteered for?"

Jerry Price looked around. "Oh, it's late Joe Appleby. Okay, buy me a drink."

A radiogram had come from Proserpina, Jerry told him, reporting an epidemic: "Larkin's disease."

Appleby whistled. Larkin's disease was a mutated virus, possibly of Martian origin; a victim's red-cell count fell rapidly, soon he was dead. The only treatment was massive transfusions while the disease ran its course. "So, m'boy, somebody has to trot out to Pluto with a blood bank."

Appleby frowned. "My pappy warned me. 'Joe,' he said, 'keep your mouth shut and never volunteer.' "

Jerry grinned. "We didn't exactly volunteer."

"How long is the boost? Eighteen days or so? I've got social obligations Earthside."

"Eighteen days at one-g—but this will be higher. They are running out of blood donors."

"How high? A g-and-a-half?"

Price shook his head. "I'd guess two gravities."

"Two g's!"

"What's hard about that? Men have lived through a lot more."

"Sure, for a short pull-out—not for days on end. Two g's strains your heart if you stand up."

"Don't moan, they won't pick you—I'm more the hero type. While you're on leave, think of me out in those lonely wastes, a grim-jawed angel of mercy. Buy me another drink."

Appleby decided that Jerry was right; with only two pilots needed he stood a good chance of catching the next Earth shuttle. He got out his little black book and was picking phone numbers when a messenger arrived. "Lieutenant Appleby, sir?" Joe admitted it.

"The-Commodore's-compliments-and-will-you-report -at-once,-sir?"

"On my way." Joe caught Jerry's eye. "Who is what type?"

Jerry said, "Shall I take care of your social obligations?"

"Not likely!"

"I was afraid not. Good luck, boy."

With Commodore Berrio was the flight surgeon and an older lieutenant. Berrio said, "Sit down, Appleby. You know Lieutenant Kleuger? He's your skipper. You will be co-pilot."

"Very good, sir."

"Appleby, Mr. Kleuger is the most experienced torch pilot available. You were picked because medical records show you have exceptional tolerance for acceleration. This is a high-boost trip."

"How high, sir?"

Berrio hesitated. "Three and one-half gravities."

Three and a half g's! That wasn't a boost—that was a pullout. Joe heard the surgeon protest, "I'm sorry, sir, but three gravities is all I can approve."

Berrio frowned. "Legally, it's up to the captain. But three hundred lives depend on it."

Kleuger said, "Doctor, let's see that curve." The surgeon slid a paper across the desk; Kleuger moved it so that Joe could see it. "Here's the scoop, Appleby—"

A curve started high, dropped very slowly, made a sudden "knee" and dropped rapidly. The surgeon put his finger on the "knee." "Here," he said soberly, "is where the donors are suffering from loss of blood as much as the patients. After that it's hopeless, without a new source of blood."

"How did you get this curve?" Joe asked.

"It's the empirical equation of Larkin's disease applied to two hundred eighty-nine people."

Appleby noted vertical lines each marked with an acceleration and a time. Far to the right was one marked: "1 g— 18 days." That was the standard trip; it would arrive after the epidemic had burned out. Two gravities cut it to twelve days seventeen hours; even so, half the colony would be dead. Three g's was better but still bad. He could see why the Commodore wanted them to risk three-and-a-half kicks; that line touched the "knee," at nine days fifteen

hours. That way they could save almost everybody
. . . but, oh, brother!

The time advantage dropped off by inverse squares.
Eighteen days required one gravity, so nine days
took four, while four-and-a-half days required a fan-
tastic sixteen gravities. But someone had drawn a
line at "16 g—4.5 days." "Hey! This plot must be for
a robot-torch—that's the ticket! Is there one available?"

Berrio said gently, "Yes. But what are its chances?"

Joe shut up. Even between the inner planets ro-
bots often went astray. In four-billion-odd miles the
chance that one could hit close enough to be caught
by radio control was slim. "We'll try," Berrio promised. "If it succeeds, I'll call you at once." He looked
at Kleuger. "Captain, time is short. I must have your
decision."

Kleuger turned to the surgeon. "Doctor, why not
another half gravity? I recall a report on a chimpanzee who was centrifuged at high g for an amazingly
long time."

"A chimpanzee is not a man."

Joe blurted out, "How much did this chimp stand,
Surgeon?"

"Three and a quarter gravities for twenty-seven
days."

"He *did?* What shape was he in when the test
ended?"

"He wasn't," the doctor grunted.

Kleuger looked at the graph, glanced at Joe, then
said to the Commodore, "The boost will be at three
and one-half gravities, sir."

Berrio merely said, "Very well, sir. Hurry over to
sick bay. You haven't much time."

Forty-seven minutes later they were being packed
into the scout torchship *Salamander*. She was in
orbit close by; Joe, Kleuger, and their handlers
came by tube linking the hub of the Station to her
airlock. Joe was weak and dopey from a thorough

washing-out plus a dozen treatments and injections. A good thing, he thought, that light-off would be automatic.

The ship was built for high boost; controls were over the pilots' tanks, where they could be fingered without lifting a hand. The flight surgeon and an assistant fitted Kleuger into one tank while two medical technicians arranged Joe in his. One of them asked, "Underwear smooth? No wrinkles?"

"I guess."

"I'll check." He did so, then arranged fittings necessary to a man who must remain in one position for days. "The nipple left of your mouth is water; the two on your right are glucose and bouillon."

"No solids?"

The surgeon turned in the air and answered, "You don't need any, you won't want any, and you mustn't have any. And be careful in swallowing."

"I've boosted before."

"Sure, sure. But be careful."

Each tank was like an oversized bathtub filled with a liquid denser than water. The top was covered by a rubbery sheet, gasketed at the edges; during boost each man would float with the sheet conforming to his body. The *Salamander* being still in free orbit, everything was weightless and the sheet now served to keep the fluid from floating out. The attendants centered Appleby against the sheet and fastened him with sticky tape, then placed his own acceleration collar, tailored to him, behind his head. The surgeon came over and inspected. "You okay?"

"Sure."

"Mind that swallowing." He added, "Okay, Captain. Permission to leave your ship, sir?"

"Certainly. Thank you, Surgeon."

"Good luck." He left with the technicians.

The room had no ports and needed none. The area in front of Joe's face was filled with screens, instruments, radar, and data displays; near his forehead was his eyepiece for the coelostat. A light blinked green as the passenger tube broke its anchors; Kleuger caught Joe's eye in a mirror mounted opposite them. "Report, Mister."

"Minus seven minutes oh four. Tracking. Torch warm and idle. Green for light-off."

"Stand by while I check orientation." Kleuger's eyes disappeared into his coelostat eyepiece. Presently he said, "Check me, Joe."

"Aye aye, sir." Joe twisted a knob and his eyepiece swung down. He found three star images brought together perfectly in the cross hairs. "Couldn't be better, Skipper."

"Ask for clearance."

"Salamander to Control—clearance requested to Proserpina. Automatic light-off on tape. All green."

"Control to Salamander. You are cleared. Good luck!"

"Cleared, Skipper. Minus three. . . . *Double oh!*" Joe thought morosely that he should be half way to Earth now. Why the hell did the military always get stuck with these succor-&-rescue jobs?

When the counter flashed the last thirty seconds he forgot his foregone leave. The lust to travel possessed him. To go, no matter where, anywhere . . . go! He smiled as the torch lit off.

Then weight hit him.

At three and one-half gravities he weighed six hundred and thirty pounds. It felt as if a load of sand had landed on him, squeezing his chest, making him helpless, forcing his head against his collar. He strove to relax, to let the supporting liquid hold him together. It was all right to tighten up for a pull-out, but for a long boost one must relax. He breathed shallowly and slowly; the air was pure oxygen, little lung action was needed. But he labored just to breathe. He could feel his heart struggling to pump blood grown heavy through squeezed vessels. This is awful he admitted. I'm not sure I can take it. He had once had four g for nine minutes but he had forgotten how bad it was.

"Joe! *Joe!*"

He opened his eyes and tried to shake his head. "Yes, Skipper." He looked for Kleuger in the mirror; the pilot's face was sagging and drawn, pulled into the mirthless grin of high acceleration.

"Check orientation!"

Joe let his arms float as he worked controls with leaden fingers. "Dead on, Skipper."

"Very well. Call Luna."

Earth Station was blanketed by their torch but the Moon was on their bow. Appleby called Luna tracking center and received their data on the departure plus data relayed from Earth Station. He called figures and times to Kleuger, who fed them into the computer. Joe then found that he had forgotten, while working, his unbearable weight. It felt worse than ever. His neck ached and he suspected that there was a wrinkle under his left calf. He wiggled in the tank to smooth it, but it made it worse. "How's she look, Skipper?"

"Okay. You're relieved, Joe. I'll take first watch."

"Right, Skipper." He tried to rest—as if a man could when buried under sandbags. His bones ached and the wrinkle became a nagging nuisance. The pain in his neck got worse; apparently he had wrenched it at light-off. He turned his head, but there were just two positions—bad and worse. Closing his eyes, he attempted to sleep. Ten minutes later he was wider awake than ever, his mind on three things, the lump in his neck, the irritation under his leg, and the squeezing weight.

Look, bud, he told himself, this is a long boost. Take it easy, or adrenalin exhaustion will get you. As the book says, "*The ideal pilot is relaxed and unwor-*

ried. Sanguine in temperament, he never borrows trouble." Why, you chair-warming so-and-so! Were *you* at three and a half g's when you wrote that twaddle?

Cut it out, boy! He turned his mind to his favorite subject—girls, bless their hearts. Such self-hypnosis he had used to pass many a lonely million miles. Presently he realized wryly that his phantom harem had failed him. He could not conjure them up, so he banished them and spent his time being miserable.

He awoke in a sweat. His last dream had been a nightmare that he was headed out to Pluto at an impossibly high boost.

My God! So he was!

The pressure seemed worse. When he moved his head there was a stabbing pain down his side. He was panting and sweat was pouring off. It ran into his eyes; he tried to wipe them, found that his arm did not respond and that his fingertips were numb. He inched his arm across his body and dabbed at his eyes; it did not help.

He stared at the elapsed time dial of the integrating accelerograph and tried to remember when he was due on watch. It took a while to understand that six and a half hours had passed since light-off. He then realized with a jerk that it was long past time to relieve the watch. Kleuger's face in the mirror was still split in the grin of high g; his eyes were closed. "Skipper!" Joe shouted. Kleuger did not stir. Joe felt for the alarm button, thought better of it. Let the poor goop sleep!

But somebody had to feed the hogs—better get the clouds out of his brain. The accelerometer showed three and a half exactly; the torch dials were all in operating range; the radiometer showed leakage less than ten percent of danger level.

The integrating accelerograph displayed elapsed time, velocity, and distance, in dead-reckoning for empty space. Under these windows were three more which showed the same by the precomputed tape controlling the torch; by comparing, Joe could tell how results matched predictions. The torch had been lit off for less than seven hours, speed was nearly two million miles per hour and they were over six million miles out. A third display corrected these figures for the Sun's field, but Joe ignored this; near Earth's orbit the Sun pulls only one two-thousandth of a gravity—a gnat's whisker, allowed for in precomputation. Joe merely noted that tape and D.R. agreed; he wanted an outside check.

Both Earth and Moon now being blanketed by the same cone of disturbance, he twisted knobs until their radar beacon beamed toward Mars and let it pulse the signal meaning "Where am I?" He did not wait for an answer; Mars was eighteen minutes away by radio. He turned instead to the coelostat. The triple image had wandered slightly but the error was too small to correct.

He dictated what he had done into the log, whereupon he felt worse. His ribs hurt, each breath carried the stab of pleurisy. His hands and feet felt "pins-and-needles" from scanty circulation. He wiggled them, which produced crawling sensations and wearied him. So he held still and watched the speed soar. It increased seventy-seven miles per hour every second, more than a quarter million miles per hour every hour. For once he envied rocketship pilots; they took forever to get anywhere but they got there in comfort.

Without the torch, men would never have ventured much past Mars. $E = Mc^2$, mass is energy, and a pound of sand equals fifteen billion horsepower-hours. An atomic rocketship uses but a fraction of one percent of that energy, whereas the new torchers used better than eighty percent. The conversion chamber of a torch was a tiny sun; particles expelled from it approached the speed of light.

Appleby was proud to be a torcher, but not at the moment. The crick had grown into a splitting head-ache, he wanted to bend his knees and could not, and he was nauseated from the load on his stomach. Kleuger seemed able to sleep through it, damn his eyes! How did they expect a man to *stand* this? Only eight hours and already he felt done in, bushed—how could he last nine days?

Later—time was beginning to be uncertain—some indefinite time later he heard his name called. "Joe! *Joe!*"

Couldn't a man die in peace? His eyes wandered around, found the mirror; he struggled to focus. "Joe! You've got to relieve me—I'm groggy."

"Aye aye, sir."

"Make a check, Joe. I'm too goofed up to do it."

"I already did, sir."

"*Huh?* When?"

Joe's eyes swam around to the elapsed-time dial. He closed one eye to read it. "Uh, about six hours ago."

"What? *What time is it?*"

Joe didn't answer. He wished peevishly that Kleuger would go away. Kleuger added soberly, "I must have blacked out, kid. What's the situation?" Presently he insisted, "Answer me, Mister."

"Huh? Oh, we're all right—down the groove. Skip-per, is my left leg twisted? I can't see it."

"Eh? Oh, never mind your leg! What were the figures?"

"What figures?"

" 'What figures?' Snap out of it, Mister! You're on duty."

A fine one to talk, Joe thought fretfully. If that's how he's going to act, I'll just close my eyes and ignore him.

Kleuger repeated, "The figures, Mister."

"Huh? Oh, play 'em off the log if you're so damned eager!" He expected a blast at that, but none came. When next he opened his eyes Kleuger's eyes were closed. He couldn't recall whether the Skipper had played his figures back or not—nor whether he had logged them. He decided that it was time for another check but he was dreadfully thirsty; he needed a drink first. He drank carefully but still got a drop down his windpipe. A coughing spasm hurt him all over and left him so weak that he had to rest.

He pulled himself together and scanned the dials. Twelve hours and—No, wait a minute! One *day* and twelve hours—that *couldn't* be right. But their speed was over ten million miles per hour and their distance more than ninety million miles from Earth; they were beyond the orbit of Mars. "Skipper! Hey! Lieutenant Kleuger!"

Kleuger's face was a grinning mask. In dull panic Joe tried to find their situation. The coelostat showed them balanced; either the ship had wobbled back, or Kleuger had corrected it. Or had he himself? He decided to run over the log and see. Fumbling among buttons he found the one to rewind the log.

Since he didn't remember to stop it the wire ran all the way back to light-off, then played back, zipping through silent stretches and slowing for speech. He listened to his record of the first check, then found that Phobos Station, Mars, had answered with a favorable report—to which a voice added, *"Where's the fire?"*

Yes, Kleuger had corrected balance hours earlier. The wire hurried through a blank spot, slowed again— Kleuger had dictated a letter to someone; it was unfinished and incoherent. Once Kleuger had stopped to shout, *"Joe! Joe!"* and Joe heard himself answer, *"Oh shut up!"* He had no memory of it.

There was something he should do but he was too

tired to think and he hurt all over—except his legs, he couldn't feel them. He shut his eyes and tried not to think. When he opened them the elapsed time was turning three days; he closed them and leaked tears.

A bell rang endlessly; he became aware that it was the general alarm, but he felt no interest other than a need to stop it. It was hard to find the switch, his fingers were numb. But he managed it and was about to rest from the effort, when he heard Kleuger call him. "Joe!"

"Huh?"

"Joe—don't go back to sleep or I'll turn the alarm on again. You hear me?"

"Yeah—" So Kleuger had done that—why, damn him!

"Joe, I've got to talk to you. I can't stand any more."

" 'Any more' what?"

"High boost. I can't take any more—it's killing me."

"Oh, rats!" Turn on that loud bell, would he?

"I'm dying, Joe. I can't see—my eyes are shot. Joe, I've got to shut down the boost. I've got to."

"Well, what's stopping you?" Joe answered irritably.

"Don't you see, Joe? You've got to back me up. We tried and we couldn't. We'll both log it. Then it'll be all right."

"Log what?"

"Eh? Dammit, Joe, pay attention. I can't talk much. You've got to say—to say that the strain became unendurable and you advised me to shut down. I'll confirm it and it will be all right." His labored whisper was barely audible.

Joe couldn't figure out what Kleuger meant. He couldn't remember why Kleuger had put them in high boost anyhow. *"Hurry,* Joe."

There he went, nagging him! Wake him up and

then nag him—to hell with him. "Oh, go back to sleep!" He dozed off and was again jerked awake by the alarm. This time he knew where the switch was and flipped it quickly. Kleuger switched it on again, Joe turned it off. Kleuger quit trying and Joe passed out.

He came awake in free fall. He was still realizing the ecstasy of being weightless when he managed to reorient; he was in the *Salamander,* headed for Pluto. Had they reached the end of the run? No, the dial said four days and some hours. Had the tape broken? The autopilot gone haywire? He then recalled the last time he had been awake.

Kleuger had shut off the torch!

The stretched grin was gone from Kleuger's face, the features seemed slack and old. Joe called out, "Captain! Captain Kleuger!" Kleuger's eyes fluttered and lips moved but Joe heard nothing. He slithered out of the tank, moved in front of Kleuger, floated there. "Captain, can you hear me?"

The lips whispered, "I had to, boy. I saved us. Can you get us back, Joe?" His eyes opened but did not track.

"Captain, listen to me. I've got to light off again."

"Huh? No, Joe, no!"

"I've got to."

"*No!* That's an order, Mister."

Appleby stared, then with a judo chop caught the sick man on the jaw. Kleuger's head bobbed loosely. Joe pulled himself between the tanks, located a three-position switch, turned it from "Pilot & Co-Pilot" to "Co-Pilot Only"; Kleuger's controls were now dead. He glanced at Kleuger, saw that his head was not square in his collar, so he taped him properly into place, then got back in his tank. He settled his head and fumbled for the switch that would put the autopilot back on tape. There was some reason why they must finish this run—but for the life of him he could not remember why. He squeezed the switch and weight pinned him down.

He was awakened by a dizzy feeling added to the pressure. It went on for seconds, he retched futilely. When the motion stopped he peered at the dials. The *Salamander* had just completed the somersault from acceleration to deceleration. They had come half way, about, eighteen hundred million miles; their speed was over three million miles per hour and beginning to drop. Joe felt that he should report it to the skipper—he had no recollection of any trouble with him. "Skipper! Hey!" Kleuger did not move. Joe called again, then resorted to the alarm.

The clangor woke, not Kleuger, but Joe's memory. He shut it off, feeling soul sick. Topping his physical misery was shame and loss and panic as he recalled the shabby facts. He felt that he ought to log it but could not decide what to say. Beaten and ever lower in mind he gave up and tried to rest.

He woke later with something gnawing at his mind . . . something he should do for the Captain . . . something about a cargo robot—

That was it! If the robot-torch had reached Pluto, they could quit! Let's see—elapsed-time from light-off was over five days. Yes, if it ever got there, then—

He ran the wire back, listened for a recorded message. It was there: *"EarthStation to Salamander— Extremely sorry to report that robot failed rendezvous. We are depending on you.—Berrio."*

Tears of weakness and disappointment sped down his cheeks, pulled along by three and one-half gravities.

It was on the eighth day that Joe realized that Kleuger was dead. It was not the stench—he was unable to tell that from his own ripe body odors. Nor was it that the Captain had not roused since flipover; Joe's time sense was so fogged that he did not realize this. But he had dreamt that Kleuger was shouting for him to get up, to stand up—"Hurry up, Joe!" But the weight pressed him down.

So sharp was the dream that Joe tried to answer after he woke up. Then he looked for Kleuger in the mirror. Kleuger's face was much the same, but he knew with sick horror that the captain was dead. Nevertheless he tried to arouse him with the alarm. Presently he gave up; his fingers were purple and he could feel nothing below his waist; he wondered if he were dying and hoped that he was. He slipped into that lethargy which had become his normal state.

He did not become conscious when, after more than nine days, the autopilot quenched the torch. Awareness found him floating in midroom, having somehow squirmed out of his station. He felt deliciously lazy and quite hungry; the latter eventually brought him awake.

His surroundings put past events somewhat into place. He pulled himself to his tank and examined the dials. Good grief!—it had been two hours since the ship had gone into free fall. The plan called for approach to be computed before the tape ran out, corrected on entering free fall, a new tape cut and fed in without delay, then let the autopilot make the approach. He had done nothing and wasted two hours.

He slid between tank and controls, discovering then that his legs were paralyzed. No matter—legs weren't needed in free fall, nor in the tank. His hands did not behave well, but he could use them. He was stunned when he found Kleuger's body, but steadied down and got to work. He had no idea where he was; Pluto might be millions of miles away, or almost in his lap—perhaps they had spotted him and were already sending approach data. He decided to check the wire.

He found their messages at once:

"Proserpina to Salamander—Thank God you are

coming. Here are your elements at quench out—": followed by time reference, range-and-bearing figures, and doppler data.

And again: *"Here are later and better figures, Salamander—hurry!"*

And finally, only a few minutes before: *"Salamander, why the delay in light-off? Is your computer broken down? Shall we compute a ballistic for you?"*

The idea that anyone but a torcher could work a torch ballistic did not sink in. He tried to work fast, but his hands bothered him—he punched wrong numbers and had to correct them. It took him a half hour to realize that the trouble was not just his fingers. Ballistics, a subject as easy for him as checkers, was confused in his mind.

He could not work the ballistic.

"Salamander to Proserpina—Request ballistic for approach into parking orbit around Pluto."

The answer came so quickly that he knew that they had not waited for his okay. With ponderous care he cut the tape and fed it into the autopilot. It was then that he noticed the boost . . . four point oh three.

Four gravities for the approach—

He had assumed that the approach would be a normal one—and so it might have been if he had not wasted three hours.

But it wasn't fair! It was too much to expect. He cursed childishly as he settled himself, fitted the collar, and squeezed the button that turned control to the autopilot. He had a few minutes of waiting time; he spent it muttering peevishly. They could have figured him a better ballistic—hell, he should have figured it. They were always pushing him around. Good old Joe, anybody's punching bag! That so-and-so Kleuger over there, grinning like a fool and leaving

the work for him—if Kleuger hadn't been so confounded eager—

Acceleration hit him and he blacked out.

When the shuttle came up to meet him, they
found one man dead, one nearly dead, and the cargo
of whole blood.

The supply ship brought pilots for the *Salamander*
and fetched Appleby home. He stayed in sick bay
until ordered to Luna for treatment; on being de-
tached he reported to Berrio, escorted by the flight
surgeon. The Commodore let him know brusquely
that he had done a fine job, a damn fine job! The
interview ended and the surgeon helped Joe to stand;
instead of leaving Joe said, "Uh, Commodore?"

"Yes, son?"

"Uh, there's one thing I don't understand, uh,
what I don't understand is, uh, this: why do I have to
go, uh, to the geriatrics clinic at Luna City? That's
for old people, uh? That's what I've always understood—the way I understand it. Sir?"

The surgeon cut in, "I told you, Joe. They have
the very best physiotherapy. We got special permission for you."

Joe looked perplexed. "Is that right, sir? I feel
funny, going to an old folks', uh, hospital?"

"That's right, son."

Joe grinned sheepishly. "Okay, sir, uh, if you say
so."

They started to leave. "Doctor—stay a moment.
Messenger, help Mr. Appleby."

"Joe, can you make it?"

"Uh, sure! My legs are lots better—see?" He went
out, leaning on the messenger.

Berrio said, "Doctor, tell me straight: will Joe get
well?"

"No, sir."

"Will he get better?"

"Some, perhaps. Lunar gravity makes it easy to get the most out of what a man has left."

"But will his mind clear up?"

The doctor hesitated. "It's this way, sir. Heavy acceleration is a speeded-up aging process. Tissues break down, capillaries rupture, the heart does many times its proper work. And there is hypoxia, from failure to deliver enough oxygen to the brain."

The Commodore struck his desk an angry blow. The surgeon said gently, "Don't take it so hard, sir."

"Damn it, man—think of the way he was. Just a kid, all bounce and vinegar—now look at him! He's an old man—senile."

"Look at it this way," urged the surgeon, "you expended one man, but you saved two hundred and seventy."

" 'Expended one man'? If you mean Kleuger, he gets a medal and his wife gets a pension. That's the best any of us can expect. I wasn't thinking of Kleuger."

"Neither was I," answered the surgeon.

Goldfish Bowl

Goldfish Bowl

On the horizon lay the immobile cloud which capped the incredible waterspouts known as the Pillars of Hawaii.

Captain Blake lowered his binoculars. "There they stand, gentlemen."

In addition to the naval personnel of the watch, the bridge of the hydrographic survey ship U. S. S. *Mahan* held two civilians; the captain's words were addressed to them. The elder and smaller of the pair peered intently through a spyglass he had borrowed from the quartermaster. "I can't make them out," he complained.

"Here—try my glasses, doctor," Blake suggested, passing over his binoculars. He turned to the officer of the deck and added, "Have the forward range finder manned, if you please, Mr. Mott." Lieutenant Mott caught the eye of the bos'n's mate of the watch, listening from a discreet distance, and jerked a thumb upward. The petty officer stepped to the microphone, piped a shrill stand-by, and the metallic voice of the loud-speaker filled the ship, drowning out the next words of the captain:

"Raaaaange one! Maaaaaaaan and cast loose!"

183

"I asked," the captain repeated, "if that was any better."

"I think I see them," Jacobson Graves acknowledged. "Two dark vertical stripes, from the cloud to the horizon."

"That's it."

The other civilian, Bill Eisenberg, had taken the telescope when Graves had surrendered it for the binoculars. "I got 'em, too," he announced. "There's nothing wrong with this 'scope, Doc. But they don't look as big as I had expected," he admitted.

"They are still beyond the horizon," Blake explained. "You see only the upper segments. But they stand just under eleven thousand feet from water line to cloud—if they are still running true to form."

Graves looked up quickly. "Why the mental reservation? Haven't they been?"

Captain Blake shrugged. "Sure. Right on the nose. But they ought not to be there at all—four months ago they did not exist. How do I know what they will be doing today—or tomorrow?"

Graves nodded. "I see your point—and agree with it. Can we estimate their height from the distance?"

"I'll see." Blake stuck his head into the charthouse. "Any reading, Archie?"

"Just a second, captain." The navigator stuck his face against a voice tube and called out, "Range!"

A muffled voice replied, "Range one—no reading."

"Something greater than twenty miles," Blake told Graves cheerfully. "You'll have to wait, doctor."

Lieutenant Mott directed the quartermaster to make three bells; the captain left the bridge, leaving word that he was to be informed when the ship approached the critical limit of three miles from the Pillars. Somewhat reluctantly, Graves and Eisenberg followed him down; they had barely time enough to dress before dining with the captain.

Captain Blake's manners were old-fashioned; he

did not permit the conversation to turn to shop talk until the dinner had reached the coffee and cigars stage. "Well, gentlemen," he began, as he lit up, "just what is it you propose to do?"

"Didn't the Navy Department tell you?" Graves asked with a quick look.

"Not much. I have had one letter, directing me to place my ship and command at your disposal for research concerning the Pillars, and a dispatch two days ago telling me to take you aboard this morning. No details."

Graves looked nervously at Eisenberg, then back to the captain. He cleared his throat. "Uh—we propose, captain, to go up the Kanaka column and down the Wahini."

Blake gave him a sharp look, started to speak, reconsidered, and started again. "Doctor—you'll forgive me, I hope; I don't mean to be rude—but that sounds utterly crazy. A fancy way to commit suicide."

"It may be a little dangerous—"

"Hummph!"

"—but we have the means to accomplish it, if, as we believe to be true, the Kanaka column supplies the water which becomes the Wahini column on the return trip." He outlined the method. He and Eisenberg totaled between them nearly twenty-five years of bathysphere experience, eight for Eisenberg, seventeen for himself. They had brought aboard the *Mahan*, at present in an uncouth crate on the fantail, a modified bathysphere. Externally it was a bathysphere with its anchor weights removed; internally it much more nearly resembled some of the complicated barrels in which foolhardy exhibitionists have essayed the spectacular, useless trip over Niagara Falls. It would supply air, stuffy but breathable, for forty-eight hours; it held water and concentrated food for at least that period; there were even rude but adequate sanitary arrangements.

But its principal feature was an anti-shock harness, a glorified corset, a strait jacket, in which a man could hang suspended clear of the walls by means of a network of Gideon cord and steel springs. In it, a man might reasonably hope to survive most violent pummeling. He could perhaps be shot from a cannon, bounced down a hillside, subjected to the sadistic mercy of a baggage smasher, and still survive with bones intact and viscera unruptured.

Blake poked a finger at a line sketch with which Graves had illustrated his description. "You actually intend to try to ascend the Pillars in that?"

Eisenberg replied. "Not him, captain. Me."

Graves reddened. "My damned doctor—"

"*And* your colleagues," Eisenberg added. "It's this way, captain: there's nothing wrong with Doc's nerve, but he has a leaky heart, a pair of submarine ears, and a set of not-so-good arteries. So the Institute has delegated me to kinda watch over him."

"Now look here," Graves protested, "Bill, you're not going to be stuffy about this. I'm an old man; I'll never have another such chance."

"No go," Eisenberg denied. "Captain, I wish to inform you that the Institute vested title of record to that gear we brought aboard in me, just to keep the old war horse from doing anything foolish."

"That's your pidgin," Blake answered testily. "My instructions are to facilitate Dr. Graves' research. Assuming that one or the other of you wish to commit suicide in that steel coffin, how do you propose to enter the Kanaka Pillar?"

"Why, that's your job, captain. You put the sphere into the up column and pick it up again when it comes down the down column."

Blake pursed his lips, then slowly shook his head. "I can't do that."

"Huh? Why not?"

"I will not take my ship closer than three miles to

the Pillars. The *Mahan* is a sound ship, but she is not built for speed. She can't make more than twelve knots. Some place inside that circle the surface current which feeds the Kanaka column will exceed twelve knots. I don't care to find out where, by losing my ship.

"There have been an unprecedented number of unreported fishing vessels out of the islands lately. I don't care to have the *Mahan* listed."

"You think they went up the column?"

"I do."

"But, look, captain," suggested Bill Eisenberg, "you wouldn't have to risk the ship. You could launch the sphere from a power boat."

Blake shook his head. "Out of the question," he said grimly. "Even if the ship's boats were built for the job, which they aren't, I will not risk naval personnel. This isn't war."

"I wonder," said Graves softly.

"What's that?"

Eisenberg chuckled. "Doc has a romantic notion that all the odd phenomena turned up in the past few years can be hooked together into one smooth theory with a single, sinister cause—everything from the Pillars to LaGrange's fireballs."

"LaGrange's fireballs? How could there be any connection there? They are simply static electricity, allee samee heat lightning. I know; I've seen 'em."

The scientists were at once attentive, Graves' pique and Eisenberg's amusement alike buried in truth-tropism "You did? When? Where?"

"Golf course at Hilo. Last March. I was—"

"*That* case! That was one of the disappearance cases!"

"Yes, of course. I'm trying to tell you. I was standing in a sand trap near the thirteenth green, when I happened to look up—" A clear, balmy island day.

No clouds, barometer normal, light breeze. Nothing to suggest atmospheric disturbance, no maxima of sunspots, no static on the radio. Without warning a half dozen or more, giant fireballs—ball "lightning" on a unprecedented scale—floated across the golf course in a sort of skirmish line, a line described by some observers as mathematically even—an assertion denied by others.

A woman player, a tourist from the mainland, screamed and began to run. The flanking ball nearest her left its place in line and danced after her. No one seemed sure that the ball touched her—Blake could not say although he had watched it happen—but when the ball had passed on, there she lay on the grass, dead.

A local medico of somewhat flamboyant reputation insisted that he found evidence in the cadaver of both coagulation and electrolysis, but the jury that sat on the case followed the coroner's advice in calling it heart failure, a verdict heartily approved by the local chamber of commerce and tourist bureau.

The man who disappeared did not try to run; his fate came to meet him. He was a caddy, a Japanese-Portygee-Kanaka mixed breed, with no known relatives, a fact which should have made it easy to leave his name out of the news reports had not a reporter smelled it out. "He was standing on the green, not more than twenty-five yards away from me," Blake recounted, "when the fireballs approached. One passed on each side of me. My skin itched, and my hair stood up. I could smell ozone. I stood still—"

"That saved you," observed Graves.

"Nuts," said Eisenberg. "Standing in the dry sand of the trap was what saved him."

"Bill, you're a fool," Graves said wearily. "These fireball things perform with intelligent awareness."

Blake checked his account. "Why do you assume that, doctor?"

"Never mind, for the moment, please. Go on with your story."

"Hm-m-m. Well, they passed on by me. The caddy fellow was directly in the course of one of them. I don't believe he saw it—back toward it, you see. It reached him, enveloped him, passed on—but the boy was gone."

Graves nodded. "That checks with the accounts I have seen. Odd that I did not recall your name from the reports."

"I stayed in the background," Blake said shortly. "Don't like reporters."

"Hm-m-m. Anything to add to the reports that did come out? Any errors in them?"

"None that I can recall. Did the reports mention the bag of golf clubs he was carrying?"

"I think not."

"They were found on the beach, six miles away."

Eisenberg sat up. "That's news," he said. "Tell me: Was there anything to suggest how far they had fallen? Were they smashed or broken?"

Blake shook his head. "They weren't even scratched, nor was the beach sand disturbed. But they were—ice-cold."

Graves waited for him to go on; when the captain did not do so he inquired, "What do you make of it?"

"Me? I make nothing of it."

"How do you explain it?"

"I don't. Unclassified electrical phenomena. However, if you want a rough guess, I'll give you one. This fireball is a static field of high potential. It englobes the caddy and charges him, whereupon he bounces away like a pith ball—electrocuted, incidentally. When the charge dissipates, he falls into the sea."

"So? There was a case like it in Kansas, rather too far from the sea."

"The body might simply never have been found."

"They never are. But even so—how do you account for the clubs being deposited so gently? And why were they cold?"

"Dammit, man, *I* don't know! I'm no theoretician; I'm a maritime engineer by profession, an empiricist by disposition. Suppose you tell me."

"All right—but bear in mind that my hypothesis is merely tentative, a basis for investigation. I see in these several phenomena, the Pillars, the giant fireballs, a number of other assorted phenomena which should never have happened, but did—including the curious case of a small mountain peak south of Boulder, Colorado, which had its tip leveled off 'spontaneously'—I see in these things evidence of intelligent direction, a single conscious cause." He shrugged. "Call it the 'X' factor. I'm looking for X."

Eisenberg assumed a look of mock sympathy. "Poor old Doc," he sighed. "Sprung a leak at last."

The other two ignored the crack. Blake inquired, "You are primarily an ichthyologist, aren't you?"

"Yes."

"How did you get started along this line?"

"I don't know. Curiosity, I suppose. My boisterous young friend here would tell you that ichthyology is derived from 'icky.' "

Blake turned to Eisenberg. "But aren't *you* an ichthyologist?"

"Hell, no! I'm an oceanographer specializing in ecology."

"He's quibbling," observed Graves. "Tell Captain Blake about Cleo and Pat."

Eisenberg looked embarrassed. "They're damned nice pets," he said defensively.

Blake looked puzzled; Graves explained. "He kids me, but *his* secret shame is a pair of goldfish. Goldfish! You'll find 'em in the washbasin in his stateroom this minute."

"Scientific interest?" Blake inquired with a dead pan.

"Oh, no! He thinks they are devoted to him."

"They're damned nice pets," Eisenberg insisted. "They don't bark, they don't scratch, they don't make messes. And Cleo does so have expression!"

In spite of his initial resistance to their plans Blake cooperated actively in trying to find a dodge whereby the proposed experiment could be performed without endangering naval personnel or matcrial. IIe liked these two; he understood their curious mixture of selfless recklessness and extreme caution; it matched his own—it was professionalism, as distinguished from economic motivation.

He offered the services of his master diver, an elderly commissioned warrant officer, and his technical crew in checking their gear. "You know," he added, "there is some reason to believe that your bathysphere could make the round trip, aside from the proposition that what goes up must come down. You know of the VJ-14?"

"Was that the naval plane lost in the early investigation?"

"Yes." He buzzed for his orderly. "Have my writer bring up the jacket on the VJ-14," he directed.

Attempts to reconnoiter the strange "permanent" cloud and its incredible waterspouts had been made by air soon after its discovery. Little was learned. A plane would penetrate the cloud. Its ignition would fail; out it would glide, unharmed, whereupon the engines would fire again. Back into the cloud—engine failure. The vertical reach of the cloud was greater than the ceiling of any plane.

"The VJ-14," Blake stated, referring occasionally to the file jacket which had been fetched, "made an air reconnaissance of the Pillars themselves on 12 May, attended by the U. S. S. Pelican. Besides the pilot and radioman she carried a cinematographer and a chief aerographer. Mm-m-m—only the last two entries seem to be pertinent: 'Changing course. Will fly between the Pillars—14,' and '0913—Ship does not respond to controls—14.' Telescopic observation from the *Pelican* shows that she made a tight upward spiral around the Kanaka Pillar, about one and a half turns, and was sucked into the column itself. Nothing was seen to fall.

"Incidentally the pilot, Lieutenant—m-m-m-m, yes—Mattson—Lieutenant Mattson was exonerated posthumously by the court of inquiry. Oh, yes, here's the point pertinent to our question: From the log of the *Pelican:* '1709—Picked up wreckage identified as part of VJ-14. See additional sheet for itemized description.' We needn't bother with that. Point is, they picked it up four miles from the base of the Wahini Pillar on the side away from the Kanaka. The inference is obvious and your scheme might work. Not that you'd live through it."

"I'll chance it," Eisenberg stated.

"Mm-m-m—yes. But I was going to suggest we send up a dead load, say a crate of eggs packed into a hogshead." The buzzer from the bridge sounded; Captain Blake raised his voice toward the brass funnel of a voice tube in the overhead. "Yes?"

"Eight o'clock, Captain. Eight o'clock lights and galley fires out; prisoners secured."

"Thank you, sir." Blake stood up. "We can get together on the details in the morning."

A fifty-foot motor launch bobbed listlessly astern the *Mahan*. A nine-inch coir line joined it to its mother ship; bound to it at fathom intervals was a telephone line ending in a pair of headphones worn by a signalman seated in the stern sheets of the launch. A pair of flags and a spyglass lay on the thwart beside him; his blouse had crawled up, exposing part of the lurid cover of a copy of *Dynamic Tales*, smuggled along as a precaution against boredom.

Already in the boat were the coxswain, the engineman, the boat officer, Graves, and Eisenberg. With them, forward in the boat, was a breaker of water rations, two fifty-gallon drums of gasoline—and a hogshead. It contained not only a carefully packed crate of eggs but also a jury-rigged smoke-signal device, armed three ways—delayed action set for eight, nine and ten hours; radio relay triggered from the ship; and simple salt-water penetration to complete an electrical circuit. The torpedo gunner in charge of diving hoped that one of them might work and thereby aid in locating the hogshead. He was busy trying to devise more nearly foolproof gear for the bathysphere.

The boat officer signaled ready to the bridge. A megaphoned bellow responded, "Pay her out handsomely!" The boat drifted slowly away from the ship and directly toward the Kanaka Pillar, three miles away.

The Kanaka Pillar loomed above them, still nearly a mile away but loweringly impressive nevertheless. The place where it disappeared in cloud seemed almost overhead, falling toward them. Its five-hundred-foot-thick trunk gleamed purplish-black, more like polished steel than water.

"Try your engine again, coxswain."

"Aye, aye, sir!" The engine coughed, took hold; the engineman eased in the clutch, the screw bit in, and the boat surged forward, taking the strain off the towline. "Slack line, sir."

"Stop your engine." The boat officer turned to his passengers. "What's the trouble, Mr. Eisenberg? Cold feet?"

"No, dammit—seasick. I *hate* a small boat."

"Oh, that's too bad. I'll see if we haven't got a pickle in that chow up forward."

"Thanks, but pickles don't help me. Never mind, I can stand it."

The boat officer shrugged, turned and let his eye travel up the dizzy length of the column. He whistled, something which he had done every time he had looked at it. Eisenberg, made nervous by his nausea, was beginning to find it cause for homicide. "*Whew!* You really intend to try to go up that thing, Mr. Eisenberg?"

"I do!"

The boat officer looked startled at the tone, laughed uneasily, and added, "Well, you'll be worse than seasick, if you ask me."

Nobody had. Graves knew his friend's temperament; he made conversation for the next few minutes.

"Try your engine, coxswain." The petty officer acknowledged, and reported back quickly:

"Starter doesn't work, sir."

"Help the engineman get a line on the flywheel. I'll take the tiller."

The two men cranked the engine over easily, but got no answering cough. "Prime it!" Still no results.

The boat officer abandoned the useless tiller and jumped down into the engine space to lend his muscle to heaving on the cranking line. Over his shoulder he ordered the signalman to notify the ship.

"Launch Three, calling bridge. Launch Three, calling bridge. Bridge—reply! Testing—testing." The signalman slipped a phone off one ear. "Phone's dead, sir."

"Get busy with your flags. Tell'em to haul us in!" The officer wiped sweat from his face and straightened up. He glanced nervously at the current *slap-slapping* against the boat's side.

Graves touched his arm. "How about the barrel?"

"Put it over the side if you like. I'm busy. Can't you raise them, Sears?"

"I'm trying, sir."

"Come on, Bill," Graves said to Eisenberg. The two of them slipped forward in the boat, threading their way past the engine on the side away from the three men sweating over the flywheel. Graves cut the hogshead loose from its lashings, then the two attempted to get a purchase on the awkward, unhandy object. It and its light load weighed less than two hundred pounds, but it was hard to manage, especially on the uncertain footing of heaving floorboards.

They wrestled it outboard somehow, with one smashed finger for Eisenberg, a badly banged shin for Graves. It splashed heavily, drenching them with sticky salt water, and bobbed astern, carried rapidly toward the Kanaka Pillar by the current which fed it.

"Ship answers, sir!"

"Good! Tell them to haul us in—*carefully*." The boat officer jumped out of the engine space and ran forward, where he checked again the secureness with which the towline was fastened.

Graves tapped him on the shoulder. "Can't we stay here until we see the barrel enter the column?"

"No! Right now you had better pray that that line holds, instead of worrying about the barrel—or we go up the column, too. Sears, has the ship acknowledged?"

"Just now, sir."

"Why a coir line, Mr. Parker?" Eisenberg inquired, his nausea forgotten in the excitement. "I'd rather depend on steel, or even good stout Manila."

"Because coir floats, and the others don't," the officer answered snappishly. "Two miles of line would drag us to the bottom. *Sears!* Tell them to ease the strain. We're shipping water."

"Aye, aye, sir!"

The hogshead took less than four minutes to reach the column, enter it, a fact which Graves ascertained by borrowing the signalman's glass to follow it on the last leg of its trip—which action won him a dirty look from the nervous boat officer. Some minutes later, when the boat was about five hundred yards farther from the Pillar than it had been at nearest approach, the telephone came suddenly to life. The starter of the engine was tested immediately; the engine roared into action.

The trip back was made with engine running to take the strain off the towline—at half speed and with some maneuvering, in order to avoid fouling the screw with the slack bight of the line.

The smoke signal worked—one circuit or another. The plume of smoke was sighted two miles south of the Wahini Pillar, elapsed time from the moment the vessel had entered the Kanaka column just over eight hours.

Bill Eisenberg climbed into the saddle of the exerciser in which he was to receive antibends treatment—thirty minutes of hard work to stir up his circulation while breathing an atmosphere of helium and oxygen, at the end of which time the nitrogen normally dissolved in his blood stream would be largely replaced by helium. The exerciser itself was simply an old bicycle mounted on a stationary platform. Blake looked it over. "You needn't have bothered to bring this," he remarked. "We've a better one aboard. Standard practice for diving operations these days."

"We didn't know that," Graves answered. "Anyhow, this one will do. All set, Bill?"

"I guess so." He glanced over his shoulder to where the steel bulk of the bathysphere lay, uncrated, checked and equipped, ready to be swung outboard by the boat crane. "Got the gasket-sealing compound?"

"Sure. The Iron Maiden is all right. The gunner and I will seal you in. Here's your mask."

Eisenberg accepted the inhaling mask, started to strap it on, checked himself. Graves noticed the look on his face. "What's the trouble, son?"

"Doc . . . uh—"

"Yes?"

"I say—you'll look out for Cleo and Pat, won't you?"

"Why, sure. But they won't need anything in the length of time you'll be gone."

"Um-m-m, no, I suppose not. But you'll look out for 'em?"

"Sure."

"O.K." Eisenberg slipped the inhaler over his face, waved his hand to the gunner waiting by the gas bottles. The gunner eased open the cut-off valves, the gas lines hissed, and Eisenberg began to pedal like a six-day racer.

With thirty minutes to kill, Blake invited Graves to go forward with him for a smoke and a stroll on the fo'c's'le. They had completed about twenty turns when Blake paused by the wildcat, took his cigar from his mouth and remarked, "Do you know, I believe he has a good chance of completing the trip."

"So? I'm glad to hear that."

"Yes, I do, really. The success of the trial with the dead load convinced me. And whether the smoke gear works or not, if that globe comes back down the Wahini Pillar, *I'll find it.*"

"I know you will. It was a good idea of yours, to paint it yellow."

"Help us to spot it, all right. I don't think he'll learn anything, however. He won't see a thing through those ports but blue water, from the time he enters the column to the time we pick him up."

"Perhaps so."

"What else *could* he see?"

"I don't know. Whatever it is that *made* those Pillars, perhaps."

Blake dumped the ashes from his cigar carefully over the rail before replying. "Doctor, I don't understand you. To my mind, those Pillars are a natural, even though strange, phenomenon."

"And to me it's equally obvious that they are not 'natural.' They exhibit intelligent interference with the ordinary processes of nature as clearly as if they had a sign saying so hung on them."

"I don't see how you can say that. Obviously, they are not man-made."

"No."

"Then who did make them—if they were made?"

"I don't know."

Blake started to speak, shrugged, and held his tongue. They resumed their stroll. Graves turned aside to chuck his cigarette overboard, glancing outboard as he did so.

He stopped, stared, then called out: "Captain Blake!"

"Eh?" The captain turned and looked where Graves pointed. "Great God! Fireballs!"

"That's what I thought."

"They're some distance away," Blake observed, more to himself than to Graves. He turned decisively. "Bridge!" he shouted. "Bridge! Bridge ahoy!"

"Bridge, aye aye!"

"Mr. Weems—pass the word: 'All hands, below decks.' Dog down all ports. Close all hatches. And close up the bridge itself! Sound the general alarm."

"Aye aye, sir!"

"Move!" Turning to Graves, he added, "Come inside." Graves followed him; the captain stopped to dog down the door by which they entered, himself. Blake pounded up the inner ladders to the bridge, Graves in his train. The ship was filled with the whine of the bos'n pipe, the raucous voice of the loud-speaker, the clomp of hurrying feet, and the monotonous, menacing *cling-cling-cling!* of the general alarm.

The watch on the bridge were still struggling with

the last of the heavy glass shutters of the bridge when the captain burst into their midst. "I'll take it, Mr. Weems," he snapped. In one continuous motion he moved from one side of the bridge to the other, letting his eye sweep the port side aft, the fo'c's'le, the starboard side aft, and finally rest on the fireballs—distinctly nearer and heading straight for the ship. He cursed. "Your friend did not get the news," he said to Graves. He grasped the crank which could open or close the after starboard shutter of the bridge.

Graves looked past his shoulder, saw what he meant—the afterdeck was empty, save for one lonely figure pedaling away on the stationary bicycle. The LaGrange fireballs were closing in.

The shutter stuck, jammed tight, would not open. Blake stopped trying, swung quickly to the loud-speaker control panel, and cut in the whole board without bothering to select the proper circuit. "Eisenberg! *Get below!*"

Eisenberg must have heard his name called, for he turned his head and looked over his shoulder—Graves saw distinctly—just as the fireball reached him. It passed on, and the saddle of the exerciser was empty.

The exerciser was undamaged, they found, when they were able to examine it. The rubber hose to the inhaler mask had been cut smoothly. There was no blood, no marks. Bill Eisenberg was simply gone.

"I'm going up."

"You are in no physical shape to do so, doctor."

"You are in no way responsible, Captain Blake."

"I know that. You may go if you like—after we have searched for your friend's body."

"Search be damned! I'm going up to *look* for him."

"Huh? Eh? How's that?"

"If you are right, he's dead, and there is no point in searching for his body. If I'm right, there is just an outside chance of finding him—up there!" He pointed toward the cloud cap of the Pillars.

Blake looked him over slowly, then turned to the master diver. "Mr. Hargreave, find an inhaler mask for Dr. Graves."

They gave him thirty minutes of conditioning against the caisson disease while Blake looked on with expressionless silence. The ship's company, bluejackets and officers alike, stood back and kept quiet; they walked on eggs when the Old Man had that look.

Exercise completed, the diver crew dressed Graves rapidly and strapped him into the bathysphere with dispatch, in order not to expose him too long to the nitrogen in the air. Just before the escape port was dogged down Graves spoke up. "Captain Blake."

"Yes, doctor?"

"Bill's goldfish—will you look out for them?"

"Certainly, doctor."

"Thanks."

"Not at all. Are you ready?"

"Ready."

Blake stepped forward, stuck an arm through the port of the sphere and shook hands with Graves. "Good luck." He withdrew his arm. "Seal it up."

They lowered it over the side; two motor launches nosed it half a mile in the direction of the Kanaka Pillar where the current was strong enough to carry it along. There they left it and bucked the current back to the ship, and were hoisted in.

Blake followed it with his glasses from the bridge. It drifted slowly at first, then with increased speed as it approached the base of the column. It whipped into rapid motion the last few hundred yards; Blake saw a flash of yellow just above the water line, then nothing more.

Eight hours—no plume of smoke. Nine hours, ten hours, nothing. After twenty-four hours of steady patrol in the vicinity of the Wahini Pillar, Blake radioed the Bureau.

Four days of vigilance—Blake knew that the bathysphere's passenger must be dead; whether by suffocation, drowning, implosion, or other means was not important. He so reported and received orders to proceed on duty assigned. The ship's company was called to quarters; Captain Blake read the service for the dead aloud in a harsh voice, dropped over the side some rather wilted hibiscus blooms—all that his steward could produce at the time—and went to the bridge to set his course for Pearl Harbor.

On the way to the bridge he stopped for a moment at his cabin and called to his steward: "You'll find some goldfish in the stateroom occupied by Mr. Eisenberg. Find an appropriate container and place them in my cabin."

"Yes, suh, Cap'n."

When Bill Eisenberg came to his senses he was in a Place.

Sorry, but no other description is suitable; it lacked features. Oh, not entirely, of course—it was not dark where he was, nor was it in a state of vacuum, nor was it cold, nor was it too small for comfort. But it did lack features to such a remarkable extent that he had difficulty in estimating the size of the place. Consider—stereo vision, by which we estimate the size of things *directly*, does not work beyond twenty feet or so. At greater distances we depend on previous knowledge of the true size of familiar objects, usually making our estimates subconsciously—a man *so high* is about *that far* away, and vice versa.

But the Place contained no familiar objects. The ceiling was a considerable distance over his head, too far to touch by jumping. The floor curved up to join the ceiling and thus prevented further lateral progress of more than a dozen paces or so. He would become aware of the obstacle by losing his balance.

(He had no reference lines by which to judge the vertical; furthermore, his sense of innate balance was affected by the mistreatment his inner ears had undergone through years of diving. It was easier to sit than to walk, nor was there any reason to walk, after the first futile attempt at exploration.)

When he first woke up he stretched and opened his eyes, looked around. The lack of detail confused him. It was as if he were on the inside of a giant eggshell, illuminated from without by a soft, mellow, slightly amber light. The formless vagueness bothered him; he closed his eyes, shook his head, and opened them again—no better.

He was beginning to remember his last experience before losing consciousness—the fireball swooping down, his frenzied, useless attempt to duck, the "Hold your hats, boys!" thought that flashed through his mind in the long-drawn-out split second before contact. His orderly mind began to look for explanations. Knocked cold, he thought, and my optic nerve paralyzed. Wonder if I'm blind for good.

Anyhow, they ought not to leave him alone like this in his present helpless condition. "Doc!" he shouted. "Doc Graves!"

No answer, no echo—he became aware that there was *no* sound, save for his own voice, none of the random little sounds that fill completely the normal "dead" silence. This place was as silent as the inside of a sack of flour. Were his ears shot, too?

No, he had heard his own voice. At that moment he realized that he was looking at his own hands. Why, there was nothing wrong with his eyes—he could see them plainly!

And the rest of himself, too. He was naked.

It might have been several hours later, it might have been moments, when he reached the conclusion that he was dead. It was the only hypothesis which seemed to cover the facts. A dogmatic agnostic by faith, he had expected no survival after death; he had expected to go out like a light, with a sudden termination of consciousness. However, he had been subjected to a charge of static electricity more than sufficient to kill a man; when he regained awareness, he found himself without all the usual experience which makes up living. Therefore—he was dead. Q.E.D.

To be sure, he seemed to have a body, but he was acquainted with the subjective-objective paradox. He still had memory, the strongest pattern in one's memory is body awareness. This was not his body, but his detailed sensation memory of it. So he reasoned. Probably, he thought, my dreambody will slough away as my memory of the object-body fades.

There was nothing to do, nothing to experience, nothing to distract his mind. He fell asleep at last, thinking that, if this were death, it was damned dull!

He awoke refreshed, but quite hungry and extremely thirsty. The matter of dead, or not-dead, no longer concerned him; he was interested in neither theology nor metaphysics. He was hungry.

Furthermore, he experienced on awakening a phenomenon which destroyed most of the basis for his intellectual belief in his own death—it had never reached the stage of emotional conviction. Present there with him in the Place he found material objects other than himself, objects which could be seen and touched.

And eaten.

Which last was not immediately evident, for they did not look like food. There were two sorts. The first was an amorphous lump of nothing in particular, resembling a grayish cheese in appearance, slightly greasy to the touch, and not appetizing. The second sort was a group of objects of uniform and delightful appearance. They were spheres, a couple of dozen; each one seemed to Bill Eisenberg to be a duplicate of a crystal ball he had once purchased—true Brazilian rock crystal the perfect beauty of which he had not been able to resist; he had bought it and smuggled it home to gloat over in private.

The little spheres were like that in appearance. He touched one. It was smooth as crystal and had the same chaste coolness, but it was soft as jelly. It quivered like jelly, causing the lights within it to dance delightfully, before resuming its perfect roundness.

Pleasant as they were, they did not look like food, whereas the cheesy, soapy lump might be. He broke off a small piece, sniffed it, and tasted it tentatively. It was sour, nauseating, unpleasant. He spat it out, made a wry face, and wished heartily that he could brush his teeth. If that was food, he would have to be much hungrier—

He turned his attention back to the delightful little spheres of crystallike jelly. He balanced them in his palms, savoring their soft, smooth touch. In the heart of each he saw his own reflection, imagined in miniature, made elfin and graceful. He became aware almost for the first time of the serene beauty of the human figure, almost any human figure, when viewed as a composition and not as a mass of colloidal detail.

But thirst became more pressing than narcissist admiration. It occurred to him that the smooth, cool spheres, if held in the mouth, might promote salivation, as pebbles will. He tried it; the sphere he selected struck against his lower teeth as he placed it in his mouth, and his lips and chin were suddenly wet, while drops trickled down his chest. The spheres were water, nothing but water, no cellophane skin, no container of any sort. Water had been delivered to him, neatly packaged, by some esoteric trick of surface tension.

He tried another, handling it more carefully to insure that it was not pricked by his teeth until he had it in his mouth. It worked; his mouth was filled with cool, pure water—too quickly; he choked. But he had caught on to the trick; he drank four of the spheres.

His thirst satisfied, he became interested in the strange trick whereby water became its own container. The spheres were tough; he could not squeeze them into breaking down, nor did smashing them hard against the floor disturb their precarious balance. They bounced like golf balls and came up for more. He managed to pinch the surface of one between thumb and fingernail. It broke down at once, and the water trickled between his fingers—water alone, no skin nor foreign substance. It seemed that a cut alone could disturb the balance of tensions; even wetting had no effect, for he could hold one carefully in his mouth, remove it, and dry it off on his own skin.

He decided that, since his supply was limited, and no more water was in prospect, it would be wise to conserve what he had and experiment no further.

The relief of thirst increased the demands of hunger. He turned his attention again to the other substance and found that he could force himself to chew and swallow. It might not be food, it might even be poison, but it filled his stomach and stayed the pangs. He even felt well fed, once he had cleared out the taste with another sphere of water.

After eating he rearranged his thoughts. He was not dead, or, if he were, the difference between living and being dead was imperceptible, verbal. OK, he was alive. But he was shut up alone. Somebody knew where he was and was aware of him, for he had been supplied with food and drink—mysteriously but cleverly. *Ergo*—he was a prisoner, a word which implies a warden.

Whose prisoner? He had been struck by a La-Grange fireball and had awakened in his cell. It looked, he was forced to admit, as if Doc Graves had been right; the fireballs were intelligently controlled. Furthermore, the person or persons behind them had novel ideas as to how to care for prisoners as well as strange ways of capturing them.

Eisenberg was a brave man, as brave as the ordinary run of the race from which he sprang—a race as foolhardy as Pekingese dogs. He had the high degree of courage so common in the human race, a race capable of conceiving death, yet able to face its probability daily, on the highway, on the obstetrics table, on the battlefield, in the air, in the subway—and to face lightheartedly the certainty of death in the end.

Eisenberg was apprehensive, but not panic-stricken. His situation was decidedly interesting; he was no longer bored. If he were a prisoner, it seemed likely that his captor would come to investigate him presently, perhaps to question him, perhaps to attempt to use him in some fashion. The fact that he had been saved and not killed implied some sort of plans for his future. Very well, he would concentrate on meeting whatever exigency might come with a calm and resourceful mind. In the meantime, there was nothing he could do toward freeing himself; he had satisfied himself of that. This was a prison which would baffle Houdini—smooth continuous walls, no way to get a purchase.

He had thought once that he had a clue to escape; the cell had sanitary arrangements of some sort, for that which his body rejected went elsewhere. But he got no further with that lead; the cage was self-cleaning—and that was that. He could not tell how it was done. It baffled him.

Presently he slept again.

*   *   *

When he awoke, one element only was changed—
the food and water had been replenished. The "day"
passed without incident, save for his own busy fruitless thoughts.

And the next "day." And the next.

He determined to stay awake long enough to find
out how food and water were placed in his cell. He
made a colossal effort to do so, using drastic mea-
sures to stimulate his body into consciousness. He
bit his lips, he bit his tongue. He nipped the lobes of
his ear viciously with his nails. He concentrated on
difficult mental feats.

Presently he dozed off; when he awoke, the food
and water had been replenished.

The waking periods were followed by sleep, renewed hunger and thirst, the satisfying of same, and
more sleep. It was after the sixth or seventh sleep
that he decided that some sort of a calendar was
necessary to his mental health. He had no means of
measuring time except by his sleeps; he arbitrarily
designated them as days. He had no means of keeping records, save his own body. He made that do. A
thumbnail shred, torn off, made a rough tattooing
needle. Continued scratching of the same area on his
thigh produced a red welt which persisted for a day
or two, and could be renewed. Seven welts made a
week. The progression of such welts along ten fingers and ten toes gave him the means to measure
twenty weeks—which was a much longer period than
he anticipated any need to measure.

He had tallied the second set of seven thigh welts
on the ring finger of his left hand when the next
event occurred to disturb his solitude. When he
awoke from the sleep following said tally, he became
suddenly and overwhelmingly aware that he was not
alone!

There was a human figure sleeping beside him. When he had convinced himself that he was truly wide awake—his dreams were thoroughly populated —he grasped the figure by the shoulder and shook it. "Doc!" he yelled. "Doc! Wake up!"

Graves opened his eyes, focused them, sat up, and put out his hand. "Hi, Bill," he remarked. "I'm damned glad to see you."

"Doc!" He pounded the older man on the back. "Doc! For Criminy sake! You don't know how glad *I* am to see *you*."

"I can guess."

"Look, Doc—where have you been? How did you get here? Did the fireballs snag you, too?"

"One thing at a time, son. Let's have breakfast." There was a double ration of food and water on the "floor" near them. Graves picked up a sphere, nicked it expertly, and drank it without losing a drop. Eisenberg watched him knowingly.

"You've been here for some time."

"That's right."

"Did the fireballs get you the same time they got me?"

"No." He reached for the food. "I came up the Kanaka Pillar."

"What!"

"That's right. Matter of fact, I was looking for you."

"The hell you say!"

"But I do say. It looks as if my wild hypothesis was right; the Pillars and the fireballs are different manifestations of the same cause—X!"

It seemed almost possible to hear the wheels whir in Eisenberg's head. "But, Doc . . . look here, Doc, that means your whole hypothesis was correct. Somebody *did* the whole thing. Somebody has us locked up here now."

"That's right." He munched slowly. He seemed tired, older and thinner than the way Eisenberg remembered him. "Evidence of intelligent control. Always was. No other explanation."

"But *who*?"

"Ah!"

"Some foreign power? Are we up against something utterly new in the way of an attack?"

"Hummph! Do you think the Russians, for instance, would bother to serve us water like *this*?" He held up one of the dainty little spheres.

"Who, then?"

"I wouldn't know. Call 'em Martians—that's a convenient way to think of them."

"Why Martians?"

"No reason. I said that was a convenient way to think of them."

"Convenient how?"

"Convenient because it keeps you from thinking of them as human beings—which they obviously aren't. Nor animals. Something very intelligent, but not animals, because they are smarter than we are. Martians."

"But . . . but—Wait a minute. Why do you assume that your X people aren't human? Why not humans who have a lot of stuff on the ball that we don't have? New scientific advances?"

"That's a fair question," Graves answered, picking his teeth with a forefinger. "I'll give you a fair answer. Because in the present state of the world we know pretty near where all the best minds are and what they are doing. Advances like these couldn't be hidden and would be a long time in developing. X indicates evidence of a half a dozen different lines of development that are clear beyond our ken and which would require years of work by hundreds of researchers, to say the very least. *Ipso facto,* nonhuman science.

"Of course," he continued, "if you want to postulate a mad scientist and a secret laboratory, I can't argue with you. But I'm not writing Sunday supplements."

Bill Eisenberg kept very quiet for some time, while he considered what Graves said in the light of his own experience. "You're right, Doc," he finally admitted. "Shucks—you're usually right when we have an argument. It has to be Martians. Oh, I don't mean inhabitants of Mars; I mean some form of intelligent life from outside this planet."

"Maybe."

"But you just said so!"

"No, I said it was a convenient way to look at it."

"But it has to be, by elimination."

"Elimination is a tricky line of reasoning."

"What else could it be?"

"Mm-m-m. I'm not prepared to say just what I do think—yet. But there are stronger reasons than we have mentioned for concluding that we are up against nonhumans. Psychological reasons."

"What sort?"

"X doesn't treat prisoners in any fashion that arises out of human behavior patterns. Think it over."

They had a lot to talk about; much more than X, even though X was a subject they were bound to return to. Graves gave Bill a simple bald account of how he happened to go up the Pillar—an account which Bill found very moving for what was left out, rather than told. He felt suddenly very humble and unworthy as he looked at his elderly, frail friend. "Doc, you don't look well."

"I'll do."

"That trip up the Pillar was hard on you. You shouldn't have tried it."

Graves shrugged. "I made out all right." But he

had not, and Bill could see that he had not. The old man was "poorly."

They slept and they ate and they talked and they slept again. The routine that Eisenberg had grown used to alone continued, save with company. But Graves grew no stronger.

"Doc, it's up to us to do something about it."

"About what?"

"The whole situation. This thing that has happened to us is an intolerable menace to the whole human race. We don't know what may have happened down below—"

"Why do you say 'down below?'"

"Why, you came up the Pillar."

"Yes, true—but I don't know when or how I was taken out of the bathysphere, nor where they may have taken me. But go ahead. Let's have your idea."

"Well, but—OK—we don't know what may have happened to the rest of the human race. The fireballs may be picking them off one at a time, with no chance to fight back and no way of guessing what has been going on. We have some idea of the answer. It's up to us to escape and warn them. There may be some way of fighting back. It's our duty; the whole future of the human race may depend on it."

Graves was silent so long after Bill had finished his tocsin that Bill began to feel embarrassed, a bit foolish. But when he finally spoke it was to agree. "I think you are right, Bill. I think it quite possible that you are right. Not necessarily, but distinctly possible. And that possibility does place an obligation on us to all mankind. I've known it. I knew it before we got into this mess, but I did not have enough data to justify shouting, 'Wolf!'

"The question is," he went on, "how can we give such a warning—now?"

"We've got to escape!"

"Ah!"

"There *must* be some way."

"Can you suggest one?"

"Maybe. We haven't been able to find any way in or out of this place, but there must be a way—has to be; we were brought in. Furthermore, our rations are put inside every day—somehow. I tried once to stay awake long enough to see how it was done, but I fell asleep—"

"So did I."

"Uh-huh. I'm not surprised. But there are two of us now; we could take turns, watch on and watch off, until something happened."

Graves nodded. "It's worth trying."

Since they had no way of measuring the watches, each kept the vigil until sleepiness became intolerable, then awakened the other. But nothing happened. Their food ran out, was not replaced. They conserved their water balls with care, were finally reduced to one, which was not drunk because each insisted on being noble about it—the other must drink it! But still no manifestation of any sort from their unseen captors.

After an unmeasured and unestimated length of time—but certainly long, almost intolerably long—at a time when Eisenberg was in a light, troubled sleep, he was suddenly awakened by a touch and the sound of his name. He sat up, blinking, disoriented. "Who? What? Wha'sa matter?"

"I must have dozed off," Graves said miserably. "I'm sorry, Bill." Eisenberg looked where Graves pointed. Their food and water had been renewed.

Eisenberg did not suggest a renewal of the experiment. In the first place, it seemed evident that their keepers did not intend for them to learn the combination to their cell and were quite intelligent enough to outmaneuver their necessarily feeble attempts. In the second place, Graves was an obviously sick man; Eisenberg did not have the heart to suggest another long, grueling, half-starved vigil.

But, lacking knowledge of the combination, it appeared impossible to break jail. A naked man is a particularly helpless creature; lacking materials wherewith to fashion tools, he can do little. Eisenberg would have swapped his chances for eternal bliss for a diamond drill, an acetylene torch, or even a rusty, secondhand chisel. Without tools of some sort it was impressed on him that he stood about as much chance of breaking out of his cage as his goldfish, Cleo and Patra, had of chewing their way out of a glass bowl.

"Doc."

"Yes, son."

"We've tackled this the wrong way. We know that X is intelligent; instead of trying to escape, we should be trying to establish communication."

"How?"

"I don't know. But there must be *some* way."

But if there was, he could never conjure it up. Even if he assumed that his captors could see and hear him, how was he to convey intelligence to them by word or gesture? Was it theoretically possible for any nonhuman being, no matter how intelligent, to find a pattern of meaning in human speech symbols, if he encountered them without context, without background, without pictures, without *pointing?* It is certainly true that the human race, working under much more favorable circumstances, has failed almost utterly to learn the languages of the other races of animals.

What should he do to attract their attention, stimulate their interest? Recite the "Gettysburg Address?" Or the multiplication table? Or, if he used gestures, would deaf-and-dumb language mean any more, or any less, to his captors than the sailor's hornpipe?

*   *   *

"Doc."

"What is it, Bill?" Graves was sinking; he rarely initiated a conversation these "days."

"Why are we here? I've had it in the back of my mind that *eventually* they would take us out and do something with us. Try to question us, maybe. But it doesn't look like they meant to."

"No, it doesn't."

"Then why are we here? Why do they take care of us?"

Graves paused quite a long time before answering: "I think that they are expecting us to reproduce."

"What!"

Graves shrugged.

"But that's ridiculous."

"Surely. But would they know it?"

"But they are intelligent."

Graves chuckled, the first time he had done so in many sleeps "Do you know Roland Young's little verse about the flea:

> " '*A funny creature is the Flea*
> *You cannot tell the She from He.*
> *But He can tell—and so can She.*'

"After all, the visible differences between men and women are quite superficial and almost negligible— except to men and women!"

Eisenberg found the suggestion repugnant, almost revolting; he struggled against it. "But look, Doc— even a little study would show them that the human race is divided up into sexes. After all, we aren't the first specimens they've studied."

"Maybe they don't study us."

"Huh?"

"Maybe we are just—pets."

Pets! Bill Eisenberg's morale had stood up well in

the face of danger and uncertainty. This attack on it was more subtle. Pets! He had thought of Graves and himself as prisoners of war, or, possibly, objects of scientific research. But pets!

"I know how you feel," Graves went on, watching his face. "It's . . . it's *humiliating* from an anthropocentric viewpoint. But I think it may be true. I may as well tell you my own private theory as to the possible nature of X, and the relation of X to the human race. I haven't up to now, as it is almost sheer conjecture, based on very little data. But it does cover the known facts.

"I conceive of the X creatures as being just barely aware of the existence of men, unconcerned by them, and almost completely uninterested in them."

"But they hunt us!"

"Maybe. Or maybe they just pick us up occasionally by accident. A lot of men have dreamed about an impingement of nonhuman intelligences on the human race. Almost without exception the dream has taken one of two forms, invasion and war, or exploration and mutual social intercourse. Both concepts postulate that nonhumans are enough like us either to fight with us or talk to us—treat us as equals, one way or the other.

"I don't believe that X is sufficiently interested in human beings to want to enslave them, or even exterminate them. They may not even study us, even when we come under their notice. They may lack the scientific spirit in the sense of having a monkeylike curiosity about everything that moves. For that matter, how thoroughly do *we* study other life forms? Did you ever ask your goldfish for their views on goldfish poetry or politics? Does a termite think that a woman's place is in the home? Do beavers prefer blondes or brunettes?"

"You are joking."

"No, I'm not. Maybe the life forms I mentioned

don't have such involved ideas. My point is: if they did, or do, we'd never guess it. I don't think X conceives of the human race as intelligent."

Bill chewed this for a while, then added: "Where do you think they came from, Doc? Mars, maybe? Or clear out of the Solar System?"

"Not necessarily. Not even probably. It's my guess that they came from the same place we did—*from up out of the slime of this planet.*"

"Really, Doc—"

"I mean it. And don't give me that funny look. I may be sick, but I'm not balmy. *Creation took eight days!*"

"Huh?"

"I'm using biblical language. 'And God blessed them, and God said unto them, Be fruitful and multiply, and replenish the earth, and subdue it: and have dominion over the fish of the sea, and over the fowl of the air, and over every living thing that moveth upon the earth.' And so it came to pass. But nobody mentioned the stratosphere."

"Doc—are you sure you feel all right?"

"Dammit—quit trying to psychoanalyze me! I'll drop the allegory. What I mean is: We aren't the latest nor the highest stage in evolution. First the oceans were populated. Then lungfish to amphibian, and so on up, until the continents were populated, and, in time, man ruled the surface of the earth—or thought he did. But did evolution stop there? I think not. Consider—from a fish's point of view air is a hard vacuum. From our point of view the upper reaches of the atmosphere, sixty, seventy, maybe a hundred thousand feet up seem like a vacuum and unfit to sustain life. But it's not vacuum. It's thin, yes, but there is matter there and radiant energy. Why not life, intelligent life, highly evolved as it would have to be—but evolved from the same ancestry as ourselves and fish? We wouldn't see it happen; man hasn't been aware, in a scientific sense, that long. When our granddaddies were swinging in the trees, it had already happened."

Eisenberg took a deep breath. "Just wait a minute, Doc. I'm not disputing the theoretical possibility of your thesis, but it seems to me it is out on direct evidence alone. We've never seen them, had no direct evidence of them. At least, not until lately. And we *should* have seen them."

"Not necessarily. Do ants see men? I doubt it."

"Yes—but, consarn it, a man has better eyes than an ant."

"Better eyes for what? For his own needs. Suppose the X creatures are too high up, or too tenuous, or too fast-moving for us to notice them. Even a thing as big and as solid and as slow as an airplane can go up high enough to pass out of sight, even on a clear day. If X is tenuous and even semitransparent, we never *would* see them—not even as occultations of stars, or shadows against the moon—though as a matter of fact there have been some very strange stories of just that sort of thing."

Eisenberg got up and stomped up and down. "Do you mean to suggest," he demanded, "that creatures so insubstantial they can float in a soft vacuum built the Pillars?"

"Why not? Try explaining how a half-finished, naked embryo like *homo sapiens* built the Empire State Building."

Bill shook his head. "I don't get it."

"You don't try. Where do you think *this* came from?" Graves held up one of the miraculous little water spheres. "My guess is that life on this planet is split three ways, with almost no intercourse between the three. Ocean culture, land culture, and another—call it stratoculture. Maybe a fourth, down under the crust—but we don't know. We know a little about life under the sea, because we are curious. But how much do they know of us? Do a few dozen bathysphere descents constitute an invasion? A fish that sees our bathysphere might go home and take to his bed with a sick headache, but he wouldn't talk about it, and he wouldn't be believed if he did. If a lot of fish see us and swear out affidavits, along comes a fish-psychologist and explains it as mass hallucination.

"No, it takes something at least as large and solid and permanent as the Pillars to have any effect on orthodox conceptions. Casual visitations have no real effect."

Eisenberg let his thoughts simmer for some time before commenting further. When he did, it was half to himself. "I don't believe it. I won't believe it!"

"Believe what?"

"Your theory. Look, Doc—if you are right, don't you see what it means? We're helpless, we're outclassed."

"I don't think they will bother much with human beings. They haven't, up till now."

"But that isn't it. Don't you see? We've had some dignity as a race. We've striven and accomplished things. Even when we failed, we had the tragic satisfaction of knowing that we were, nevertheless, superior and more able than the other animals. We've had faith in the race—we would accomplish great things yet. But if we are just one of the lower animals ourselves, what does our great work amount to? Me, I couldn't go on pretending to be a 'scientist' if I thought I was just a fish, mucking around in the bottom of a pool. My work wouldn't *signify* anything."

"Maybe it doesn't."

"No, maybe it doesn't." Eisenberg got up and paced the constricted area of their prison. "Maybe not. But I won't surrender to it. I *won't!* Maybe you're right. Maybe you're wrong. It doesn't seem to matter very much *where* the X people came from. One way or the other, they are a threat to our own kind. Doc, we've got to get out of here and warn them!"

"How?"

Graves was comatose a large part of the time before he died. Bill maintained an almost continuous watch over him, catching only occasional cat naps. There was little he could do for his friend, even though he did watch over him, but the spirit behind it was comfort to them both.

But he was dozing when Graves called his name. He woke at once, though the sound was a bare whisper. "Yes, Doc?"

"I can't talk much more, son. Thanks for taking care of me."

"Shucks, Doc."

"Don't forget what you're here for. Some day you'll get a break. Be ready for it and don't muff it. People have to be warned."

"I'll do it, Doc. I swear it."

"Good boy." And then almost inaudibly, "G'night son"

Eisenberg watched over the body until it was quite cold and had begun to stiffen. Then, exhausted by his long vigil and emotionally drained, he collapsed into a deep sleep. When he woke up the body was gone.

It was hard to maintain his morale, after Graves was gone. It was all very well to resolve to warn the rest of mankind at the first possible chance, but there was the endless monotony to contend with. He had not even the relief from boredom afforded the condemned prisoner—the checking off of limited days.

Even his "calendar" was nothing but a counting of his sleeps.

He was not quite sane much of the time, and it was the twice-tragic insanity of intelligence, aware of its own instability. He cycled between periods of elation and periods of extreme depression, in which he would have destroyed himself, had he the means.

During the periods of elation he made great plans for fighting against the X creatures—after he escaped. He was not sure how or when, but, momentarily, he was sure. He would lead the crusade himself; rockets could withstand the dead zone of the Pillars and the cloud; atomic bombs could destroy the dynamic balance of the Pillars. They would harry them and hunt them down; the globe would once again be the kingdom of man, to whom it belonged.

During the bitter periods of relapse he would realize clearly that the puny engineering of mankind would be of no force against the powers and knowledge of the creatures who built the Pillars, who kidnaped himself and Graves in such a casual and mysterious a fashion. They were outclassed. Could codfish plan a sortie against the city of Boston? Would it matter if the chattering monkeys in Guatemala passed a resolution to destroy the navy?

They were outclassed. The human race had reached its highest point—the point at which it began to be aware that it was not the highest race, and the knowledge was death to it, one way or the other—the mere knowledge alone, even as the knowledge was now destroying him, Bill Eisenberg, himself. Eisenberg—*homo piscis*. Poor fish!

His overstrained mind conceived a means by which he might possibly warn his fellow beings. He could not escape as long as his surroundings remained unchanged. That was established and he accepted it; he no longer paced his cage. But certain things *did* leave his cage: left-over food, refuse—and Graves' body. If he died, his own body would be removed, he felt sure. Some, at least, of the things which had gone up the Pillars had come down again—he knew that. Was it not likely that the X creatures disposed of any heavy mass for which they had no further use by dumping it down the Wahini Pillar? He convinced himself that it was so.

Very well, his body would be returned to the surface, eventually. How could he use it to give a message to his fellow men, if it were found? He had no writing materials, nothing but his own body.

But the same make-do means which served him as a calendar gave him a way to write a message. He could make welts on his skin with a shred of thumbnail. If the same spot were irritated over and over again, not permitted to heal, scar tissue would form. By such means he was able to create permanent tattooing.

The letters had to be large; he was limited in space to the fore part of his body; involved argument was impossible. He was limited to a fairly simple warning. If he had been quite right in his mind, perhaps he would have been able to devise a more cleverly worded warning—but then he was not.

In time, he had covered his chest and belly with cicatrix tattooing worthy of a bushman chief. He was thin by then and of an unhealthy color; the welts stood out plainly.

His body was found floating in the Pacific, by Portuguese fishermen who could not read the message, but who turned it in to the harbor police of Honolulu. They, in turn, photographed the body, fingerprinted it, and disposed of it. The fingerprints were checked in Washington, and William Eisenberg, scientist, fellow of many distinguished societies, and high type of *homo sapiens,* was officially dead for the second time, with a new mystery attached to his name.

The cumbersome course of official correspondence unwound itself and the record of his reappearance reached the desk of Captain Blake, at a port in the South Atlantlc. Photographs of the body were attached to the record, along with a short official letter telling the captain that, in view of his connection with the case, it was being provided for his information and recommendation.

Captain Blake looked at the photographs for the dozenth time. The message told in scar tissue was plain enough: "BEWARE—CREATION TOOK EIGHT DAYS." But what did it mean?

Of one thing he was sure—Eisenberg had not had those scars on his body when he disappeared from the *Mahan*.

The man had lived for a considerable period after he was grabbed up by the fireball—that was certain. And he had learned something. What? The reference to the first chapter of Genesis did not escape him; it was not such as to be useful.

He turned to his desk and resumed making a draft in painful longhand of his report to the bureau. "—the message in scar tissue adds to the mystery, rather than clarifying it. I am now forced to the opinion that the Pillars and the LaGrange fireballs are connected in some way. The patrol around the Pillars should not be relaxed. If new opportunities or methods for investigating the nature of the Pillars should develop, they should be pursued thoroughly. I regret to say that I have nothing of the sort to suggest—"

He got up from his desk and walked to a small aquarium supported by gimbals from the inboard bulkhead, and stirred up the two goldfish therein with a forefinger. Noticing the level of the water, he turned to the pantry door. "Johnson, you've filled this bowl too full again. Pat's trying to jump out again!"

"I'll fix it, captain." The steward came out of the pantry with a small pan. ("Don't know why the Old Man keeps these tarnation fish. He ain't interested in 'em—*that's certain*.") Aloud he added: "That Pat fish don't want to stay in there, captain. Always trying to jump out. And he don't *like* me, captain."

"What's that?" Captain Blake's thoughts had already left the fish; he was worrying over the mystery again.

"I say that fish don't *like* me, captain. Tries to bite my finger every time I clean out the bowl."

"Don't be silly, Johnson."

Project Nightmare

Project Nightmare

"Four's your point. Roll 'em!"

"Anybody want a side bet on double deuces?"

No one answered; the old soldier rattled dice in a glass, pitched them against the washroom wall. One turned up a deuce; the other spun. Somebody yelled, "It's going to five! Come, Phoebe!"

It stopped—a two. The old soldier said, "I told you not to play with me. Anybody want cigarette money?"

"Pick it up, Pop. We don't—oh, oh! 'Ten*shun!*"

In the door stood a civilian, a colonel, and a captain. The civilian said, "Give the money back, Two-Gun."

"Okay, Prof." The old-soldier extracted two singles. "That much is mine."

"Stop!" objected the captain. "I'll impound that for evidence. Now, you men—"

The colonel stopped him. "Mick. Forget that you're adjutant. Private Andrews, come along." He went out; the others followed. They hurried through the enlisted men's club, out into desert sunshine and across the quadrangle.

The civilian said, "Two-Gun, what the deuce!"

"Shucks, Prof, I was just practicing."

"Why don't you practice against Grandma Wilkins?"
The soldier snorted. "Do I look silly?"

The colonel put in, "You're keeping a crowd of generals and V.I.P.s waiting. That isn't bright."

"Colonel Hammond, I was told to wait in the club."

"But not in its washroom. Step it up!"

They went inside headquarters to a hall where guards checked their passes before letting them in. A civilian was speaking: "—and that's the story of the history-making experiments at Duke University. Doctor Reynolds is back; he will conduct the demonstrations."

The officers sat down in the rear; Dr. Reynolds went to the speaker's table. Private Andrews sat down with a group set apart from the high brass and distinguished civilians of the audience. A character who looked like a professional gambler—and was—sat next to two beautiful redheads, identical twins. A fourteen-year-old Negro boy slumped in the next chair; he seemed asleep. Beyond him a most wideawake person, Mrs. Anna Wilkins, tatted and looked around. In the second row were college students and a drab middleaged man.

The table held a chuck-a-luck cage, packs of cards, scratch pads, a Geiger counter, a lead carrying case. Reynolds leaned on it and said, "Extra-Sensory Perception, or E.S.P., is a tag for little-known phenomena—telepathy, clairvoyance, clairaudience, precognition, telekinesis. They exist; we can measure them; we know that some people are thus gifted. But we don't know how they work. The British, in India during World War One, found that secrets were being stolen by telepathy." Seeing doubt in their faces Reynolds added, "It is conceivable that a spy five hundred miles away is now 'listening in'—and picking your brains of top-secret data."

Doubt was more evident. A four-star Air Force general said, "One moment, Doctor—if true, what can we do to stop it?"

"Nothing."

"That's no answer. A lead-lined room?"

"We've tried that, General. No effect."

"Jamming with high frequencies? Or whatever 'brain waves' are?"

"Possibly, though I doubt it. If E.S.P. becomes militarily important you may have to operate with all facts known. Back to our program: These ladies and gentlemen are powerfully gifted in telekinesis, the ability to control matter at a distance. Tomorrow's experiment may not succeed, but we hope to convince the doubting Thomases"—he smiled at a man in the rear—"that it is worth trying."

The man he looked at stood up. "General Hanby!"

An Army major general looked around. "Yes, Doctor Withers?"

"I asked to be excused. My desk is loaded with urgent work—and these games have nothing to do with me."

The commanding general started to assert himself; the four-star visitor put a hand on his sleeve. "Doctor Withers, my desk in Washington is piled high, but I am here because the President sent me. Will you please stay? I want a skeptical check on my judgment."

Withers sat down, still angry. Reynolds continued: "We will start with E.S.P. rather than telekinesis— which is a bit different, anyhow." He turned to one of the redheads. "Jane, will you come here?"

The girl answered, "I'm Joan. Sure."

"All right—Joan. General LaMott, will you draw something on this scratch pad?"

The four-star flyer cocked an eyebrow. "Anything?"

"Not too complicated."

"Right, Doctor." He thought, then began a cartoon of a girl, grinned and added a pop-eyed wolf. Shortly he looked up. "Okay?"

Joan had kept busy with another pad; Reynolds took hers to the general. The sketches were alike—except that Joan had added four stars to the wolf's shoulders. The general looked at her; she looked demure. "I'm convinced," he said drily. "What next?"

"That could be clairvoyance or telepathy," Reynolds lectured. "We will now show direct telepathy." He called the second twin to him, then said, "Doctor Withers, will you help us?"

Withers still looked surly. "With what?"

"The same thing—but Jane will watch over your shoulder while Joan tries to reproduce what you draw. Make it something harder."

"Well . . . okay." He took the pad, began sketching a radio circuit while Jane watched. He signed it with a "Clem," the radioman's cartoon of the little fellow peering over a fence.

"That's fine!" said Reynolds. "Finished, Joan?"

"Yes, Doctor." He fetched her pad; the diagram was correct—but Joan had added to "Clem" a wink.

Reynolds interrupted awed comment with, "I will skip card demonstrations and turn to telekinesis. Has anyone a pair of dice?" No one volunteered; he went on, "We have some supplied by your physics department. This chuck-a-luck cage is signed and sealed by them and so is this package." He broke it open, spilled out a dozen dice. "Two-Gun, how about some naturals?"

"I'll try, Prof."

"General LaMott, please select a pair and put them in this cup."

The general complied and handed the cup to Andrews. "What are you going to roll, soldier?"

"Would a sixty-five suit the General?"

"If you can."

"Would the General care to put up a five spot, to make it interesting?" He waited, wide-eyed and innocent.

LaMott grinned. "You're faded, soldier." He peeled out a five; Andrews covered it, rattled the cup and rolled. One die stopped on the bills—a five. The other bounced against a chair—a six.

"Let it ride, sir?"

"I'm not a sucker twice. Show us some naturals."

"As you say, sir." Two-Gun picked up the money, then rolled 6-1, 5-2, 4-3, and back again. He rolled several 6-1s, then got snake eyes. He tried again, got acey-deucey. He faced the little old lady. "Ma'am," he said, "if you want to roll, why don't you get down here and do the work?"

"Why, Mr. Andrews!"

Reynolds said hastily, "You'll get your turn, Mrs. Wilkins."

"I don't know what you gentlemen are talking about." She resumed tatting.

Colonel Hammond sat down by the redheads. "You're the January Twins—aren't you?"

"Our public!" one answered delightedly.

"The name is 'Brown,' " said the other.

" 'Brown,' " he agreed, "but how about a show for the boys?"

"Dr. Reynolds wouldn't like it," the first said dutifully.

"I'll handle him. We don't get USO; security regulations are too strict. How about it, Joan?"

"I'm Jane. Okay, if you fix it with Prof."

"Good girls!" He went back to where Grandma Wilkins was demonstrating selection—showers of sixes in the chuck-a-luck cage. She was still tatting. Dr. Withers watched glumly. Hammond said, "Well, Doc?"

"These things are disturbing," Withers admitted,

"but it's on the molar level—nothing affecting the elementary particles."

"How about those sketches?"

"I'm a physicist, not a psychologist. But the basic particles—electrons, neutrons, protons—can't be affected except with apparatus designed in accordance with the laws of radioactivity!"

Dr. Reynolds was in earshot; at Withers' remark he said, "Thank you, Mrs. Wilkins. Now, ladies and gentlemen, another experiment. Norman!"

The colored boy opened his eyes. "Yeah, Prof?"

"Up here. And the team from your physics laboratory, please. Has anyone a radium-dial watch?"

Staff technicians hooked the Geiger counter through an amplifier so that normal background radioactivity was heard as occasional clicks, then placed a radium-dial watch close to the counter tube; the clicks changed to hail-storm volume. "Lights out, please," directed Reynolds.

The boy said, "Now, Prof?"

"Wait, Norman. Can everyone see the watch?" The silence was broken only by the rattle of the amplifier, counting radioactivity of the glowing figures. "Now, Norman!"

The shining figures quenched out; the noise died to sparse clicks.

The same group was in a blockhouse miles out in the desert; more miles beyond was the bomb proving site; facing it was a periscope window set in concrete and glazed with solid feet of laminated filter glass. Dr. Reynolds was talking with Major General Hanby. A naval captain took reports via earphones and speaker horn; he turned to the C.O. "Planes on station, sir."

"Thanks, Dick."

The horn growled, "Station Charlie to Control; we fixed it."

The navy man said to Hanby, "All stations ready, range clear."

"Pick up the count."

"All stations, stand by to resume count at minus seventeen minutes. Time station, pick up the count. This is a live run. Repeat, this is a live run."

Hanby said to Reynolds, "Distance makes no difference?"

"We could work from Salt Lake City once my colleagues knew the setup." He glanced down. "My watch must have stopped."

"Always feels that way. Remember the metronome on the first Bikini test? It nearly drove me nuts."

"I can imagine. Um, General, some of my people are high-strung. Suppose I *ad lib?*"

Hanby smiled grimly. "We always have a pacifier for visitors. Doctor Withers, ready with your curtain raiser?"

The chief physicist was bending over a group of instruments; he looked tired. "Not today," he answered in a flat voice. "Satterlee will make it."

Satterlee came forward and grinned at the brass and V.I.P.'s and at Reynolds' operators. "I've been saving a joke for an audience that can't walk out. But first—" He picked up a polished metal sphere and looked at the E.S.P. adepts. "You saw a ball like this on your tour this morning. That one was plutonium; it's still out there waiting to go *bang!* in about . . . eleven minutes. This is merely steel—unless someone has made a mistake. That would be a joke—we'd laugh ourselves to bits!"

He got no laughs, went on: "But it doesn't weigh enough; we're safe. This dummy has been prepared so that Dr. Reynolds' people will have an image to help them concentrate. It looks no more like an atom bomb than I look like Stalin, but it represents—if it were plutonium—what we atom tinkerers call a 'subcritical mass.' Since the spy trials everybody knows how an atom bomb works. Plutonium gives off neutrons at a constant rate. If the mass is small, most of them escape to the outside. But if it is large enough, or a critical mass, enough are absorbed by other nuclei to start a chain reaction. The trick is to assemble a critical mass quickly—then run for your life! This happens in microseconds; I can't be specific without upsetting the security officer.

"Today we will find out if the mind can change the rate of neutron emission in plutonium. By theories sound enough to have destroyed two Japanese cities, the emission of any particular neutron is pure chance, but the total emission is as invariable as the stars in their courses. Otherwise it would be impossible to make atom bombs.

"By standard theory, theory that works, that subcritical mass out there is no more likely to explode than a pumpkin. Our test group will try to change that. They will concentrate, try to increase the probability of neutrons' escaping, and thus set off that sphere as an atom bomb."

"Doctor Satterlee?" asked a vice admiral with wings. "Do you think it can be done?"

"*Absolutely not!*" Satterlee turned to the adepts. "No offense intended, folks."

"Five minutes!" announced the navy captain.

Satterlee nodded to Reynolds. "Take over. And good luck."

Mrs. Wilkins spoke up. "Just a moment, young man. These 'neuter' things. I—"

"Neutrons, madam."

"That's what I said. I don't quite understand. I suppose that sort of thing comes in high school, but I only finished eighth grade. I'm sorry."

Satterlee looked sorry, too, but he tried. "—and each of these nuclei is potentially able to spit out one of these little neutrons. In that sphere out there"—he held up the dummy—"There are, say, five thousand billion trillion nuclei, each one—"

"My, that's quite a lot, isn't it?"

"Madam, it certainly is. Now—"

"Two minutes!"

Reynolds interrupted. "Mrs. Wilkins, don't worry. Concentrate on that metal ball out there and think about those neutrons, each one ready to come out. When I give the word, I want you all—you especially, Norman—to think about that ball, spitting sparks like a watch dial. Try for more sparks. Simply try. If you fail, no one will blame you. Don't get tense."

Mrs. Wilkins nodded. "I'll try." She put her tatting down and got a faraway look.

At once they were blinded by unbelievable radiance bursting through the massive filter. It beat on them, then died away.

The naval captain said, "What the hell!" Someone screamed, "It's gone, it's gone!"

The speaker brayed: "Fission at minus one minute thirty-seven seconds. Control, what went wrong. It looks like a hydrogen—"

The concussion wave hit and all sounds were smothered. Lights went out, emergency lighting clicked on. The blockhouse heaved like a boat in a heavy sea. Their eyes were still dazzled, their ears assaulted by cannonading afternoise, and physicists were elbowing flag officers at the port, when an anguished soprano cut through the din. "Oh, *dear!*"

Reynolds snapped, "What's the matter, Grandma? You all right?"

"Me? Oh, yes, yes—but I'm so sorry. I didn't mean to do it."

"Do what?"

"I was just feeling it out, thinking about all those little bitty neuters, ready to spit. But I didn't mean to make it go off—not till you told us to."

"Oh." Reynolds turned to the rest. "Anyone else jump the gun?"

No one admitted it. Mrs. Wilkins said timidly, "I'm sorry, Doctor. Have they got another one? I'll be more careful."

Reynolds and Withers were seated in the officers' mess with coffee in front of them; the physicist paid no attention to his. His eyes glittered and his face twitched. "No limits! Calculations show over *ninety per cent* conversion of mass to energy. You know what that *means?* If we assume—no, never mind. Just say that we could make every bomb the size of a pea. No tamper. No control circuits. Nothing but . . ." He paused. "Delivery would be fast, small jets—just a pilot, a weaponeer, and one of your 'operators.' No limit to the number of bombs. No nation on earth could—"

"Take it easy," said Reynolds. "We've got only a few telekinesis operators. You wouldn't risk them in a plane."

"But—"

"You don't need to. Show them the bombs, give them photos of the targets, hook them by radio to the weaponeer. That spreads them thin. And we'll test for more sensitive people. My figures show about one in eighteen hundred."

" 'Spread them thin,'" repeated Withers. "Mrs. Wilkins could handle dozens of bombs, one after another—couldn't she?"

"I suppose so. We'll test."

"We will indeed!" Withers noticed his coffee, gulped it. "Forgive me, Doctor; I'm punchy. I've had to revise too many opinions."

"I know. I was a behaviorist."

Captain Mikeler came in, looked around and came over. "The General wants you both," he said softly. "Hurry."

They were ushered into a guarded office. Major General Hanby was with General LaMott and Vice Admiral Keithley; they looked grim. Hanby handed them message flimsies. Reynolds saw the stamp TOP SECRET and handed his back. "General, I'm not cleared for this."

"Shut up and read it."

Reynolds skipped the number groups: "—(PARAPH-RASED) RUSSIAN EMBASSY TODAY HANDED STATE ULTI-MATUM: DEMANDS USA CONVERT TO 'PEOPLE'S REPUB-LIC' UNDER POLITICAL COMMISSARS TO BE ASSIGNED BY USSR. MILITARY ASSURANCES DEMANDED. NOTE CLAIMS MAJOR US CITIES (LIST SEPARATE) ARE MINED WITH ATOMIC BOMBS WHICH THEY THREATENED TO SET OFF BY RADIO IF TERMS ARE NOT MET BY SIXTEEN HUNDRED FRIDAY EST."

Reynolds reread it—"SIXTEEN HUNDRED FRIDAY" —two P.M. day after tomorrow, local time. Our cities booby-trapped with A-bombs? Could they do that? He realized that LaMott was speaking. "We must assume that the threat is real. Our free organization makes it an obvious line of attack."

The admiral said, "They may be bluffing."

The air general shook his head. "They know the President won't surrender. We can't assume that Ivan is stupid."

Reynolds wondered why he was being allowed to hear this. LaMott looked at him. "Admiral Keithley and I leave for Washington at once. I have delayed to ask you this: your people set off an atom bomb. *Can they keep bombs from going off?*"

Reynolds felt his time sense stretch as if he had all year to think about Grandma Wilkins, Norman, his other paranormals. "Yes," he answered.

LaMott stood up. "Your job, Hanby. Coming, Admiral?"

"Wait!" protested Reynolds. "Give me one bomb

and Mrs. Wilkins—and I'll sit on it. But how many cities? Twenty? Thirty?"

"Thirty-eight."

"Thirty-eight bombs—or more. Where are they? What do they look like? How long will this go on? It's impossible."

"Of course—but do it anyhow. Or try. Hanby, tell them we're on our way, will you?"

"Certainly, General."

"Good-by, Doctor. Or so long, rather."

Reynolds suddenly realized that these two were going back to "sit" on one of the bombs, to continue their duties until it killed them. He said quickly, "We'll try. We'll certainly try."

Thirty-eight cities . . . forty-three hours . . . and seventeen adepts. Others were listed in years of research, but they were scattered through forty-one states. In a dictatorship secret police would locate them at once, deliver them at supersonic speeds. But this was America.

Find them! Get them here! *Fast!* Hanby assigned Colonel Hammond to turn Reynolds' wishes into orders and directed his security officer to delegate his duties, get on the phone and use his acquaintance with the F.B.I., and other security officers, and through them with local police, to cut red tape and *find those paranormals*. Find them, convince them, bring pressure, start them winging toward the proving ground. By sundown, twenty-three had been found, eleven had been convinced or coerced, two had arrived. Hanby phoned Reynolds, caught him eating a sandwich standing up. "Hanby speaking. The President just phoned."

"The President?"

"LaMott got in to see him. He's dubious, but he's authorized an all-out try, short of slowing down conventional defense. One of his assistants left National

Airport by jet plane half an hour ago to come here and help. Things will move faster."

But it did not speed things up, as the Russian broadcast was even then being beamed, making the crisis public; the President went on the air thirty minutes later. Reynolds did not hear him; he was busy. Twenty people to save twenty cities—and a world. But how? He was sure that Mrs. Wilkins could smother any A-bomb she had seen; he hoped the others could. But a hidden bomb in a far-off city—find it mentally, think about it, quench it, not for the microsecond it took to set one off, but for the billions of microseconds it might take to uncover it—was it possible?

What would help? Certain drugs—caffeine, benzedrine. They must have quiet, too. He turned to Hammond. "I want a room and bath for each one."

"You've got that."

"No, we're doubled up, with semi-private baths."

Hammond shrugged. "Can do. It means booting out some brass."

"Keep the kitchen manned. They must not sleep, but they'll have to eat. Fresh coffee all the time and cokes and tea—anything they want. Can you put the room phones through a private switchboard?"

"Okay. What else?"

"I don't know. We'll talk to them."

They all knew of the Russian broadcast, but not what was being planned; they met his words with uneasy silence. Reynolds turned to Andrews. "Well, Two-Gun?"

"Big bite to chew, Prof."

"Yes. Can you chew it?"

"Have to, I reckon."

"Norman?"

"Gee, Boss! How can I when I can't see 'em?"

"Mrs. Wilkins couldn't see that bomb this morning. You can't see radioactivity on a watch dial; it's too small. You just see the dial and think about it. Well?"

The Negro lad scowled. "Think of a shiny ball in a city somewhere?"

"Yes. No, wait—Colonel Hammond, they need a visual image and it won't be that. There are atom bombs here—they must *see* one."

Hammond frowned. "An American bomb meant for dropping or firing won't look like a Russian bomb rigged for placement and radio triggering."

"What will they look like?"

"G-2 ought to know. I hope. We'll get some sort of picture. A three-dimensional mock-up, too. I'd better find Withers and the General." He left.

Mrs. Wilkins said briskly, "Doctor, I'll watch Washington, D.C."

"Yes, Mrs. Wilkins. You're the only one who has been tested, even in reverse. So you guard Washington; it's of prime importance."

"No, no, that's not why. It's the city I can *see* best."

Andrews said, "She's got something, Prof. I pick Seattle."

By midnight Reynolds had his charges, twenty-six by now, tucked away in the officers' club. Hammond and he took turns at a switchboard rigged in the upper hall. The watch would not start until shortly before deadline. Fatigue reduced paranormal powers, sometimes to zero; Reynolds hoped that they were getting one last night of sleep.

A microphone had been installed in each room; a selector switch let them listen in. Reynolds disliked this but Hammond argued, "Sure, it's an invasion of privacy. So is being blown up by an A-bomb." He dialed the switch. "Hear that? Our boy Norman is sawing wood." He moved it again. "Private 'Two-

Gun' is still stirring. We can't let them sleep, once it starts, so we have to spy on them."

"I suppose so."

Withers came upstairs. "Anything more you need?"

"I guess not," answered Reynolds. "How about the bomb mock-up?"

"Before morning."

"How authentic is it?"

"Hard to say. Their agents probably rigged firing circuits from radio parts bought right here; the circuits could vary a lot. But the business part—well, we're using real plutonium."

"Good. We'll show it to them after breakfast."

Two-Gun's door opened. "Howdy, Colonel. Prof— it's there."

"What is?"

"The bomb. Under Seattle. I can feel it."

"*Where is it?*"

"It's down—it *feels* down. And it feels wet, somehow. Would they put it in the Sound?"

Hammond jumped up. "In the harbor—and shower the city with radioactive water!" He was ringing as he spoke. "Get me General Hanby!"

"Morrison here," a voice answered. "What is it, Hammond?"

"The Seattle bomb—have them dredge for it. It's in the Sound, or somewhere under water."

"Eh? How do you know?"

"One of Reynolds' magicians. Do it!" He cut off.

Andrews said worriedly, "Prof, I can't *see* it—I'm not a 'seeing-eye.' Why don't you get one? Say that little Mrs. Brentano?"

"Oh, my God! Clairvoyants—we need them, too."

Withers said, "Eh, Doctor? Do you think—"

"No, I don't, or I would have thought of it. How do they search for bombs? What instruments?"

"Instruments? A bomb in its shielding doesn't even

affect a Geiger counter. You have to open things and look."

"How long will that take? Say for New York!"

Hammond said, "Shut up! Reynolds, where are these clairvoyants?"

Reynolds chewed his lip. "They're scarce."

"Scarcer than us dice rollers," added Two-Gun. "But get that Brentano kid. She found keys I had lost digging a ditch. Buried three feet deep—and me searching my quarters."

"Yes, yes, Mrs. Brentano." Reynolds pulled out a notebook.

Hammond reached for the switchboard. "Morrison? Stand by for more names—and even more urgent than the others."

More urgent but harder to find; the Panic was on. The President urged everyone to keep cool and stay home, whereupon thirty million people stampeded. The ticker in the P.I.O. office typed the story: "NEW YORK NY—TO CLEAR JAM CAUSED BY WRECKS IN OUT-BOUND TUBE THE INBOUND TUBE OF HOLLAND TUNNEL HAS BEEN REVERSED. POLICE HAVE STOPPED TRYING TO PREVENT EVACUATION. BULLDOZERS WORKING TO REOPEN TRIBOROUGH BRIDGE, BLADES SHOVING WRECKED CARS AND HUMAN HAMBURGER. WEEHAWKEN FERRY DISASTER CONFIRMED: NO PASSENGER LIST YET—FLASH— GEORGE WASHINGTON BRIDGE GAVE WAY AT 0353 EST, WHETHER FROM OVERLOAD OR SABOTAGE NOT KNOWN, MORE MORE MORE— FLASH—

It was repeated everywhere. The Denver-Colorado Springs highway had one hundred thirty-five deaths by midnight, then reports stopped. A DC-7 at Burbank ploughed into a mob which had broken through the barrier. The Baltimore-Washington highway was clogged both ways; Memorial Bridge was out of service. The five outlets from Los Angeles were solid with creeping cars. At four A.M. EST the President declared martial law; the order had no immediate effect.

By morning Reynolds had thirty-one adepts assigned to twenty-four cities. He had a stomach-churning ordeal before deciding to let them work only cities known to them. The gambler, Even-Money Karsch, had settled it: "Doc, I know when I'm hot. Minneapolis *has* to be mine." Reynolds gave in, even though one of his students had just arrived from there; he put them both on it and prayed that at least one would be "hot." Two clairvoyants arrived; one, a blind newsdealer from Chicago, was put to searching there; the other, a carnie mentalist, was given the list and told to find bombs wherever she could. Mrs. Brentano had remarried and moved; Norfolk was being combed for her.

At one fifteen P.M., forty-five minutes before deadline, they were in their rooms, each with maps and aerial views of his city, each with photos of the mocked-up bomb. The club was clear of residents; the few normals needed to coddle the paranormals kept carefully quiet. Roads nearby were blocked; air traffic was warned away. Everything was turned toward providing an atmosphere in which forty-two people could sit still and *think*.

At the switchboard were Hammond, Reynolds, and Gordon McClintock, the President's assistant. Reynolds glanced up. "What time is it?"

"One thirty-seven," rasped Hammond. "Twenty-three minutes."

"One thirty-eight," disagreed McClintock. "Reynolds, how about Detroit? You *can't* leave it unguarded."

"Whom can I use? Each is guarding the city he knows best."

"Those twin girls—I heard them mention Detroit."

"They've played everywhere. But Pittsburgh is their home."

"Switch one of them to Detroit."

Reynolds thought of telling him to go to Detroit himself. "They work together. You want to get them upset and lose both cities?"

Instead of answering McClintock said, "And who's watching Cleveland?"

"Norman Johnson. He lives there and he's our second strongest operator."

They were interrupted by voices downstairs. A man came up, carrying a bag, and spotted Reynolds. "Oh, hello, Doctor. What is this? I'm on top priority work—tank production—when the F.B.I. grabs me. You are responsible?"

"Yes. Come with me." McClintock started to speak, but Reynolds led the man away. "Mr. Nelson, did you bring your family?"

"No, they're still in Detroit. Had I known—"

"Please! Listen carefully." He explained, pointed out a map of Detroit in the room to which they went, showed him pictures of the simulated bomb. "You understand?"

Nelson's jaw muscles were jumping. "It seems impossible."

"It *is* possible. You've got to think about that bomb—or bombs. Get in touch, squeeze them, keep them from going off. You'll have to stay awake."

Nelson breathed gustily. "I'll stay awake."

"That phone will get you anything you want. Good luck."

He passed the room occupied by the blind clairvoyant; the door was open. "Harry, it's Prof. Getting anything?"

The man turned to the voice. "It's in the Loop. I could walk to it if I were there. A six-story building."

"That's the best you can do?"

"Tell them to try the attic. I get warm when I go up."

"Right away!" He rushed back, saw that Hanby

had arrived. Swiftly he keyed the communications office. "Reynolds speaking. The Chicago bomb is in a six-story building in the Loop area, probably in the attic. No—that's all. G'bye!"

Hanby started to speak; Reynolds shook his head and looked at his watch. Silently the General picked up the phone. "This is the commanding officer. Have any flash sent here." He put the phone down and stared at his watch.

For fifteen endless minutes they stood silent. The General broke it by taking the phone and saying, "Hanby. Anything?"

"No, General. Washington is on the wire."

"Eh? You say Washington?"

"Yes, sir. Here's the General, Mr. Secretary."

Hanby sighed. "Hanby speaking, Mr. Secretary. You're all right? Washington . . . is all right?"

They could hear the relayed voice. "Certainly certainly. We're past the deadline. But I wanted to tell you: Radio Moscow is telling the world that our cities are in flames."

Hanby hesitated. "None of them are?"

"Certainly not. I've a talker hooked in to GHQ, which has an open line to every city listed. All safe. I don't know whether your freak people did any good but, one way or another, it was a false—" The line went dead.

Hanby's face went dead with it. He jiggled the phone. "I've been cut off!"

"Not here, General—at the other end. Just a moment."

They waited. Presently the operator said, "Sorry, sir. I can't get them to answer."

"Keep trying!"

It was slightly over a minute—it merely seemed longer—when the operator said, "Here's your party, sir."

"That you, Hanby?" came the voice. "I suppose

we'll have phone trouble just as we had last time. Now, about these ESP people: while we are grateful and all that, nevertheless I suggest that nothing be released to the papers. Might be misinterpreted."

"Oh. Is that an order, Mr. Secretary?"

"Oh, no, no! But have such things routed through my office."

"Yes, sir." He cradled the phone.

McClintock said, "You shouldn't have rung off, General. I'd like to know whether the Chief wants this business continued."

"Suppose we talk about it on the way back to my office." The General urged him away, turned and gave Reynolds a solemn wink.

Trays were placed outside the doors at six o'clock; most of them sent for coffee during the evening. Mrs. Wilkins ordered tea; she kept her door open and chatted with anyone who passed. Harry the newsboy was searching Milwaukee; no answer had been received from his tip about Chicago. Mrs. Ekstein, or "Princess Cathay" as she was billed, had reported a "feeling" about a house trailer in Denver and was now poring over a map of New Orleans. With the passing of the deadline panic abated; communications were improving. The American people were telling each other that they had known that those damned commies were bluffing.

Hammond and Reynolds sent for more coffee at three A.M.; Reynolds' hand trembled as he poured. Hammond said, "You haven't slept for two nights. Get over on that divan."

"Neither have you."

"I'll sleep when you wake up."

"I *can't* sleep. I'm worrying about what'll happen when *they* get sleepy." He gestured at the line of doors.

"So am I."

At seven A.M. Two-Gun came out. "Prof, they got

it. The bomb. It's gone. Like closing your hand on nothing."

Hammond grabbed the phone. "Get me Seattle—the F.B.I. office."

While they waited, Two-Gun said, "What now, Prof?"

Reynolds tried to think. "Maybe you should rest."

"Not until this is over. Who's got Toledo? I know that burg."

"Uh . . . young Barnes."

Hammond was connected; he identified himself, asked the question. He put the phone down gently. "They *did* get it," he whispered. "It was in the lake."

"I told you it was wet," agreed Two-Gun. "Now, about Toledo—"

"Well . . .tell me when you've got it and we'll let Barnes rest."

McClintock rushed in at seven thirty-five, followed by Hanby. "Doctor Reynolds! Colonel Hammond!"

"*Sh!* Quiet! You'll disturb them."

McClintock said in a lower voice, "Yes, surely—I was excited. This is important. They located a bomb in Seattle and—"

"Yes. Private Andrews told us."

"Huh? How did *he* know?"

"Never mind," Hanby intervened. "The point is, they found the bomb already triggered. Now we *know* that your people are protecting the cities."

"Was there any doubt?"

"Well . . . yes."

"But there isn't now," McClintock added. "I must take over." He bent over the board. "Communications? Put that White House line through here."

"Just what," Reynolds said slowly, "do you mean by 'take over?' "

"Eh? Why, take charge on behalf of the President. Make sure these people don't let down an instant!"

"But what do you propose to *do?*"

Hanby said hastily, "Nothing, Doctor. We'll just keep in touch with Washington from here."

They continued the vigil together; Reynolds spent the time hating McClintock's guts. He started to take coffee, then decided on another benzedrine tablet instead. He hoped his people were taking enough of it—and not too much. They all had it, except Grandma Wilkins, who wouldn't touch it. He wanted to check with them but knew that he could not—each bomb was bound only by a thread of thought; a split-split second of diversion might be enough.

The outside light flashed; Hanby took the call. "Congress has recessed," he announced, "and the President is handing the Soviet Union a counter ultimatum; locate and disarm any bombs or be bombed in return." The light flashed again; Hanby answered. His face lit up. "Two more found," he told them. "One in Chicago, right where your man said; the other in Camden."

"Camden? How?"

"They rounded up the known Communists, of course. This laddie was brought back there for questioning. He didn't like that; he knew that he was being held less than a mile from the bomb. Who is on Camden?"

"Mr. Dimwiddy."

"The elderly man with the bunions?"

"That's right—retired postman. General, do we assume that there is only one bomb per city?"

McClintock answered, "Of course not! These people must—"

Hanby cut in, "Central Intelligence is assuming so, except for New York and Washington. If they had more bombs here, they would have added more cities."

Reynolds left to take Dimwiddy off watch. McClin-

tock, he fumed, did not realize that people were
flesh and blood.

Dimwiddy was unsurprised. "A while ago the pressure let up, then—well, I'm afraid I dozed. I had a
terrible feeling that I had let it go off, then I knew it
hadn't." Reynolds told him to rest, then be ready to
help out elsewhere. They settled on Philadelphia;
Dimwiddy had once lived there.

The watch continued. Mrs. Ekstein came up with
three hits, but no answers came back; Reynolds still
had to keep those cities covered. She then complained that her "sight" had gone; Reynolds went to
her room and told her to nap, not wishing to consult
McClintock.

Luncheon trays came and went. Reynolds continued worrying over how to arrange his operators to let
them rest. Forty-three people and thirty-five cities—if
only he had two for every city! Maybe any of them
could watch any city? No, he could not chance it.

Barnes woke up and took back Toledo; that left
Two-Gun free. Should he let him take Cleveland?
Norman had had no relief and Two-Gun had once
been through it, on a train. The colored boy was
amazing but rather hysterical, whereas Two-Gun—
well, Reynolds felt that Two-Gun would last, even
through a week of no sleep.

No! He couldn't trust Cleveland to a man who had
merely passed through it. But with Dimwiddy on
Philadelphia, when Mary Gifford woke he could put
her on Houston and that would let Hank sleep before shifting him to Indianapolis and that would let
him—

A chess game, with all pawns queens and no mistakes allowed.

McClintock was twiddling the selector switch, listening in. Suddenly he snapped, "Someone is asleep!"

Reynolds checked the number.

"Of course, that's the twins' room; they take turns. You may hear snores in 21 and 30 and 8 and 19. It's okay; they're off watch."

"Well, all right." McClintock seemed annoyed.

Reynolds bent back to his list. Shortly McClintock snorted, "Who's in room 12?"

"Uh? Wait—that's Norman Johnson, Cleveland."

"*You mean he's on watch?*"

"Yes." Reynolds could hear the boy's asthmatic breathing, felt relieved.

"He's asleep!"

"No, he's not."

But McClintock was rushing down the corridor. Reynolds took after him; Hammond and Hanby followed. Reynolds caught up as McClintock burst into room 12. Norman was sprawled in a chair, eyes closed in his habitual attitude. McClintock rushed up, slapped him. "Wake up!"

Reynolds grabbed McClintock. "You bloody fool!"

Norman opened his eyes, then burst into tears. "It's *gone!*"

"Steady, Norman. It's all right."

"No, no! It's gone—and my mammy's gone with it!"

McClintock snapped, "Concentrate, boy! Get back on it!"

Reynolds turned on him. "Get out. Get out before I punch you."

Hanby and Hammond were in the door; the General cut in with a hoarse whisper, "Pipe down, Doctor, bring the boy."

Back at the board the outside light was flashing. Hanby took the call while Reynolds tried to quiet the boy. Hanby listened gravely, then said, "He's right. Cleveland just got it."

McClintock snapped, "He went to sleep. He ought to be shot."

"Shut up," said Hanby.

"But—"

Reynolds said, "Any others, General?"

"Why would there be?"

"All this racket. It may have disturbed a dozen of them."

"Oh, we'll see." He called Washington again. Presently he sighed. "No, just Cleveland. We were . . . lucky."

"General," McClintock insisted, "he was asleep."

Hanby looked at him. "Sir, you may be the President's deputy but you yourself have no military authority. Off my post."

"But I am directed by the President to—"

"Off my post, sir! Go back to Washington. *Or to Cleveland.*"

McClintock looked dumbfounded. Hanby added, "You're worse than bad—you're a fool."

"The President will hear of this."

"Blunder again and the President won't live that long. Get out."

By nightfall the situation was rapidly getting worse. Twenty-seven cities were still threatened and Reynolds was losing operators faster than bombs were being found. Even-Money Karsch would not relieve when awakened. "See that?" he said, rolling dice. "Cold as a well-digger's feet. I'm through." After that Reynolds tested each one who was about to relieve, found that some were tired beyond the power of short sleep to restore them—they were "cold."

By midnight there were eighteen operators for nineteen cities. The twins had fearfully split up; it had worked. Mrs. Wilkins was holding both Washington and Baltimore; she had taken Baltimore when he had no one to relieve there.

But now he had no one for relief anywhere and three operators—Nelson, Two-Gun and Grandma Wilkins—had had no rest. He was too fagged to worry; he simple knew that whenever one of them, reached his limit, the United States would lose a city. The panic had resumed after the bombing of Cleveland; roads again were choked. The disorder made harder the search for bombs. But there was nothing he could do.

Mrs. Ekstein still complained about her sight but kept at it. Harry the newsboy had had no luck with Milwaukee, but there was no use shifting him; other cities were "dark" to him. During the night Mrs. Ekstein pointed to the bomb in Houston. It was, she said, in a box underground. A coffin? Yes, there was a headstone; she was unable to read the name.

Thus, many recent dead in Houston were disturbed. But it was nine Sunday morning before Reynolds went to tell Mary Gifford that she could rest—or relieve for Wilmington, if she felt up to it. He found her collapsed and lifted her onto the bed, wondering if she had known the Houston bomb was found.

Eleven cities now and eight people. Grandma Wilkins held four cities. No one else had been able to double up. Reynolds thought dully that it was a miracle that they had been able to last at all; it surpassed enormously the best test performance.

Hammond looked up as he returned. "Make any changes?"

"No. The Gifford kid is through. We'll lose half a dozen cities before this is over."

"Some of them must be damn near empty by now."

"I hope so. Any more bombs found?"

"Not yet. How do you feel, Doc?"

"Three weeks dead." Reynolds sat down wearily. He was wondering if he should wake some of those sleeping and test them again when he heard a noise below; he went to the stairwell.

Up came an M.P. captain. "They said to bring her here."

Reynolds looked at the woman with him. "Dorothy Brentano!"

"Dorothy Smith now."

He controlled his trembling and explained what was required. She nodded. "I figured that out on the plane. Got a pencil? Take this: St. Louis—a river warehouse with a sign reading 'Bartlett & Sons, Jobbers.' Look in the loft. And Houston—no, they got that one. Baltimore—it's in a ship at the docks, the S.S. *Gold Coast*. What other cities? I've wasted time feeling around where there was nothing to find."

Reynolds was already shouting for Washington to answer.

Grandma Wilkins was last to be relieved; Dorothy located one in the Potomac—and Mrs. Wilkins told her sharply to keep trying. There were four bombs in Washington, which Mrs. Wilkins had known all along. Dorothy found them in eleven minutes.

Three hours later Reynolds showed up in the club messroom, not having been able to sleep. Several of his people were eating and listening to the radio blast about our raid on Russia. He gave it a wide berth; they could blast Omsk and Tomsk and Minsk and Pinsk; today he didn't care. He was sipping milk and thinking that he would never drink coffee again when Captain Mikeler bent over his table.

"The General wants you. Hurry!"

"Why?"

"I said, Hurry! Where's Grandma Wilkins—oh—see her. Who is Mrs. Dorothy Smith?"

Reynolds looked around. "She's with Mrs. Wilkins."

Mikeler rushed them to Hanby's office. Hanby merely said, "Sit over there. And you ladies, too. Stay in focus."

Reynolds found himself looking into a television screen at the President of the United States. He looked as weary as Reynolds felt, but he turned on his smile. "You are Doctor Reynolds?"

"Yes, Mr. President!"

"These ladies are Mrs. Wilkins and Mrs. Smith?"

"Yes, sir."

The President said quietly, "You three and your colleagues will be thanked by the Republic. And by me, for myself. But that must wait. Mrs. Smith, there are more bombs—in Russia. Could your strange gift find them there?"

"Why, I don't—I can try!"

"Mrs. Wilkins, could you set off those Russian bombs while they are still far away?"

Incredibly, she was still bright-eyed and chipper. "Why, Mr. President!"

"Can you?"

She got a far-away look. "Dorothy and I had better have a quiet room somewhere. And I'd like a pot of tea. A large pot."

Water Is for Washing

Water Is for Washing

He judged that the Valley was hotter than usual—
but, then, it usually was. Imperial Valley was a natural hothouse, two hundred and fifty feet below sea
level, diked from the Pacific Ocean by the mountains
back of San Diego, protected from the Gulf of Baja
California by high ground on the south. On the east,
the Chocolate Mountains walled off the rushing Colorado River.

He parked his car outside the Barbara Worth Hotel in El Centro and went into the bar. "Scotch."

The bartender filled a shot glass, then set a glass of
ice water beside it. "Thanks. Have one?"

"Don't mind if I do."

The customer sipped his drink, then picked up the
chaser. "That's just the right amount of water in the
right place. I've got hydrophobia."

"Huh?"

"I hate water. Darn near drowned when I was a
kid. Afraid of it ever since."

"Water ain't fit to drink," the bartender agreed,
"but I do like to swim."

"Not for me. That's why I like the Valley. They
restrict the stuff to irrigation ditches, washbowls,

257

bathtubs, and glasses. I always hate to go back to Los Angeles."

"If you're afraid of drowning," the barkeep answered, "you're better off in L.A. than in the Valley. We're below sea level here. Water all around us, higher than our heads. Suppose somebody pulled out the cork?"

"Go frighten your grandmother. The Coast Range is no cork."

"Earthquake."

"That's crazy. Earthquakes don't move mountain ranges."

"Well, it wouldn't necessarily take a quake. You've heard about the 1905 flood, when the Colorado River spilled over and formed the Salton Sea? But don't be too sure about quakes; valleys below sea level don't just grow—*something* has to cause them. The San Andreas Fault curls around this valley like a question mark. Just imagine the shake-up it must have taken to drop thousands of square miles below the level of the Pacific."

"Quit trying to get my goat. That happened thousands of years ago. Here." He laid a bill on the bar and left. Joykiller! A man like that shouldn't be tending bar.

The thermometer in the shaded doorway showed 118 degrees. The solid heat beat against him, smarting his eyes and drying his lungs, even while he remained on the covered sidewalk. His car, he knew, would be too hot to touch; he should have garaged it. He walked around the end of it and saw someone bending over the lefthand door. He stopped. "What the hell do you think you're doing?"

The figure turned suddenly, showing pale, shifty eyes. He was dressed in a business suit, dirty and unpressed. He was tieless. His hands and nails were dirty, but not with the dirt of work; the palms were uncalloused. A weak mouth spoiled features otherwise satisfactory. "No harm intended," he apologized. "I just wanted to read your registration slip. You're from Los Angeles. Give me a lift back to the city, pal."

The car owner ignored him and glanced around inside the automobile. "Just wanted to see where I was from, eh? Then why did you open the glove compartment? I ought to run you in." He looked past the vagrant at two uniformed deputy sheriffs sauntering down the other side of the street. "On your way, bum."

The man followed the glance, then faded swiftly away in the other direction. The car's owner climbed in, swearing at the heat, then checked the glove compartment. The flashlight was missing.

Checking it off to profit-and-loss, he headed for Brawley, fifteen miles north. The heat was oppressive, even for Imperial Valley. Earthquake weather, he said to himself, giving vent to the Californian's favorite superstition, then sternly denied it—that dumb fool gin peddler had put the idea in his mind. Just an ordinary Valley day, a little hotter, maybe.

His business took him to several outlying ranchos between Brawley and the Salton Sea. He was heading back toward the main highway on a worn gravel mat when the car began to waltz around as if he were driving over corduroy. He stopped the car, but the shaking continued, accompanied by a bass grumble.

Earthquake! He burst out of the car possessed only by the primal urge to get out in the open, to escape the swaying towers, the falling bricks. But there were no buildings here—nothing but open desert and irrigated fields.

He went back to the car, his stomach lurching to every following temblor. The right front tire was flat. Stone-punctured, he decided, when the car was bounced around by the first big shock.

Changing that tire almost broke his heart. He was faint from heat and exertion when he straightened up from it.

Another shock, not as heavy as the first, but heavy, panicked him again and he began to run, but he fell, tripped by the crazy galloping of the ground. He got up and went back to the car.

It had slumped drunkenly, the jack knocked over by the quake.

He wanted to abandon it, but the dust from the shocks had closed in around him like fog, without fog's blessed coolness. He knew he was several miles from town and doubted his ability to make it on foot.

He got to work, sweating and gasping. One hour and thirteen minutes after the initial shock the spare tire was in place. The ground still grumbled and shook from time to time. He resolved to drive slowly and thereby keep the car in control if another bad shock came along. The dust forced him to drive slowly, anyhow.

Moseying back toward the main highway, he was regaining his calm, when he became aware of a train in the distance. The roar increased, over the noise of the car—an express train, he decided, plunging down the valley. The thought niggled at the back of his mind for a moment, until he realized why the sound seemed wrong: Trains should not race after a quake; they should creep along, the crew alert for spread rails.

The sound was recast in his mind. *Water!*

Out of the nightmare depths of his subconscious, out of the fright of his childhood, he placed it. This was the sound after the dam broke, when, as a kid, he had been so nearly drowned. Water! A great wall of water, somewhere in the dust, hunting for him, hunting for *him!*

His foot jammed the accelerator down to the floorboards; the car bucked and promptly stalled. He started it again and strove to keep himself calm. With no spare tire and a bumpy road he could not afford the risk of too much speed. He held himself down to a crawling thirty-five miles an hour, tried to estimate the distance and direction of the water, and prayed.

The main highway jumped at him in the dust and he was almost run down by a big car roaring past to the north. A second followed it, then a vegetable truck, then the tractor unit of a semi-trailer freighter.

It was all he needed to know. He turned north.

He passed the vegetable truck and a jalopy-load of Okiestyle workers, a family. They shouted at him, but he kept going. Several cars more powerful than his passed him and he passed in turn several of the heaps used by the itinerant farm workers. After that he had the road to himself. Nothing came from the north.

The trainlike rumble behind him increased.

He peered into the rear-view mirror but could see nothing through the dusty haze.

There was a child sitting beside the road and crying—a little girl about eight. He drove on past, hardly aware of her, then braked to a stop. He told himself that she must have folks around somewhere, that it was no business of his. Cursing himself, he backed and turned, almost drove past her in the dust, then managed to turn around without backing and pulled up beside her. "Get in!"

She turned a dirty, wet, tragic face, but remained seated. "I can't. My foot hurts."

He jumped out, scooped her up and dumped her in the righthand seat, noting as he did so that her right foot was swollen. "How did you do it?" he demanded, as he threw in the clutch.

"When the *thing* happened. Is it broke?" She was not crying now. "Are you going to take me home?"

"I—I'll take care of you. Don't ask questions."

"All right," she said doubtfully. The roar behind them was increasing. He wanted to speed up but the haze and the need to nurse his unreliable spare tire held him back. He had to swerve suddenly when a figure loomed up in the dust—a Nisei boy, hurrying toward them.

The child beside him leaned out. "That's Tommy!"

"Huh? Never mind. Just a goddam Jap."

"That's Tommy Hayakawa. He's in my class." She added. "Maybe he's looking for me."

He cursed again, under his breath, and threw the car into a turn that almost toppled it. Then he was heading back, into that awful sound.

"There he is," the child shrieked. "Tommy! Oh, Tommy!"

"Get in," he commanded, when he had stopped the car by the boy.

"Get in, Tommy," his passenger added.

The boy hesitated; the driver reached past the little girl, grabbed the boy by his shirt and dragged him in. "Want to be drowned, you fool?"

He had just shifted into second, and was still accelerating, when another figure sprang up almost in front of the car—a man, waving his arms. He caught a glimpse of the face as the car gained speed. It was the sneak thief.

His conscience was easy about that one, he thought as he drove on. Good riddance! Let the water get him.

Then the horror out of his own childhood welled up in him and he saw the face of the tramp again, in a horrible fantasy. He was struggling in the water, his bloodshot eyes bulging with terror, his gasping mouth crying wordlessly for help.

The driver was stopping the car. He did not dare

turn; he backed the car, at the highest speed he could manage. It was no great distance, or else the vagrant had run after them.

The door was jerked open and the tramp lurched in. "Thanks, pal," he gasped. "Let's get out of here!"

"Right!" He glanced into the mirror, then stuck his head out and looked behind. Through the haze he saw it, a leadblack wall, thirty—or was it a hundred?—feet high, rushing down on them, overwhelming them. The noise of it pounded his skull.

He gunned the car in second, then slid into high and gave it all he had, careless of the tires. "How we doing?" he yelled.

The tramp looked out the rear window. "We're gaining. Keep it up."

He skidded around a wreck on the highway, then slowed a trifle, aware that the breakneck flight would surely lose them the questionable safety of the car if he kept it up. The little girl started to cry.

"Shut up!" he snapped.

The Nisei boy twisted around and looked behind. "What is it?" he asked in an awed voice.

The tramp answered him. "The Pacific Ocean has broken through."

"It can't be!" cried the driver. "It must be the Colorado River."

"That's no river, Mac. That's the Gulf. I was in a cantina in Centro when it came over the radio from Calexico. Warned us that the ground had dropped away to the south. Tidal wave coming. Then the station went dead." He moistened his lips. "That's why I'm here."

The driver did not answer. The vagrant went on nervously, "Guy I hitched with went on without me, when he stopped for gas in Brawley." He looked back again. "I can't see it any more."

"We've gotten away from it?"

"Hell, no. It's just as loud. I just can't see it through the murk."

They drove on. The road curved a little to the right and dropped away almost imperceptibly.

The bum looked ahead. Suddenly he yelled. "Hey! Where you going?"

"Huh?"

"You got to get off the highway, man! We're dropping back toward the Salton Sea—the lowest place in the Valley."

"There's no other place to go. We *can't* turn around."

"You can't go ahead. It's suicide!"

"We'll outrun it. North of the Salton, it's high ground again."

"Not a chance. Look at your gas gauge."

The gauge was fluttering around the left side of the dial. Two gallons, maybe less. Enough to strand them by the sunken shores of the Salton Sea. He stared at it in an agony of indecision.

"Gotta cut off to the left," his passenger was saying. "Side road. Follow it up toward the hills."

"Where?"

"Coming up. I know this road. I'll watch for it."

When he turned into the side road, he realized sickly that his course was now nearly parallel to the hungry flood south of them. But the road climbed.

He looked to the left and tried to see the black wall of water, the noise of which beat loud in his ears, but the road demanded his attention. "Can you see it?" he yelled to the tramp.

"Yes! Keep trying, pal!"

He nodded and concentrated on the hills ahead. The hills must surely be above sea level, he told himself. On and on he drove, through a timeless waste of dust and heat and roar. The grade increased, then suddenly the car broke over a rise and headed down into a wash—a shallow arroyo that should have been dry, but was not.

He was into water before he knew it, hub high and higher. He braked and tried to back. The engine coughed and stalled.

The tramp jerked open the door, dragged the two children out, and, with one under each arm, splashed his way back to higher ground. The driver tried to start the car, then saw frantically that the rising water was up above the floorboards. He jumped out, stumbled to his knees in water waist-deep, got to his feet, and struggled after them.

The tramp had set the children down on a little rise and was looking around. "We got to get out of here," the car owner gasped.

The tramp shook his head. "No good. Look around you."

To the south, the wall of water had broken around the rise on which they stood. A branch had sluiced between them and the hills, filling the wash in which the car lay stalled. The main body of the rushing waters had passed east of them, covering the highway they had left, and sweeping on toward the Salton Sea.

Even as he watched, the secondary flood down the wash returned to the parent body. They were cut off, surrounded by the waters.

He wanted to scream, to throw himself into the opaque turbulence and get it over. Perhaps he did scream. He realized that the tramp was shaking him by the shoulder.

"Take it easy, pal. We've got a couple of throws left."

"Huh?" He wiped his eyes. "What do we do?"

"I want my mother," the little girl said decisively.

The tramp reached down and patted her absent-mindedly.

Tommy Hayakawa put his arm around her. "I'll take care of you, Laura," he said gravely.

The water was already over the top of the car and rising. The boiling head of the flood was well past them; its thunder was lessening; the waters rose quietly—but they rose.

"We can't stay here," he persisted.

"We'll have to," the tramp answered. . . .

Their living space grew smaller, hardly thirty feet by fifty. They were not alone now. A coyote, jack rabbits, creepers, crawlers, and gnawers, all the poor relations of the desert, were forced equally back into the narrowing circle of dry land. The coyote ignored the rabbits; they ignored the coyote. The highest point of their island was surmounted by a rough concrete post about four feet high, an obelisk with a brass plate set in its side. He read it twice before the meaning of the words came to him.

It was a bench mark, stating, as well as latitude and longitude, that this spot, this line engraved in brass, was "sea level." When it soaked into his confused brain he pointed it out to his companion. "Hey! Hey, look! We're going to make it! The water won't come any higher!"

The tramp looked. "Yes, I know. I read it. But it doesn't mean anything. That's the level it used to be before the earthquake."

"But—"

"It may be higher—or lower. We'll find out."

The waters still came up. They were ankle-deep at sundown. The rabbits and the other small things were gradually giving up. They were in an unbroken waste of water, stretching from the Chocolate Mountains beyond where the Salton Sea had been, to the nearer hills on the west. The coyote slunk up against their knees, dog fashion, then appeared to make up its mind, for it slipped into the water and struck out toward the hills. They could see its out-thrust head for a long time, until it was just a dot on the water in the gathering darkness.

When the water was knee-deep, each man took one of the children in his arms. They braced themselves against the stability of the concrete post, and waited, too tired for panic. They did not talk. Even the children had not talked much since abandoning the car.

It was getting dark. The tramp spoke up suddenly. "Can you pray?"

"Uh—not very well."

"Okay. I'll try, then." He took a deep breath. "Merciful Father, Whose all-seeing eye notes even the sparrow in its flight, have mercy on these Thy unworthy servants. Deliver them from this peril, if it be Thy will." He paused, and then added, "And make it as fast as You can, please. Amen."

The darkness closed in, complete and starless. They could not see the water, but they could feel it and hear it. It was warm—it felt no worse when it soaked their armpits than it had around their ankles. They had the kids on their shoulders now, with their backs braced against the submerged post. There was little current.

Once something bumped against them in the darkness—a dead steer, driftwood, a corpse—they had no way of knowing. It nudged them and was gone. Once he thought he saw a light, and said suddenly to the tramp, "Have you still got that flashlight you swiped from me?"

There was a long silence and a strained voice answered, "You recognized me."

"Of course. Where's the flashlight?"

"I traded it for a drink in Centro."

"But, look, Mac," the voice went on reasonably, "If I hadn't borrowed it, it would be in your car. It wouldn't be here. And if I *did* have it in my pocket, it'd be soaked and wouldn't work."

"Oh, forget it!"

"Okay." There was silence for a while, then the voice went on, "Pal, could you hold both the kids a while?"

"I guess so. Why?"

"This water is still coming up. It'll be over our heads, maybe. You hang onto the kids; I'll boost myself up on the post. I'll sit on it and wrap my legs around it. Then you hand me the kids. That way we gain maybe eighteen inches or two feet."

"And what happens to me?"

"You hang onto my shoulders and float with your head out of the water."

"Well—we'll try it."

It worked. The kids clung to the tramp's sides, supported by water and by his arms. The driver hung onto the tramp where he could, first to his belt, then, as the waters rose and his toes no longer touched bottom, to the collar of his coat. They were still alive.

"I wish it would get light. It's worse in the darkness."

"Yeah," said the tramp. "If it was light, maybe somebody 'ud see us."

"How?"

"Airplane, maybe. They always send out airplanes, in floods."

He suddenly began to shake violently, as the horror came over him, and the memory of another flood when there had been no rescuing airplanes.

The tramp said sharply, "What's the matter, Mac? Are you cracking up?"

"No, I'm all right. I just hate water."

"Want to swap around? You hold the kids for a while and I'll hang on and float."

"Uh . . .. No, we might drop one. Stay where you are."

"We can make it. The change'll do you good." The tramp shook the children. "Hey, wake up! Wake up, honey—and hold tight."

The kids were transferred to his shoulders while he gripped the post with his knees and the tramp steadied him with an arm. Then he eased himself cautiously onto the top of the post, as the tramp got off and floated free, save for one anchoring hand. "You all right?" he said to the tramp.

The hand squeezed his shoulder in the darkness. "Sure. Got a snootful of water."

"Hang on."

"Don't worry—I will!"

He was shorter than the tramp; he had to sit erect to keep his head out of water. The children clung tightly. He kept them boosted high.

Presently the tramp spoke. "You wearing a belt?"

"Yes. Why?"

"Hold still." He felt a second hand fumbling at his waist, then his trousers loosened as the belt came away. "I'm going to strap your legs to the post. That's the bad part about it; your legs cramp. Hold tight now. I'm going under."

He felt hands under water, fumbling at his legs. Then there was the tension of the belt being tightened around his knees. He relaxed to the pressure. It *was* a help; he found he could hold his position without muscular effort.

The tramp broke water near him. "Where are you?" the voice was panicky.

"Here! Over here!" he tried to peer into the inky darkness; it was hopeless. "Over this way!" The splashing seemed to come closer. He shouted again, but no hand reached out of the darkness. He continued to shout, then shouted and listened intermittently. It

seemed to him that he heard splashing long after the
sound had actually ceased.

He stopped shouting only when his voice gave
out. Little Laura was sobbing on his shoulder. Tommy
was trying to get her to stop. He could tell from their
words that they had not understood what had happened and he did not try to explain.

When the water dropped down to his waist, he
moved the kids so that they sat on his lap. This let
him rest his arms, which had grown almost unbearably tired as the receding water ceased to support
the weight of the children. The water dropped still
more, and the half dawn showed him that the ground
beneath him was, if not dry, at least free from flood.

He shook Tommy awake. "I can't get down, kid.
Can you unstrap me?"

The boy blinked and rubbed his eyes. He looked
around and seemed to recall his circumstances without dismay. "Sure. Put me down."

The boy loosened the buckle after some difficulty
and the man cautiously unwound himself from his
perch. His legs refused him when he tried to stand;
they let him and the girl sprawl in the mud.

"Are you hurt?" he asked her as he sat up.

"No," she answered soberly.

He looked around. It was getting steadily lighter
and he could see the hills to the west; it now appeared that the water no longer extended between
the hills and themselves. To the east was another
story; the Salton Sea no longer existed as such. An
unbroken sheet of water stretched from miles to the
north clear to the southern horizon.

His car was in sight; the wash was free of water
except for casual pools. He walked down toward the
automobile, partly to take the knots out of his legs,
partly to see if the car could ever be salvaged. It was
there that he found the tramp.

*   *   *

The body lay wedged against the right rear wheel, as if carried down there by undertow.

He walked back toward the kids. "Stay away from the car," he ordered. "Wait here. I've got something to do." He went back to the car and found the keys still in the ignition lock. He opened the trunk with some difficulty and got out a short spade he kept for desert mishaps.

It was not much of a grave, just a shallow trench in the wet sand, deep enough to receive and cover a man, but he promised himself that he would come back and do better. He had no time now. The waters, he thought, would be back with high tide. He must get himself and the children to the hills.

Once the body was out of sight, he called out to the boy and the girl, "You can come here now." He had one more chore. There was drift about, yucca stalks, bits of wood. He selected two pieces of unequal length, then dug around in his tool chest for bits of wire. He wired the short piece across the longer, in a rough cross, then planted the cross in the sand near the head of the grave.

He stepped back and looked at it, the kids at his side.

His lips moved silently for a moment, then he said, "Come on, kids. We got to get out of here." He picked up the little girl, took the boy by the hand, and they walked away to the west, the sun shining on their backs.

continued ☞

DAVID WEBER

The Honor Harrington series: *(cont.)*

Field of Dishonor

Honor goes home to Manticore—and fights for her life on a battlefield she never trained for, in a private war that offers just two choices: death—or a "victory" that can end only in dishonor and the loss of all she loves....

Flag in Exile

Hounded into retirement and disgrace by political enemies, Honor Harrington has retreated to planet Grayson, where powerful men plot to reverse the changes she has brought to their world. And for their plans to suceed, Honor Harrington must die!

Honor Among Enemies

Offered a chance to end her exile and again command a ship, Honor Harrington must use a crew drawn from the dregs of the service to stop pirates who are plundering commerce. Her enemies have chosen the mission carefully, thinking that either she will stop the raiders or they will kill her . . . and either way, her enemies will win....

In Enemy Hands

After being ambushed, Honor finds herself aboard an enemy cruiser, bound for her scheduled execution. But one lesson Honor has never learned is how to give up! One way or another, she and her crew are going home—even if they have to conquer Hell to get there!

continued ☞

PRAISE FOR
LOIS MCMASTER BUJOLD

What the critics say:

The Warrior's Apprentice: "Now here's a fun romp through the spaceways—not so much a space opera as space ballet.... it has all the 'right stuff.' A lot of thought and thoughtfulness stand behind the all-too-human characters. Enjoy this one, and look forward to the next."   —Dean Lambe, *SF Reviews*

"The pace is breathless, the characterization thoughtful and emotionally powerful, and the author's narrative technique and command of language compelling. Highly recommended."   —*Booklist*

Brothers in Arms: "... she gives it a geniune depth of character, while reveling in the wild turnings of her tale. ... Bujold is as audacious as her favorite hero, and as brilliantly (if sneakily) successful."   —*Locus*

"Miles Vorkosigan is such a great character that I'll read anything Lois wants to write about him. ... a book to re-read on cold rainy days."   —Robert Coulson, *Comics Buyer's Guide*

Borders of Infinity: "Bujold's series hero Miles Vorkosigan may be a lord by birth and an admiral by rank, but a bone disease that has left him hobbled and in frequent pain has sensitized him to the suffering of outcasts in his very hierarchical era.... Playing off Miles's reserve and cleverness, Bujold draws outrageous and outlandish foils to color her high-minded adventures."   —*Publishers Weekly*

Falling Free: "In *Falling Free* Lois McMaster Bujold has written her fourth straight superb novel. ... How to break down a talent like Bujold's into analyzable components? Best not to try. Best to say 'Read, or you will be missing something extraordinary.' "   —Roland Green, *Chicago Sun-Times*

The Vor Game: "The chronicles of Miles Vorkosigan are far too witty to be literary junk food, but they rouse the kind of craving that makes popcorn magically vanish during a double feature."   —Faren Miller, *Locus*

MORE PRAISE FOR
LOIS MCMASTER BUJOLD

What the readers say:

"My copy of *Shards of Honor* is falling apart I've reread it so often.... I'll read whatever you write. You've certainly proved yourself a grand storyteller."
—Liesl Kolbe, Colorado Springs, CO

"I experience the stories of Miles Vorkosigan as almost viscerally uplifting.... But certainly, even the weightiest theme would have less impact than a cinder on snow were it not for a rousing good story, and good storytelling with it. This is the second thing I want to thank you for.... I suppose if you boiled down all I've said to its simplest expression, it would be that I immensely enjoy and admire your work. I submit that, as literature, your work raises the overall level of the science fiction genre, and spiritually, your work cannot avoid positively influencing all who read it."
—Glen Stonebraker, Gaithersburg, MD

" 'The Mountains of Mourning' [in *Borders of Infinity*] was one of the best-crafted, and simply best, works I'd ever read. When I finished it, I immediately turned back to the beginning and read it again, and I can't remember the last time I did that."   —Betsy Bizot, Lisle, IL

"I can only hope that you will continue to write, so that I can continue to read (and of course buy) your books, for they make me laugh and cry and think ... rare indeed."   —Steven Knott, Major, USAF

What Do You Say?

Send me these books!

Shards of Honor	72087-2 ✦ $5.99	☐
Barrayar	72083-X ✦ $5.99	☐
Cordelia's Honor (trade)	87749-6 ✦ $15.00	☐
The Warrior's Apprentice	72066-X ✦ $5.99	☐
The Vor Game	72014-7 ✦ $5.99	☐
Young Miles (trade)	87782-8 ✦ $15.00	☐
Cetaganda (hardcover)	87701-1 ✦ $21.00	☐
Cetaganda (paperback)	87744-5 ✦ $5.99	☐
Ethan of Athos	65604-X ✦ $5.99	☐
Borders of Infinity	72093-7 ✦ $5.99	☐
Brothers in Arms	69799-4 ✦ $5.99	☐
Mirror Dance (paperback)	87646-5 ✦ $6.99	☐
Memory (paperback)	87845-X ✦ $6.99	☐
The Spirit Ring (paperback)	72188-7 ✦ $5.99	☐

LOIS MCMASTER BUJOLD
Only from Baen Books

If not available at your local bookstore, fill out this coupon and send a check or money order for the cover price(s) plus $1.50 s/h to Baen Books, Dept. BA, P.O. Box 1403, Riverdale, NY 10471. Delivery can take up to ten weeks.

NAME: _____

ADDRESS: _____

_____

_____

I have enclosed a check or money order in the amount of $ _____